LooseId ®

ISBN 10: 1-59632-815-0
ISBN 13: 978-1-59632-815-0
THE RIVALS: SETTLER'S MINE 1
Copyright © November 2008 by Mechele Armstrong
Originally released in e-book format in July 2007

Cover Art by April Martinez

Printed in the U.S.A. by
Lightning Source, Inc.
1246 Heil Quaker Blvd
La Vergne TN 37086
www.lightningsource.com

THE RIVALS
SETTLER'S MINE 1

Mechele Armstrong

Chapter One

"Ship's docking is complete. Welcome to Settler's Mine. A list of rules and regulations is available. Please read them carefully. Ignorance doesn't excuse you from being shot." A computer-generated voice greeted Orion as his ship's docking completed.

He rolled his eyes. Zelda always went for the dramatic. Why hadn't she used her own voice for that greeting to get the full effect? She'd shoot you, too, if you stepped out of line. He'd heard enough about her to know.

Settler's Mine.

The outpost where dreams and reality collided.

Everyone of Quatarian descent came to a mining outpost at some point in their lives. If not this one, a smaller one. Finding one's heartstone drove most to do bizarre things; even, at times, dangerous things, especially the older one got without one's stone.

A heartstone picked the Quatarian it belonged to by glowing. You couldn't screw until you found your own heartstone. Desire wasn't said to exist for someone until they held it in their hands. Once they'd found it, the search was on for their mate. They could then screw anyone, but only bond with their mate. The heartstone alerted a Quatarian to his or her mate by glowing a second time in the mate's presence and each time thereafter during moments of closeness or intense emotion. It would also grow warm to the touch and pulse, once one found a mate.

Not that he knew firsthand. And that suited him fine.

He'd heard the emotion that came with finding a mate was intense and blazing. He had no desire to get sucked into something like that. Not that one had a choice. The stone drove one's desires, then emotions, once found.

As the ship finished its interface with Settler's Mine's computers, Orion's hand went unbidden to his own heartstone hanging on a piece of rough rawhide across his high-necked shirt. Cold and lifeless, it rested against his chest much like an anchor weighing him down. His view of the heartstone? The piece of rock hadn't brought him any bliss.

Focus on what you're here for.

He had to find the girl—no, woman—who'd run away. Shouldn't be too hard to locate her, with the resources he had at his disposal. Two years at the Union Alliance Academy had netted him lots of contacts, even if he hadn't finished. That was how he'd found her destination, when most bounty hunters wouldn't have a clue where to start looking.

Then, he had to capture her. Take her back, and he'd collect a bounty worthy of a prince. Or, at least, a ruler of a small moon.

Layla.

He pulled out his scanner and pushed a few buttons to look at her profile. Her blurred picture beamed through the screen. Quite the beauty in the fuzzy image. He familiarized himself with her features.

What would she use to disguise herself? She didn't have that many resources, nor should she possess knowledge about hiding. Her body type would be easy to spot.

Ansel, the most notorious brigand this side of Bengali, wanted Layla.

It made no sense. Why such a high bounty on delivering a young woman, who wasn't a princess or of any royal blood, to a man who had no interest in women?

Heartmates among only males were rare, but it happened. It had with Ansel. He had a tri-male heartbond, not one prized by the Union Alliance, but with all of Ansel's resources, he could afford to tell them to go screw themselves. Ansel was always looking for ways to get one over on Union Alliance.

Orion blew out a breath, pocketing his scanner. His way wasn't to ask questions of his employers. People hired him to bring them other people. He didn't care or ask why. Governments hired him to bring in fugitives. He didn't care about innocence or guilt. The only thing that moved him to care was platinum. The more of it, the more he cared.

Why had the woman run here? She already had her heartstone. It showed in the picture, looped around her neck on a silver chain. But his best contacts all said Layla had hopped a freighter bound for Settler's Mine. No matter. He'd find her.

He exited his shuttle into the corridor, which would take him on a down slope into the caverns.

Crunching sounds echoed against the hard stone walls. Another shuttle docked nearby, couplings coming forth to hold it in place.

People came and went from Settler's Mine, the biggest heartstone mine in the galaxy, on a regular basis. Many races called the Quatar ancestors, which meant all mines kept busy. As this was the biggest, Settler's Mine stayed chaotic.

Orion passed by the airlock where the newest shuttle had landed, heading for the civilized pockets of the mine. Warm air rushed his face.

Layla should already be down in the mine. She'd had a couple of days' head start on him.

The shuttle probably held some sucker come to find their happiness and heartstone. Orion should tell them and everyone else here that the two didn't go hand in hand. He'd found his but hadn't located a mate. Not that he wanted to. Or so he told himself. Deep down every Quatarian, no matter how jaded, wanted their heartstone first, then wanted their mate. That desperation caused many to do extraordinary things. Or tell themselves lies that kept them warm on cold nights.

No, he'd leave it alone. He wouldn't destroy anyone's illusions. Not even he was that cruel.

A drink of Tenaglian whisky was in order before he searched for his prey. Maybe two or three. Layla wouldn't be hard to locate, capture, and bring back. He'd be back at Ansel's before the ink dried on his contract.

The airlock opened with a hiss.

A large man stepped onto the tarmac into Orion's side vision. A familiar large man.

His heart pumping faster, Orion stopped, giving the new visitor his full attention. "You've got to be kidding me." This couldn't be happening. Their eyes met. The familiar snap of annoyance at the man's presence slapped Orion.

Baltazar's lips puckered into a grin. "I was about to say the same thing."

Orion growled. "I'm here picking up a bounty. Stay out of my way. Far out of my way." Of all the outposts, why did Balt have to show up here? He'd muck everything up, as he always did.

Balt brought out the worst in Orion. He'd never decided why, other than Balt was a loud-mouthed cretin with a big, hard body build for screwing... Nope, not going there. Ever. Not enough Tenaglian whisky in the entire quadrant for that. Despite his protestations, his cock had hardened at the sight of the cretin. As it always did.

Balt's eyebrow lifted. "Me, too. On both counts." He pulled his heartstone out of his tunic, clasping it in huge hands, a habit of his, playing with it. Most people toyed with the necklace in some way. Another thing Orion didn't know the reason behind.

Orion ignored his erection as he watched the man's limber fingers roll the stone around. Damn testosterone was all it was. The arguments brought this reaction out in him whenever he saw Balt. Still, his eyes didn't leave the stone until it was tucked back inside Balt's shirt.

After a moment, they both stilled and said "Layla" at the same time.

"Bloody hell."

"Fuck." Balt stepped further away from the airlock into the corridor. "Don't you get in my way, little Kurlan."

Balt liked to pick on Orion's ancestry, Kurlan, which was a small race, and the Academy schooling he'd had. Ten to one he'd bring the highly ritualized training up next. "Don't you get in my way, you big hulking Amador. I'm bringing in this one." He folded his arms against his chest.

If only he'd brought his stun gun with him. Last time, that had netted him three blissful Balt-free days to find a capture. Amadors had a high susceptibility to tasers. It put them down for long amounts of time. If only he could have stuck around and taken advantage of the situation instead of going after a skip. Balt, tied at his mercy… It would never happen. Besides, he liked things better the other way around. Most of the time.

"The fuck you say."

Orion glared at his nemesis. They stole bounties from each other all the time. "Last time, you knocked me senseless with that big rock. Left me with that dragomoor, who decided I was a tasty snack. She singed all my hair off with her breath fire. So, it's my turn to collect *this* bounty."

"This ain't some sissy school where we take turns. It's whoever's the best." Balt grinned again. "And, that would be me."

"Ha." There was the dig about his Union Alliance Academy days. How predictable of Balt. Orion started walking for the end of the corridor. "In your dreams."

Ansel had hired them both to collect Layla. It proved how desperate the man was to get the woman, because their rivalry was legendary. Ansel knew what he was doing. It meant Orion would have to try twice as hard to get Layla before Balt, as would Balt to get to her before him, ensuring that one of them succeeded. Ansel had made sure he'd get his hands on his prize.

So much for Orion's Tenaglian whisky.

* * *

Baltazar clucked his tongue as he and Orion headed further inside the mine. It had gone from a bitch of a day to a real bastard. He glared at Orion, who glared back. Not that he couldn't handle the little pissant. What a mouth he had on him. For many things, so the rumors said. Not that Balt would ever go there. There wasn't enough tequila in the entire quadrant for that.

They stepped into the heart of Settler's Mine together. Chambers and corridors branched from the main hall in all directions.

Orion turned left, so Balt turned right. Damn the Kurlan for his stubbornness. He should leave before Balt embarrassed him. Again. Where was a rock when you needed one? He stopped. They lay all over at a mine. Maybe he should go left.

"Oh, boys…" A voice spoke from the opposite direction. "Orion. Baltazar."

Now, who would have nerve enough to call him a boy? Orion maybe, but not him. He turned, a growl reverberating in his chest. It died when he saw the cinnamon-haired beauty dressed in black leather standing between him and Orion. She commanded attention, and a growl rose up in his throat in response. He siphoned it back down.

Orion had turned at the same time he did. "Bloody hell." Orion quickly covered the swear, marching over to offer his hand to the exotic-looking woman. "Hello, Zelda. It's wonderful to finally meet you. I've heard so much about you."

Orion's hand was rough. Big for a short man. Balt was drawn to study it. He had a mark on the right one above the knuckle. So the fuck what? What was he doing staring at Orion's hand?

Shaking his head, he turned his attention to Zelda. So, this was the infamous owner of Settler's Mine. Balt had thought she'd be...shorter. She was tall for a woman. Not as tall as he was, but close enough, and he was short for an Amador. Huh, Orion had forgotten to bring that up in their earlier banter. He must be slipping.

Balt blew out a breath. He refused to do any ass kissing as the Union Alliance refugee did. "Zelda." He studied her as she nodded to him. Definitely her beauty outshone anything in the desperate mine. He'd heard she had one heartmate already. Lucky bastard. Even he saw the benefit to being heartmated to Zelda. Balt's own heartstone had come from a small mine several parsecs away, but so far, hadn't come close to finding him anyone. Not that he minded. Most of the time.

Neither of their stones glowed in response to Zelda's heartstone. Zelda wouldn't fuck with anyone besides a mate.

Not that Balt was there to fuck. He had a bounty to collect and a Kurlan to upstage.

Zelda grasped Orion's arm in hers. "Orion." She grabbed his arm as well. "Baltazar. Walk with me."

"I really should be..." Orion fidgeted.

"So should I." Balt moved to pull his arm away.

Her hand tightened onto Balt's arm, nails digging in. "I said, 'walk with me.' It's not a request."

Balt allowed himself to be led to the small bar. He could pull his arm out of her grasp. And, then, from all reports, Zelda would shoot him. Not dying seemed as if it was a good compromise for the statuesque woman. Just where did she hide the weapons in that outfit?

She directed them into the bar, to a table in the corner. The establishment had metal bars and tables. Neon lights beamed hues all over the shadowy space. She took the faux-wooden chair between them, facing the doorway.

A waitress scurried over. "What can I get for you?" She spoke in rapid-fire shots. She had a husky voice, which cut through Balt with desire.

His head lifted as their eyes met.

Her lashes lowered to shade oval, tequila-colored eyes, but not before he saw the interest mirrored there.

His favorite drink was the color of her eyes. How he'd enjoy drinking her. His cock hardened even more than it already had from earlier. A battle of wills between him and Orion usually led to a hard-on. All the adrenaline flying around. It surely wasn't anything else.

His attention came back to the tempting waitress as he appraised her, waiting for a sign she was willing. Maybe after he'd apprehended his prey, he'd make some time for a dalliance with this special one. He didn't mix business and pleasure, but her beauty called to him.

Had he seen a heartstone? He'd have to make sure she possessed one. No one could fuck anyone without one. It was against the law. Hell, men couldn't even get erections without theirs.

She wouldn't meet his eyes again, though he was positive interest had been there in hers. And that intrigued him even more. Why the elusiveness?

His gaze sought out Orion's. The Kurlan's eyes had centered on the waitress's ample cleavage. The hunger there was unmistakable.

Balt's own eyes widened even as his arousal doubled. Lacking a dick, this woman wasn't Orion's usual type. The flicker of interest from Orion surprised Balt even more than his own. What was it about this woman?

Maybe he could use this waitress to his advantage in other ways besides fucking.

"Tell Clyde to put this on my tab."

Balt watched as Zelda caught the eye of a wolfish man behind the bar. He nodded to her. Must be Clyde.

"Get what you want, boys." Zelda leaned back in her chair. "It's on me."

"Tenaglian whisky." Orion folded his hands on the table.

Balt made a face. Ratgut. That's all it was. And, it had the ability to burn certain races with a mere taste. "Tequila. Straight up."

"My usual." Zelda dismissed the waitress and turned her attention to them. "Welcome to Settler's Mine."

"So far it's been a pleasure, ma'am." Orion grinned.

Balt remained silent, waiting. Somehow a welcome didn't seem to be all the woman had in mind.

She paused a second, then continued with an arched brow. "You two fuck with each other while you're here, I'll boot you both off without the benefit of your ship."

Ah, there it came.

Orion sputtered. "Zelda, we would never…"

"I know you both from all kinds of reports. I looked you up as soon as I got your filed manifesto you were heading here. Don't tell me the fuck what you would and wouldn't do. I already know."

Balt's voice boomed louder than he meant it. "We..." What could he say? The lady wasn't a dummy. He and Orion fought whenever they were together. He'd never been sure what it was about the man that provoked him. They'd always done it. No one else incited him to both irritation and arrogance as Orion did.

Zelda didn't let him get anything out, even if he could have come up with anything. "You aren't here for your heartstones. You both already have them. Orion, from here before it was my mine. Balt, from Sarcoda. So, that means a job. Don't insult my fucking intelligence. I don't want my mine in any way harmed because you two don't play nice."

"Zelda, I'm telling you—" Orion tried to butt in.

"And I'm telling you—"

The waitress interrupted, arriving with their drinks. She quickly set the three glasses down on the table.

Balt sniffed, taking in her light scent as she leaned down to put his drink in front of him. Her skin would scorch him. Yet he wanted to touch. A lot. Being burned in her fire would be heaven.

Zelda passed a bill into the waitress's hand. "Thank you."

Orion and Balt both said at the same time, "Thank you." Orion added "love" on the end of his.

Zelda was the only woman Balt had heard Orion skip the "love" bit with. Because she'd torpedo his balls if he did that.

Zelda's mouth lifted into a little smile as if they'd impressed her with their thanks.

Balt reached toward his pocket but drew away at Zelda's frown. No sense pissing her off to touch the waitress for a second. There'd be more time later. He'd see to that.

The waitress bleated out her own thanks and headed to the other tables. Her hand remained on the pocket where that bill rested.

Zelda had given the girl an enormous tip.

Balt's eyes appraised her. The woman owned everything on the planet, yet, she'd given a large tip of appreciation to a waitress. His estimation of her went up a notch. So, she was a bitch but not a cold-blooded one as he'd heard she was.

"Now, where was I? Ah, yes, I'm telling you...don't fuck with me or my mine. Whatever business here you have, do it, and get out." She held up her glass. "You two start a fight, and I'll fucking finish it."

The three picked up their glasses and clinked them together. Then, they all tossed back the alcohol quickly.

Zelda did so as fast as Balt and Orion.

Impressive. The slow burn started in Balt's throat and wound down into his gullet. She meant what she'd said. Zelda didn't say anything she didn't mean.

"Zelda, we'll move on as soon as one of us has what we came here for." Orion put his cup gently on the table.

Balt noticed how Orion's fingers curled around the glass. Such long fingers for a Kurlan. Irritation at the attention he paid to Orion's hand filled him. "You mean after *I* collect what we came for." Balt put his crystal down on the metal table with a soft clink. That would get the other man riled. The opposite of what Zelda had told them to do, but he couldn't resist.

Orion's lips thinned. "The only way you'll be collecting it..."

"Boys." Zelda waved the hand with her drink around. "This is exactly what I'm talking about. If you're both here after the same thing, work together. But you do harm to my mine or any of my people, and I'll do harm to you. Neither of you has an extra cock, so I'd be extra careful."

Balt's hand shifted to his lap. Yeah, she meant that, too. And with her resources, she would be able to string them up by whatever appendage she chose.

"On that note," Orion hemmed. "A young woman. Blonde. Waiflike. Showed up here a few days ago. Purple eyes. Have you seen her?"

She spared Orion a withering glance. "I don't look into anyone's biz. I don't report to you or anyone else." She pushed away her chair from the table. "Are we straight, boys? You two both clear?" She stood up.

"Yes." Orion stared down into his empty glass. A copper drop remained at the bottom.

Zelda affixed Balt with her dark eyes, until he drew up his gaze from Orion to meet hers.

He nodded his agreement. So much for playing with his rival. He'd have to get down to the shitty if he wanted to bring in the bounty.

A large man with an olive complexion approached Zelda. He was almost as tall as Balt himself. "Z." He nodded to Balt and Orion. He leaned down to press an intensive kiss on her lips. Plenty of tongue and melding of mouths.

This must be Bren, Zelda's heartmate.

They pulled away from each other, eyes glowing with the knowledge that this would be continuing later.

Balt turned his gaze to Orion, whose eyes sparked for a moment as he watched. That spark ignited something in Balt's blood. When the look faded from Orion's face, Balt wanted it to come back.

He shook his head quickly back and forth to clear it.

He needed more tequila.

He motioned to the waitress. She sashayed to the bar, her ample hips moving to and fro with a little twitch.

Balt blew out a breath at the swish of her hips. Couldn't help but notice Orion doing the same thing as he watched the waitress, too.

Yes, Orion had interest in the woman.

After he'd used that to his advantage, Balt would have to make some time, when he'd secured his capture, to play with the waitress. His little head concurred with that plan.

* * *

Layla took a deep calming breath before quickly looking over to make sure no one paid her any more attention than they would a normal waitress.

Get a grip on yourself.

Mercenaries. Bounty hunters. Both of them gorgeous, but also deadly to her because of what they'd come to do.

They sat a few feet away at a table, scanning the bar with their gaze as Zelda and Bren walked away, probably to go to their quarters and have sex. They went at it as if they were Mylon rabbits, so she'd heard. So many years together and still so much attraction. That must be wonderful. Something she'd never know.

After all Layla had been through, no one would want to be a heartmate to her. They'd just as soon kill her.

Didn't matter who exactly the two men sitting at the table were. She recognized the type. She could sniff out mercenaries from ten parsecs. And there was only one reason they would descend on Settler's Mine, an outpost for finding one's heartstone. Both of them already wore theirs around their necks. Only one thing could have led them there.

Her.

At least, they couldn't be government. The Union Alliance would send an army after her, not two simple bounty catchers. That left one person they could be working for.

Ansel.

He'd told her there was nowhere in the galaxy she could run from him. This was his way of ensuring that was true.

Had they made her yet? Noticed her? Not likely, as they hadn't wrestled her to the ground to put her in cuffs. She'd paid special attention to blend in as the Coronian waitress she was supposed to be.

She looked at Clyde. "Why'd Zelda have a drink with those two?" Clyde kept his ear to the wall. Not much happened on the mine without Clyde's knowing about it.

"Oh, they're mercenaries. They have the rep of fighting all the time. So, she's making sure they won't here. Last station, they fought apprehending a skip, then got drunk, and took out over half of the bar."

"Ah." Not an intelligent reply, but, all she had right now. She'd been right. It gave her little comfort.

"You O.K.?" Clyde sniffed the air. "You seem a little off."

He could smell her fear, even if he didn't show it. Wolftons had strong senses, as did all their kind. Much stronger than most of Quatar descent and those of Union Alliance territories. What a Wolfton was doing here on Settler's Mine, she didn't have a clue. Most of them settled in forests or plains on deserted planets. They had few weaknesses…

She stiffened her shoulders. *Don't go there with Clyde.*

Clyde could also smell her arousal. The deep baritone of them both had had her oozing as if they'd touched her instead of merely speaking. *Two pretty faces. You've seen prettier before. Move along.*

Something about them interested her lusty side, even butting up again her anxiety. Too bad her arousal could never be.

There was nothing she could do about her oozing pheromones. The fear would remain inside no matter what she did. She couldn't go back. She wouldn't.

Luckily, the two hunters in front of her couldn't scent out her emotions like a Wolfton. That worked in her favor. They wouldn't scent her unexplained attraction to them either.

One looked as though he was an Amador. She'd known one... She shook off that thought. His green hair and rust-colored eyes gave it away. Though he did look small for his species. They could be as tall as nine feet, or less than seven feet. This one looked only about six foot and a few inches. Her mind ticked off an Amador's weak points, despite her denial of her talents.

The other, she couldn't be sure of his ancestry. She'd have to look it up when she had the opportunity. Jet-black hair and too-appraising green eyes. He was taller than she, but shorter than his rival. The gills on his neck, which were hidden by his high-necked shirt, should make his ancestry easy to find. She'd noticed them when she'd been setting down drinks. The gills would also be a weakness to exploit, probably why he wore the shirt he did. She added this to the list of other weaknesses she'd sized up in the few minutes she had been in his presence.

Both of them must be Quatarian, which explained their humanoid appearance and heartstones. That gave her a little more about the unknown one's weaknesses without even knowing his particular race.

She could control her actions. Nervousness in her speech or behavior would only get her caught. *Blend blend blend. Use what you know. What you were trained for. So you don't have to use the rest of your training. And forget your sexual attraction. It will only get you caught.*

Her training was the only thing she was good at. Hiding right under people's noses. If need be, killing. But only as a last resort.

Her hand started to smooth down her hips. She jerked it back. That would only call attention to the padding.

Seeking something to do with her hand, she idly reached for her heartstone, only to run her hand through her hair because it wasn't around her neck. Her stone lay hidden in her room so as to confuse anyone who knew she had one.

All of the changes she'd made to her appearance should make any photos of her out of date.

The only thing that might sell her out to them was that she'd arrived in their timeframe.

She grabbed the tequila shot, sauntered back to the table, and placed it in front of the burly man. A grin graced her face. "This one's not on Zelda's tab. Pay up."

Chapter Two

The waitress had a bemused look on her face as if she couldn't believe what he'd said. "You want me to what?'

Orion grinned at her, meeting her gaze. "I want you to seek out my friend, Balt. Spend some time with him, love."

She bent to wipe down a table, breaking their eye contact. His gaze centered on her rear as she wiggled it around as though she knew he stared. His cock, which had perked up at her husky voice, went to fully hard. His breath drew in.

He considered himself bisexual with a definite leaning toward men. Few women set his senses on fire, and never the way this one had. If circumstances had been different, he would have been seeking out her company for himself alone. Even now, his hackles rose at what he was doing, which shouldn't be his reaction. After all, this would only be a business arrangement. It wouldn't preclude him from taking it to the personal level after things were done here on Settler's Mine.

His eyes checked around her neck. Damn, no heartstone. Maybe she'd find it while he was still at the mine. He might help her dig for the jewel if it meant he could have sex with her.

He'd have been an idiot not to notice Balt's obvious attraction to the woman, and even more a rube not to exploit it. Balt would never miss an opportunity like that, which would give the other such an advantage. Balt could spend time with the woman while Orion pursued Layla at his leisure, bringing in the capture first. It was a foolproof plan, which would net him big money. And he'd still have a chance with the girl in the end. Provided she found her heartstone.

The low tones of her voice alerted him she'd spoken.

"...an odd request. Why doesn't he ask me himself if he wants to 'spend time' with me?" She moved to wipe down another table. Her fingers lingered over the wood.

They'd feel like satin running over his body. Yeah, he'd help her dig for that heartstone before he left Settler's Mine. "He's...uh, shy." He bit back a snicker.

Her eyebrow arched as she looked over at him. Her hand stopped wiping. "Amadors aren't known for being shy."

Clever lady. No, they weren't, and Balt would never fit that description. "He's special." That much was true. Balt was small for an Amador, making him noticed among those who knew Amadors. A fact which bedeviled Balt to no end. This waitress had something going on above her shoulders beyond a pretty face to have noted his lie and called him on it. How did the waitress know that? Orion's head canted to the side. "You know Amadors, Miss..."

"Besela." She went back to wiping with a shrug of her shoulders. "And I've known a little bit of every race."

Her ample breasts filled out the shirt, bouncing in a delicious manner from her movements. If only it weren't buttoned to her neck. Come to think of it, that was odd. Some cleavage showing would be more standard garb for a waitress. The more breast showing, the more tips from drunken patrons. Not to mention it would give him a peek.

Besela was a common Coronian name. Coronians were a race known for a peaceful, calm nature. They rarely fought, so they were perfect for jobs in the public eye, like waitressing. That ancestry made sense. Her dark hair, skin, eyes, rounded body, all alluded to that race. Except for her face. The angular lines of her cheeks looked sharp, not rounded, almost more like Native ancestry. Native ancestry?

His eyes narrowed as he watched her. Her body looked nothing similar to the pictures of Layla. There was an ease about her that all Coronians had. None of the nervous stiffness of Natives.

He relaxed. Layla couldn't have changed herself that much.

"I bet you have. Have you been here long?" He'd come straight back to the bar after shaking Balt off his trail. He'd do some asking around the mine once he'd set this up, about those who'd arrived over the last few days.

"Only a couple of days." She shrugged, tucking a hair behind her ear. "Saw the sign right away. Been on other rocks, too. Like this one." She pushed a chair in under a table. "Why do you want me to spend time with your friend?"

"I told you. He's shy. But he likes you, love. I'm doing him a favor."

She shot him a look, which said she didn't believe him, but didn't comment. Yes, this woman had a brain. And her mind intrigued him as much as her body. She definitely set his heart to beating on a few levels. Intelligence was something he looked for in a bedmate.

But something wasn't right with her. He frowned. Her face didn't quite look like the rest of her did. He shook that thought off. Just because she was Coronian didn't mean she had to have every trait of her race. After all, he and Balt both had quirks in their physique that were inconsistent with their heritage.

"You have a customer, Besela," the bartender said from his place at the bar as he expertly stirred a blue flaming drink.

Besela took a step away from Orion.

"Will you do it? Seek out Balt for some dinner? Talk to him?" He put on his best pleading face as she twirled to face him. It would make it so much easier for him to steal Layla's capture without Balt interfering.

She rubbed her face with a free hand as the other tossed the rag in a bucket. "What's in it for me?"

He'd waited for that question. He'd seen her reaction to the tip that Zelda had given her earlier. The woman, like so many, had a need or love of money. "A ream of platinum." This would be but a pittance against what he'd make for turning over Layla.

Her eyes widened. "All I have to do is spend time with your Amador friend? Nothing else? And, you'll pay me that much?"

He nodded. The eagerness in her voice filled him with something he couldn't quite name. If only things were different, she'd be eager over something else. "That's it."

"All right. I'll spend some time seeking out Balt."

"That's all I'm asking for, love." For now. Later, he'd ask more. His gaze traveled up and down her body. Yes, a lot more.

"I want payment up front."

His lips twitched at her cheek. "How do I know you'll do it? I don't usually pay for services until they are rendered."

"Suit yourself." She moved away from him, heading for the table where a patron waited to give her a drink order.

He admired the sway of her hips and ass as she walked away, even though she'd dismissed him outright. He straightened in his chair, cock straining against the confines of his pants.

The bartender glared at him, quiet behind the bar but watching as Orion stared after the woman's back.

He waited a second. Then, another.

She wasn't turning around to accept his offer.

He straightened up in his chair. He couldn't let this opportunity get away. "How about half?"

"All of it." She didn't miss a beat or a step, continuing to walk away from him. Bloody hell. The woman negotiated too well.

He had everything to lose. She had nothing in hand to lose. "Fine." He approached her, sliding the platinum into her hand. His finger touched hers for a millisecond, and the stroke of her skin against his jolted him. Swallowing, he attributed the current to static electricity. No mere desire could hit him that hard. "Here."

Her smile didn't reach her eyes. In fact, nothing had the whole time they'd been talking. Her eyes looked guarded, not revealing any of her emotions. The closest she'd come to showing anything was her look when he'd started talking to her and her eagerness over money. What made her so laconic and unemotional? And in need of money? "I'll start when I get off work."

"Good. Thank you, love."

After he'd captured Layla, he'd find a way to spend time with this exquisite creature alone and learn all her secrets along with every curve, heartstone or no heartstone. His cock jerked at the thought.

*　*　*

Balt sauntered into the bar and sat down after making sure she was the only waitress working. Time to make contact with her and to do that, she had to be his server. The bar must work one waitress and bartender at a time.

She shot him a slight smile and sashayed over from the bar with a clear glass filled with amber liquid. "Here you go. Tequila."

He leaned back in his chair, widening his legs. "You remembered me." He took a quick sip of his drink.

Her eyes shuttered, blocking eye contact. "You're an Amador. Not easy to forget any of them, especially you." She purred the name of his race.

His breath quickened at the seductive sound dripping from her lips. Warmth filled him as his chest expanded, though he had no illusions. She'd complimented him to pad out her tip, and it had worked. The instinctual puffing out of his chest proved that. She was a conniving wench. Just the kind he liked. Too fucking bad he had to sacrifice her to the fish to make his bounty. But he'd be a pussy not to take advantage of Orion's interest in her. Baltazar was no pussy. He'd do what needed doing to get the job done.

"Nice to know I'm not forgettable to you. Actually, I'm glad you were working. I wanted to speak with you about something. That's why I came in."

Her eyes widened slightly. "What about?" She took a little step back from his table. Her hands went to her side, drawing his gaze to those ample hips.

"What's your name?"

"Besela." Her voice sounded hesitant.

A good little Coronian name, which he'd already known from asking around the mine. Must be her ancestry, judging by most of her looks and that piece of information. She'd arrived at the mine only a few days before, putting her on a short list for Layla. But her appearance ruled her out as the woman he sought. Layla hadn't had a lot of resources to change herself so radically. "Besela. I have a business proposition for you. Can we talk about it? Maybe on your break? I'll wait around."

She licked her lips.

He widened his legs as his cock engorged. Fuck, that small tongue would be heaven rolling down him. He'd fill that small mouth to the brim. Fill her pussy up, too. His gaze drifted to her neck.

No heartstone.

No matter, she'd probably find it before he had to leave. Maybe he'd help her find it.

"I break in five."

"I'll wait."

He watched her ass sway as she walked to another table. After this was over, he would be plowing her one way or another. Didn't matter to him how she wanted it. He'd do her the way she liked it best. He took another sip, blowing out a breath. This wasn't an unusual reaction for him; he liked women and fucking. Hell, he liked men and fucking, too. But he'd not reacted this strongly to someone before.

It still puzzled him why Orion had reacted the way he did to Besela. Orion had never seemed to care for women all that much. Did Orion want to fuck her? Shouldn't that bother him as he wanted to, too? But it didn't.

Curious.

He'd had threesomes in his life. Orion, Besela, and him... No. Not just no but fuck no. No matter how good the Kurlan was supposed to be.

In five minutes, Besela came over and sat gracefully in the chair across from him. "Make it quick. I don't have much time." She carried a cup of water, which she quickly downed during his first sentence.

"I have this friend named Orion. We were in here earlier. You waited on us. I need him distracted. So I can conduct my own business here." Something struck him about her face, but he couldn't be sure what. Too angular? Her chin looked so sharp. Shouldn't it be more round to go with the rest of her?

"What does this have to do with me?" She folded her arms in front of ample tits. Were they crooked?

He lowered his head to get a better look.

"And keep your eyes on my face when I'm talking to you."

He straightened up at her comment. So, he'd been caught staring. Not the first time or the last. He must have been seeing things. No way could the right boob have been that far down. Not many would call an Amador on anything, especially when they were so little in comparison. His mouth twisted up into a grin at her feistiness. "It has to do with you, because I want you to spend some time with him. I want you to keep him out of my way."

Her eyes blinked as she sat quietly for a second. "You want me to spend time with Orion."

"Yep."

She scratched her cheek. "What's in it for me?"

His grin grew wider. She didn't disappoint him on any count. He'd known she'd want some form of payment, and he'd come prepared. "A ream of platinum." No way would she say no to that.

"You'll pay me that much, just for spending enough time with him to distract him?"

He nodded. "Nothing else is required of you." He didn't pay women to fuck anyone, not even him. A woman had to be willing. And, so far, even with his intimidating size, women didn't turn him down.

"Pay me, and I'll do it."

"Half now. Half later."

She stood up by her chair. Her face didn't change expression "All of it now."

"You get it all when you do the job." He shook his head. The woman drove a hard negotiation. Tough woman. He liked his bedmates tough. "No other deal."

"Then, I don't do the job for you. Nice talking with you, Balt." She moved away from him to the bar.

Enjoying his name rolling melodically from her lips, he watched her walk away, enjoying the show of her rolling hips.

Fuck. His head came up. How had she known his name? He hadn't mentioned it to her. Had she heard it from Zelda earlier? Did the whole fucking mine know he and Orion were there? Being that well known would make things more difficult finding Layla. She would already be in hiding. Their presence would drive her deeper in. He'd done some sweeps of the mine already, and come up with squat.

He sucked down the rest of his tequila and approached Besela. "Fine." Not his usual method, but as desperate as Layla probably was, he needed any leg up he could get over Orion. It would be worth it, especially after he was paid for the bounty. Course, if she kept the pissant out of his way, it would be worth it even without the money. "Here's the payment." He stuck it in her hand.

Their fingers met in a caress. His lingered over hers. Her skin was soft under his fingertips.

She jerked her hand away with the platinum almost as though his touch had burned her.

Her touched had seared him. "We have a deal?"

She rubbed her hand near where he'd touched. Maybe he had burned her. "Sure we do. I'll spend time with Orion as I can. I'll make reports in to you, too, about his…activities."

A bonus. He'd now know what Orion was up to. He couldn't have asked for better. "Great. Later then."

He strode off to the door of the bar to exit. Time to talk to a few more people about anyone new to the mine. Before walking through the door, he turned to watch her as she carried a tray of drinks balanced precariously on her hip. Such grace mixed with such fire. With her temperament, she'd be a hellion in bed. He couldn't wait to give her some hell back.

* * *

Layla rubbed her hand over her face as she giggled. She went to the basin to splash some water on her cheeks. Looking at herself in the mirror, she patted the damp, too dark skin. The effects should last another week, if not two. She'd be long gone from Settler's Mine by the time the toner started to fade. The makeup hadn't come cheap—it wasn't sold just anywhere—but it had been well worth it. It dyed her skin, leaving no aftertaste, wouldn't rub off, and looked authentic.

The events of the last day, especially the last few hours, had been crazy.

Two bounty hunters in pursuit of her had each hired her to keep the other distracted. So, not only would she be right under their radar, the last place they'd look, she'd be kept up on both investigations from spending time with them. That contact would alert her when it became time to bolt. The reams of platinum they'd both paid her up front would help her journey off the mine when the time came. A little bit more earned money combined with her savings and she'd have no trouble securing transport beyond the Union Alliance territories. There, she'd be safe from Ansel and the Union Alliance.

Unfricking believable.

She might escape with her life and mind intact if this all worked out. Not anything she would have believed when she'd first run. It looked as if good luck would hold while she hid here.

She grabbed a brush to pull through her hair. Only two quick swipes untangled it. She'd never get used to it being so short. Natives never cut their hair. They'd die before submitting to such a thing. She should be mourning its loss. But, of course, she'd never been a typical Native. She'd never been allowed to be.

She shifted her weight. The only drawback to all of this was her attraction to the two men. After both their visits, her sex had been slick and swollen. If only she could take advantage of what they had to offer. She'd seen their arousals and lust reflected on their faces. But, with her heartstone hidden, she couldn't. It was against the law for anyone without a heartstone to have sex. Not to mention, anything further in the bedroom, and they'd discover she was the woman they sought.

Her fingers drifted under her pants into her swollen sex. She leaned her head back as her fingers toyed in the wetness. Their fingers would fill her so much better than her own. So thick. Especially Balt's. He probably had a thick cock, too, judging from his size. And Orion's would be long. They'd both fill her while making her beg for more. Her fingers sped up the pace.

The bell sounded on her quarter door. Probably one of the men she needed to seek out. They were both intelligent men. She only had so long before they'd get suspicious about her. She didn't want either of them in her quarters. Too much would be risked. "Who's there?"

"Zelda."

Layla tensed, pulling her hand from her pants and quickly wiping it off. Now, *that* visitor hadn't been expected. Good thing she'd left the boots on, giving her several inches in height. She pressed the button unlocking the door. "Come in." No one denied Zelda entrance unless they wanted to be kicked off Settler's Mine, which Layla had no desire to be. Not right now, when things had looked up for her.

After opening the doors, the tall woman strode into Layla's little piece of the mine, while the doors hissed back into place. "Besela."

"Zelda. What a...nice surprise." She'd flown in under the radar of everyone, including the two who'd been sent after her. Surely this couldn't be about anything to do with that. Zelda couldn't suspect what everyone else didn't. Only Zelda wasn't known for social calls, so something had to be going on for her to visit Layla in her quarters. What brought her there?

Zelda smiled, showing even teeth. "Very neat quarters."

"I take care of other people's things." She'd rented this room, carved out of the rock of the mine, when she'd boarded there. She'd had very little of her own, so she was used to taking care of the things of others.

"I'm sure you do." Zelda sat down on a chair at the small table by the door. "You do good work at the bar. Clyde has nothing but praise for the way you handle the customers and yourself. He doesn't give that away easily."

"That's good to hear. Especially from Clyde." Her heart pounded. Zelda wouldn't hear it, but Clyde would. Slowly, she brought the pace down with her mind. Something she'd learned to do in training. Beating hearts could give one away.

This was a lead up to what? Zelda hadn't come there to critique her quarters or her job performance.

"Has Chumsky been bothering you at all? I'm trying to confirm something another female newcomer told me."

"No, he hasn't bothered me."

A lie. He had as soon she'd come on board, offering protection for sex. So far, she'd managed to put him off. Coronians were known peacemakers. Chumsky was shitty enough to use that to his advantage, thinking she wouldn't hit back. And as long as she wanted to blend, she couldn't. But, she didn't need the trouble ratting out Chumsky would cause. He'd get discovered in time on his own. Zelda's sharpness would ensure that.

Zelda scrutinized her for a moment, but changed the subject. "Haven't heard about you digging for your heartstone, though. Only working."

"I...I've been busy." She kept her gaze away from her bunk. Hidden under the mattress was a small box, which contained her heartstone. Yet another break with tradition. Natives especially kept their stone on at all times. But, one wore them to help locate one's heartmate or mates, and who'd want to be mated with her the way things were? No one.

She'd mentioned coming there to find her heartstone in her initial meeting with Zelda as to why she'd traveled to Settlers' Mine. Of all the lies she'd told, this one to Zelda had bothered her the most. It had seemed especially dishonest to deny her heart, to deny the stone. The stone which could pick her mate if her life ever turned normal.

Lashes crept down to hide Zelda's expressive eyes. "Usually those in search of their heartstones don't let work interfere with the search."

Her heart stopped for a second, then resumed normal operations. What Zelda said was the truth. Had anyone else noticed her lack of digging in the short time she'd been there? It hadn't occurred to her to do it. A mistake on her part. Hopefully, it was early enough, that no one had pointed out her screw-up to anyone. Like Orion and Balt. "I..."

Zelda stood. "I'm glad we had this chat, Besela. Your area is waiting for you to dig, as you know. And should you ever...need assistance, you know where to go."

Her eyes met Zelda's. Surely the woman didn't know anything. She couldn't. Zelda had displayed concern because the more people who found their heartstones here, the more would come to Settler's Mine in search of them. And, if "Besela" didn't look, she wouldn't find it. That had to be why Zelda had brought it up.

"Thank you, Zelda. I was planning to dig later today." Close call. Good thing it had come before it was too late.

Zelda nodded as she pressed the button to exit. "Oh, one more thing. Orion and Baltazar, the two bounty hunters you served earlier, are on the lookout for a runaway someone or other. I don't turn in anyone from Settler's Mine. But, a lot will. If you see anything...suspicious, you may want to...tell them."

"I'll keep that in mind." She met Zelda's eyes again, looking straight into their depths. What had clued Zelda in? Layla had no idea, but there was no other way to take this visit now. Zelda knew who and what she was. But she'd not tattle. Nor would she intervene if Layla were caught there.

Zelda continued on her way, closing the door behind her.

Layla sat down on the bed, trying to calm a heart, which now that she was alone, raced as if the hounds of hell pursued her. Of course, Ansel was a hound of hell. And he'd never give up.

She'd almost slipped up in her disguise. Swallowing, she looked at the door the other woman had disappeared through.

She couldn't screw up again.

Chapter Three

Orion saw a familiar shape scoot around the corner. A recognizable sway of hips. He hurried his steps to catch up with her. Couldn't contain the speeding up of his heart from regular to race levels. The pace shouldn't be this fast from a mere chance encounter. Wasn't like they were going to have sex in the walkway. Though he'd be willing if she made any overture. Hell, he'd do that anywhere she asked him. *Heartstone.* He had to keep repeating that. It wouldn't be as enjoyable for her without one. "Besela."

Her steps slowed down. "Orion." Her voice was like the music of the angels of old. Her lips tilted into a shy smile.

Ding. A bell went off in his chest, resounding through his body. Damn, what a smile from her could do to him. He found himself smiling back. He didn't understand his reactions to this woman. How strongly a smile from her could affect him. Sex with her might just kill him if it ever happened. Oh, it would happen, and he'd enjoy the death. He'd see to the fucking if he had to dig for that heartstone himself. "Where you headed?"

Her lips twitched merrily at him. "To...dig." She sounded confused, which puzzled him, until he looked away from her face.

"Oh." She was carrying a shovel and several other digging implements, along with a pack. Her smile had disarmed his usual scrutiny. He shook his head as he fell into step beside her. She'd be dangerous working for the enemy. One look at her and all soldiers would forget they had weapons as if she were a siren from the old tales. Sirens had seduced shipmen, making them forget all but the seductresses. "Looking for your heartstone?"

"Yeah." She pressed a strand of hair back behind her ear. It promptly sprang out again. "Need to find it."

No determination backed up her words. She stated it as if the search weren't important. Was she frustrated by the expedition? With her age, she probably was. He'd heard of Quatarians getting so disgusted by their lack of luck, they would give up. Not everyone found their heartstone, a dismal fact. She couldn't give up, not now. "Don't give up. You'll find it." *Please, Goddess, let her find it.*

One lone shoulder shrugged. "Maybe."

"Been looking a while, huh?"

"Awhile."

He heard the solid resignation in her voice. He couldn't have this woman ready to give up. He wanted her too badly. Not to mention, for all his beliefs about his own mate, hers existed somewhere out there. He could feel it. And, even with his attraction to her, he wanted her to find her mate. A hint of sadness remained in her eyes no matter the expression on her face. And he needed to ease it. In any way he could. She had to find her mate. "They say when you least expect it, your stone will pop up."

"Maybe."

He stopped short. Moved in closer to her.

She stopped to look at him. Her face slackened so he could read no expression. Her scent pervaded his senses. Her body warmth called to him to bring him even closer. They were barely touching, but it was like being submerged in a fire too hot to touch.

"Don't."

A swallow moved down her throat.

He watched it, unable to pull his eyes away from her slender neck. He'd never wanted to taste anything more.

"Don't what?"

He ran one finger up her arm to rest at her shoulder. Tremors emerged under his fingers. Like popcorn popping, pulses flew between his finger and her clothed skin. "Don't give up. You have to find your heartstone, Besela."

"It doesn't matter."

"Oh, but it does." He moved in closer, backing her against the wall. She didn't give any indication this closeness made her uncomfortable, or he'd have backed off. Her face did register puzzlement. "To me."

She stared up at him as though she hadn't comprehended his words. "Why? Why does it matter to you?"

A good question. One he had no real answer for. He didn't understand this need pulsing within him either. "Because it does." He ran his finger back down to her hand. A soft hand. Unspoiled with roughness. So different from his own tough skin. The pack of tools fell from her grasp. He bent down to pick it up. "Let me get that for you."

"Thank you." Her gaze ran down his chest and back up to his eyes. Her tongue tip came out to moisten her deep, red lips.

He moved closer, drawn in as if he were a magnet, tilting his head down. Would she accept his kiss? Only one way to find out.

Her head drew up as her lips parted for him.

As he was about to claim the promised land of her luscious mouth, his com went off.

Instantly, she pulled back.

It was a reminder of who he was supposed to meet. He'd set it himself. Bloody hell, if only he hadn't set up the damn meeting.

The moment broke apart as she stepped back from him.

"It's an alarm."

She cleared her throat. "Not a problem, I hope."

"No. I have a meeting to go to." He ran a hand down his neck. If only the reminder had been five seconds later.

"Oh. Well, don't let me keep you from it. I have to go dig." She brandished her shovel close against her.

"Yeah. You do." He moved away. "I'll see you later though." Yes, he would. He'd make sure of it. Maybe she'd even have her heartstone in hand after this mining expedition. No, he had to continue searching for Layla. Do that job before any pleasure. Layla was what his meeting was about.

"Uh…sure." Her hands tightened on her shovel. She turned to walk down into the mine. Such grace of movement.

Orion looked down at the pack in his hand. "Wait, you forgot this."

She turned and glided back across the rock floor to him. Her shoes made only small sounds.

He could watch her move all day. He held the pack out to her. "Here."

She reached to take the bag from him. Her fingers brushed across his.

Desire hummed across his senses.

She quickly pulled back as though the contact charred her. Her pack was in hand so she didn't have to reach to him again. "Thanks." Her breathing had sped up when their fingers touched. Maybe Besela was as affected by him as he was by her. Did Balt affect her that same way?

He'd have to watch and see. "You're welcome."

She turned back through the shaft.

"Besela?"

"Yes, Orion?"

"Happy hunting."

He heard her swallow as she didn't turn around, but kept walking. He watched until she disappeared into a corridor. Then, he hurried on his way. He had a job to do before he could even hope to get to the pleasure that was Besela.

* * *

Layla pushed back a loose piece of hair. She pushed her shovel forward, chipping away at the rock. Shaken by her encounter with Orion, she dug in her mine spot, trying to keep her mind from what had happened.

Digging had sucked doing this back when she had been looking for her heartstone. And, it sucked even more now. She should be seeking out one of the bounty hunters. Discovering where they were with their investigation. Spending more time with them. Damn her, because she enjoyed being in their presence.

But she needed to make a show of digging. Her story had to make sense or the bounty hunters would begin to doubt her. Little unfitting pieces would make them see through her disguise. It was always the little things that did one in.

"You need to put a little more power behind the shovel." Intruding into her thoughts, the deep voice behind her made her pause.

She swiveled her head to see Balt standing behind her with a big grin. His coppery eyes beamed at her. "That's so easy for an Amador to say." Maybe she wouldn't have to seek out the bounty hunters after all if they kept coming around her this way. When would they figure out she'd played them both? She didn't like the crimp that put in her stomach.

Chuckling, he walked over to her side. "Looking for your heartstone?" His big boots clomped on the rock pathway.

"Isn't everyone? That's why most are here. To find their heartstones and live to their fullest." She swung the pick forward to dip into the rock again, but with little force behind it. "Except you and Orion. You both have yours."

They sought out human cargo here. Her value probably exceeded the worth of some small planets. Damn the Union Alliance for forcing this and Ansel for pursuing her. But even with what Orion and Balt did, she still didn't like lying to them. Somehow lying as a part of a job seemed better than what she was doing now. Even though it was her life at stake with these lies.

"I found mine years ago." He widened his stance, watching her. "You're doing it all wrong." He came up close behind her. "Let me show you." Taking the hand with the pick in his much larger one, he covered her hand with his warm one. Rough moved against her smoothness. Light against her dark.

She couldn't keep her eyes from staring at their hands. Joined. It seemed so intimate.

Then, he moved his body close against her back.

Even more intimate. She was surrounded by him. Currents flew through her already sensitized skin. His other hand dropped down to press against her stomach, which sucked in from the contact.

His body heated hers. His hardness pressed up against her back.

Even through the layers, his cock noticeably pressed into her. Her mouth dried. She swallowed, trying to bring back some moistness. She couldn't breathe with him so close. Desire rippled through her with a molten rush. This couldn't be happening, yet, as if a switch had been hit, her whole body crinkled with awareness of Balt.

"Draw back like this." He pulled her hand back. He pressed on her side with his palm. "Then, bring it forward all the way. Like so." He tapped the rock. The impact spread through her. "That way you get the maximum for the swing."

"Oh. Thanks." She should pull away from him now. Break the contact of their bodies. Make some joke about Amadors and swinging. She couldn't. Being folded into his body made her comfortable and passionate at the same time. Her body tingled everywhere his touched. It had been so long since she'd experienced anything like this. And never had desire come on so strong, so unexpectedly.

One of his fingers moved to stroke down the back of her hand to her wrist.

Sparks moved down it in the wake of his touch. Did he feel it, too?

"Your skin is so soft. Silky." His voice sounded gravelly above her head. From the rough sound of his voice, he felt it as much as she did.

Her throat moved with a swallow. "I use lotion."

He leaned over her and inhaled. The breath tickled her head. "You smell as good as you feel."

"It's the lotion." Her breath couldn't come fast enough to suit her lungs. "I use it every day."

"It's the woman." He inhaled again. His breath rasped through his chest.

She shivered, enjoying his reactions as much as her own.

He moved closer against her with a soothing noise. "Cold? The air in the mines is always so fucking frigid."

She would burn up, not freeze. Her entire back pressed against his front. The hard erection poking her through all the layers in the back told her how much he enjoyed this closeness.

She moved a centimeter back, pressing herself even more firmly against him. His scent overwhelmed her senses.

He kissed the side of her neck as her eyes dropped closed. His hands tightened on her shoulders, holding her against him as he nipped the sensitive skin below her ear. She whimpered from the contact.

Moving up, he nipped her earlobe, before spearing her ear with his tongue. In and out, he thrust. His hips moved in time with the motion of his tongue.

She gasped. So many sensations rolled through her. She'd never wanted to be with a man more than she did at that moment. "Balt…" Her eyes flew open. What the hell was she doing? He was a fricking bounty hunter. "Balt, stop."

His mouth withdrew with one final push of his tongue into her ear canal, but he didn't release her. He crooned. "What's wrong?"

"We…can't do this." She straightened her body, pushing forward and out of his arms. Had to get away. Her body tensed. Too close. He'd been too close to so many things. She never should have let this happen. "No."

His open face scanned hers. "Should I apologize?"

She shook her head. "There's no need. I…enjoyed what happened. We just can't take it further."

"Nothing I can do to persuade you?"

"No." As much as her sex wanted to deny her words, she couldn't. If they went further, he'd discover the state-of-the-art padding, which disguised her true shape. One look at her trim torso, and he'd know exactly who she was.

His lids came down to cover his eyes. "Well, see you around then." He turned to leave her.

Even a man as big as Balt didn't like to be rejected. And for whatever reason, she couldn't leave it like this. Not with him.

Against her better judgment, she went after him. "Wait, Balt." She approached him, taking his hands in hers. "It's not you."

"Yeah. Right."

"I don't...have my heartstone." That wasn't a lie. It didn't rest around her neck. It was back in her quarters. "Sex would be dangerous for you." Again, not a lie. With Ansel after her, intercourse would be dangerous for him. But Balt would take her words another way. She couldn't tell him the truth. But at least she could give him this small piece of reasoning so he didn't think it was him. If only things were different...

His eyes looked rueful. "Yeah, I know. No fucking those without heartstones. Wasn't thinking."

Somehow it made her body clench to know he'd forgotten such a vital rule. Of course, if she truly didn't have her heartstone, her reaction would have been different. The touching wouldn't have thrilled her so much. Or made her clit pulse in time to her heart. But he didn't realize just how much their embrace had affected her. "It's O.K. I enjoyed it as much as I could." Again, not a lie. She had, except for the bad things hanging over her head.

"Good." He waved an arm. "Need more help digging?"

"Nah. I think I'm going to quit for today." She tidied up her tools.

"Besela?"

"Yes?" She turned to face him.

"Hurry up and find that heartstone."

She watched his retreating back. A soft sigh escaped her lips. Balt was dangerous to her in more ways than one. So was Orion. The sooner she left this rock, the better.

* * *

Long after his meeting, Orion tossed back a shot of Tenaglian whisky. He'd come looking for Besela for an update on their arrangement, but she hadn't been at work yet. His disappointment at her not being there took him by surprise. Somehow, his emotion wasn't because he wouldn't get a report on Balt, but because he had wanted to see her. Especially after their earlier encounter. That was unexpected. He needed to focus on his difficult case, not some female.

Nothing made sense about this whole scenario. He'd combed the mine from one end to the other and still was empty handed.

From all accounts, the woman he was after had few resources and little knowledge of how to successfully evade capture. It wasn't as if she was a trained Union Alliance spy. He lacked something, though, some knowledge of her that must be vital, or they'd have found her by now.

Had Ansel held something back? That was likely. But what was it?

He had a list of females who hadn't been at the mine long— a list of possible Laylas that grew shorter every hour as he eliminated every female he checked on.

One name kept showing up when others talked about newcomers to Settler's Mine.

Besela.

No, it couldn't be her. Layla hadn't had enough at her disposal to change herself as much as it would have taken to look like Besela. And, she'd be lying low, not working in the main Settler's Mine bar.

But why hadn't either of them found such an easy mark yet?

The picture he had of Layla's actual face wasn't the best. Why didn't Ansel have more to go on about this woman? Ansel had much at his disposal. Why hadn't he given Orion her Union Alliance files? Ansel had access to everything.

Maybe Orion should ask him, or use his own Union Alliance contacts to run a check on the woman.

Something about this case had started chafing him in all the wrong places, but he couldn't point a finger to why. He peered into his glass. No answer there.

"Drinking that ratgut again?" Balt's voice boomed in the quiet bar. He took the seat across from Orion. "You do like poisoning yourself."

Sometimes a good argument helped Orion focus on cases. The sight of Balt sitting with him didn't annoy him as it usually did. "It doesn't affect me. Why don't you try some?" Orion couldn't remember if Tenaglian whisky affected Amadors or not. Would be interesting and perhaps painful for Balt to find out. Blisters could range from small to huge after drinking the real fire water.

"Ha."

A waitress ambled over to the table. "May I get you a..."

"Tequila."

"Yes, sir." She headed for the bar at a fast pace, much faster than she'd traveled getting Orion's drink.

Orion took a long sip. "Any beads on Layla yet?"

Balt shook his head.

"Like you'd tell me."

"Hey, you're the one who asked."

The waitress set down Balt's drink in front of him. "Here you go, sir." He handed her some coin. Her fingers lingered over his, prolonging the contact.

Orion rolled his eyes at her obviousness. What was he, chopped ratgut?

"I'll be right back with your change."

"I'd like another..." But the woman had scooted away before the words were barely out of Orion's mouth.

"Haven't lost your touch with the females, I see." Balt chuckled, saluting him with the glass.

Orion regarded Balt as the waitress ran back over to give him change. Her hand lingered again, passing the money to him. Balt didn't even blink or show he'd noticed the woman's attention.

Orion's eyes narrowed as the waitress left them with a sullen look on her face. That couldn't have just happened. Balt turned down an obvious interest? "Did you become a eunuch since the last time we were together?"

"Huh?" Balt threw back the tequila shot.

Orion waved a hand toward the waitress who now served other customers. "You were being hit on." As he always was. Women gravitated for Balt. Damn irritatingly often, in fact.

"Was I?" Balt's gaze sought out the waitress only to come back to Orion. He shrugged his massive shoulders.

"You're telling me you didn't notice this?"

"Right."

"That's bull. I've never seen you not pursue a female to screw when she seeks you out. Bloody hell, I figured you'd be screwing her on the table before I left, after her fingers kept touching yours." And Orion couldn't help looking down at those thick fingers. How long and broad they were. His eyes quickly drew up before Balt noticed.

"The bar maybe. Not the table. It might break."

Orion leaned back, folding his arms across his chest. "You have another female in mind for that little scenario. You have a woman who interests you." Balt had never focused on one woman before. Who was the woman?

"Maybe so many women come after me, I've stopped noticing."

"Bloody hell. Not likely. You are not the Casanova of space."

"The what?"

"Goddess, you didn't hear a lot of the old legends. A male who liked to screw females."

Balt grinned. "Sure sounds like me." His gaze shifted to the glass by the doors at the front of the bar. And, his face went slack. He stared, watching something or someone in the corridor.

Orion quickly turned around, partially standing to see. A familiar looking head walked the other way. Dark hair sat above bouncing ass. Besela. His libido perked up as it always seemed to when she was around. His mouth twitched down into a frown as he retook his seat.

Balt didn't notice. His attention remained focused on the moving form.

Orion's plan had worked. Balt was now taken with Besela. His chest constricted unexpectedly. This should make him thrilled. Instead, something broke open inside of him. He managed to spit out, "So, that's where your mind is."

"Huh?"

"Besela." This shouldn't bother him at all. But a part of him had tensed up at the other man's interest, and the even odder thing was, not as much as usual when he found himself interested in a female. Kurlans were a possessive race. If his interest in Besela had the strength it did right now, something he'd not expected, any other man's speculation would make them subject to his wrath. Only that wasn't happening with Balt. Why was that?

"What do you mean?"

"She walked by and you about broke your neck to see her. I thought I was going to have to put you in traction, your neck moved so fast."

"So? I can appreciate a fine piece of ass when it walks by." Balt's eyes drifted again and widened. "Fuck." He got up and ran for the door.

Orion's gaze looked to where Balt's had gone and hurried to his feet to follow him. He'd rounded the corner of the deserted corridor of the mine when his heart pounded at what he saw. Redness pooled in his vision.

A man had Besela by the throat up against a wall.

* * *

Balt stalked over to where the man had Besela pinned. His heart hammered in his chest much as it had been since he'd seen the man come up to Besela, grab her arm, and force her into this shaft. If this stranger hurt the waitress, Balt would kill him. Someone who he'd only known for a few hours was in trouble but it conjured up a before unknown surge of protectiveness.

Before he could grab the man to pull him off, one of the man's hands left Besela to pull a phaser and aim it straight at Balt.

Balt stopped a foot away from the outstretched hand. The safety had been cut off, and the weapon had been set to high. Aimed right at Balt's chest, it would do some damage, especially to an Amador. Brave but no fool, Balt needed a plan.

"Get your hands off of her." He growled to back up the words, already plotting how he could get around the gun.

"Jerk off."

Balt cocked his head to the side. "What did you say to me?" His hands clenched at Besela's whimper. "Let her go." The words gritted through teeth that snapped together so tightly they might break. He wanted to lunge, get the man's hands off her. No one could touch her this way and get away with it.

"Jerk off. Cocksucker. This is between me and the lady." His large hand tightened on Besela's throat.

Balt's eyes narrowed. Out of the corner of them, he saw Orion's approach in the man's blind side. Balt nodded to him show he saw him.

Orion mouthed, "Distract him."

"Take your hands off her. Or I will pulverize you." Balt flexed his arm muscles, mostly to keep the man's attention on him so Orion could sneak up.

"Balt." Besela's voice sounded hoarse from the constriction to her throat. "Leave. I'm fine." She couldn't see Orion in the position she was in, which was a good way to keep the advantage of surprise. They would only have a split second to take control of the situation without getting themselves or Besela shot.

"No." Balt's mouth set in a firm line. No fucking way were they leaving her to fend for herself. The fool would pay for his assault on the woman.

Orion tapped the man's shoulder. The man swung his head to the side Orion was on, and Balt grabbed the gun and knocked it away before the man could react. The man released Besela just as both of them hit him at the same time in different places. He went to the ground from the shock of both blows.

Stunned, he shook his head, clearing it. "You two fucktards screwed up now. I'll have your asses for lunch over this."

"Try it." Balt and Orion spoke the same words at the same time. They'd never worked together before this way. Usually, they were too busy trying to steal the other's bounty. However, that had gone rather well.

The man went to pull something from his black vest.

Both of them scrambled toward him.

"Hands in the air where I can see them." Orion pulled his own weapon, aiming it right at the man's face.

"I'm getting out my badge, you assholes."

Orion's head came up as Balt spoke. "Badge?" Fuck. That didn't sound good. Balt's legs shifted apart. A man with a badge shouldn't be taking advantage of Besela this way. Anger bubbled up in him again erupting in another large growl.

Besela rubbed her throat. "I told you to leave me. He's the security chief on Settler's Mine."

"And, now, you two stupid asses are going to pay. For doing this to me." He lurched to his feet, smoothing down his vest. His leering at Besela made Balt want to knock him back down again. "Guess you'll be paying me double, Besela. Protection and bailing out the sad sacks. Told you, you should have paid me earlier."

Paid me earlier? Even worse than Balt had originally thought. The man had been trying to get protection payment out of Besela. Coronians were a calm, peaceful race. The asshole had been taking advantage of her instinctual non-aggressive personality.

Orion and Balt moved as one toward the man, who backed up to the wall he'd had Besela up against. "You two stay back. I'm going to cart you both to a cell. Don't make it worse on yourselves."

"You listen good, little man. To every word." Orion's teeth gritted together. "You touch her again. Talk to her again. Bloody hell, even look at her again. I'll be having your body put into a cast with traction. I swear it, by Goddess."

"And, whatever he doesn't break, I will. I bet I could separate your nuts from your body." Balt grinned without humor. "Or, at least I could have fun trying." Oh yeah, it would be fun trying. He almost wanted the man to try moving to Besela again now. But the sad sack never would. He was a coward at heart.

"I'm going to stick you both in a hole. You'll never get out again." The man pulled a knife. "You'll wish you'd never laid eyes on me by the time I'm done with you. You'll beg me to get out. Your lady friend will, too. I think I'll take her in front of your cell. With a peglight."

Now, Besela growled, but a pale imitation of Balt's own sound. Peglights were long cylindrical lights used in mining. They could go into holes to illuminate them and run a camera feed back to the user. One would more than likely tear a woman from the inside out.

Balt rumbled an incoherent noise from his chest as he took another step toward the stout man.

The man's breath came as if it were a thundering herd, bringing with it a scent of unwashed socks.

Balt could tear the man's throat out. Orion would help.

A horrible noise, which pierced all their ears, sounded. They all fell to their knees, holding their heads. Even the hawk-eyed security chief.

The sound turned off. "Now that I have your attention, what the fuck is going on here?" Zelda stalked toward them from the entrance to the corridor. Her high-heeled boots clicked on the stone.

"Zelda." The man struggled to his feet. "They attacked me. I was about to put them all in lockdown."

Her eyebrow quirked up. "Oh?"

Balt and Orion both reached their feet at the same time. And both offered a hand to Besela. They stared at each other, arms outstretched.

Balt shook his head. This was different. They were both on the same side. Somehow that seemed oddly right.

Besela took both their hands to stand.

"Is that so, Chumsky?" Zelda swept around them. "Orion? Balt? I told you to stay out of trouble." Her eyes softened and fixed on Besela. "Besela, what happened?"

"She's a lying bitch." Chumsky wiped his face with a shaking hand. "I've found evidence she's been up to no good. I came to question her on it. She..."

Zelda held up a hand. "I asked Besela. Speak again out of turn, and I'll turn on the sounder again."

Besela hesitated, taking a deep breath. "Zelda, he was hitting me up for protection. He wanted sex in exchange for his care. Because I'm alone here. He said he could make sure nothing happened to me while I was here, if I paid him. If I didn't, he said, 'Who knows what could happen'?" She took a step away from Orion and Balt. "They saw him...with his hands on me. They defended me." Her voice sounded shocked.

Course, she was no more shocked about their defense of her than Balt, because he and Orion had done some good teamwork.

"Chumsky, this is the second report like this I've had. It's enough for me. Get your things. You're out."

"You can't do that! I'm your only security chief. Settler's Mine needs one, or..."

"Bren and I will handle it just fine." She gave Chumsky a scathing look. "Keep on protesting. I'll toss you off without a ship."

Chumsky's lips pursed tightly together. His eyes screamed with indignity.

If only they'd gotten a chance to smack him around a little more. How many other loners had Chumsky done this to? Besela could have been hurt if no one had been around to protect her. Of course, anyone but Zelda would have let them get away with it by looking the other way or taking a cut.

Zelda appraised Besela. "I'm sorry about this. Next time, talk to me. I hope you listen to my advice much better than you shared."

"I…" Her head bobbed up and down. "I did listen."

Zelda shuffled Chumsky out of the corridor despite his babbling..

The three stood there in awkward silence until Besela broke it. "Thank you both. You took a risk. He could have had you thrown in jail."

She approached Orion, who leaned down, and she placed a kiss on his cheek. His hand came up as she walked away to touch where her lips had.

Balt leaned down, and she kissed his cheek as well. It burned. His cock engorged, reminding him of the kiss to her neck earlier.

She left the two of them standing there.

Orion blew out a deep breath as he watched Besela walk away.

Balt nodded. Nothing needed to be said.

"You know?" Orion walked to the entrance as Balt followed. "We made a pretty good team."

They did. But damn if he'd say it out loud. "Don't let it go to your head. I'm still going to get Layla first."

Orion snickered as Balt joined in laughing. "Dream on, big man. Dream on."

Chapter Four

Orion drummed his fingers on the metal table as he waited for Tony, the mine's tool salesman. He ignored a few irritated stares for his drumming.

Not that Layla needed a heartstone as she already had hers, but maybe her disguise had prompted her to hide her status of having one. Not something a Native, or anyone else, would usually do because of their fierce traditions, but if she were as desperate as Ansel said she was, she might. Those who dug for heartstone often needed tools.

Tony arrived on time for the meeting.

Orion ordered himself and the Octavian a drink. Drinks could sometimes loosen lips. "Thank you for meeting with me." Usually he'd schmooze some more before getting to the subject at hand, but he didn't have it in him today. "I'm looking for a woman. Maybe you've seen her coming to buy tools?" Orion displayed the blurry close up of her face on his viewer. "Have you noticed any females new to Settler's Mine? She'd be a recent arrival. Could you give me a list of names?"

Tony stared stonily at the picture as if memorizing the features. "Nawp. Haven't seen that one. I told that other fella that, too."

"What other fella?"

"The big one. With the green hair."

Orion cursed softly under his breath as their drinks arrived. Balt had already been to question Tony. Had Balt found out anything? No, he must not have, or he'd have Layla in hand and be crowing to Orion about it.

"As for new females, I've had several come to see me. I am the biggest supplier of tools on the mine. Those who need, I give." He enunciated each word and spoke with the speed of a space slug. He flipped a book open. "Let's see what we have here. Tundry." A Barbosan and not Layla. "Seione." An Amador and not Layla. "Carn." A Sicilian and not Layla.

As Tony droned the names of every female that Orion had already checked out, he continued to drum his fingers as if he could speed up the man's slow speech. "And Besela. She's a waitress at the bar. She didn't come to see me right away though. Took her time getting her tools and digging."

"How about men? Could you give me a list of those new to the station?" Layla might have changed more than her appearance to evade detection. He'd caught a woman disguised as a Barbosian male in a case earlier in the year. His face scrunched. She'd made a pretty unattractive male for a man who liked his men brawny.

The droning began again with a list of names he'd already heard many times before. All the men he'd checked out had been verified as male. None of the people mentioned had been the one person he sought. So much for a new name being tossed out.

Orion stopped drumming and got to his feet. This had been a waste of time. "Thanks for your time. Drink's on me." That should smooth over any lost schmoozing time.

Tony saluted him with the almost full glass of brandy.

Orion headed back to his quarters. This investigation had headed to exactly nowhere. He'd gotten no closer to finding Layla than he had been after arriving at the mine, despite doing lots of questioning.

What had he missed?

There had to be something.

In his small quarters, he sat down on the bunk and looked at all his scribbles from questioning people and the notations he'd made before arriving. Her arrival couldn't have been any earlier than a day, or any later than his arrival, because Orion knew when she'd left bound for the Mine. He might not have known her exact shuttle, but the times she could have left had been verified.

He'd been monitoring flights on and off of Settler's Mine through acquaintances. No one had arrived and immediately taken back off so Layla hadn't left. She had to still be on Settler's Mine.

One name kept popping up. One that he hadn't investigated.

Besela.

Hell, even the teeth didn't match. Layla had pearled-up whites, and Besela's teeth had the dinginess of a Coronian.

There are mouthpieces.

But, where would Layla get such a thing? Plus, to speak with prosthesis in, one had to practice a lot or have an obvious speech impediment. Besela spoke normally with no lisp or stutter.

And Besela. She's a waitress at the bar. She didn't come to see me right away though. Took her time.

Tony's words struck him now that he had time to mull things over. Maybe visiting Tony hadn't been a waste of time. He scratched his head.

Why would Besela not have started digging right away for her heartstone? Why wait? That behavior didn't check with everything else he knew. Anyone, especially someone of her age, would be frantic to find their heartstone. So why didn't she act more desperate? Why wasn't her every waking moment spent searching for it?

It wasn't much of an oddity, but right now, he'd take any lead, no matter how small it seemed.

Perhaps it was time to stop ignoring what stared him in the face, despite his attraction to the woman, and eliminate her with detective work and not speculation. Sometimes hiding in the open worked better than hiding in the shadows.

He didn't want Layla to be Besela.

Didn't want to deliver her to Ansel.

His hands clenched.

Perhaps it was time to check on Besela, and see if he could find answers to his questions. He had to know for sure.

* * *

Balt watched as Orion hurried past him. *Hmm. Where's the little bastard going?* He got up to follow. Time to pump him for information anyway. How much time did Balt have before Orion came to the same conclusions he had? Orion might be a pain in the ass but the Kurlan had a head about him. He'd have to be quick to stay one step ahead, so he collected the reward and not Orion.

"So what's up?" Balt fell into step beside the marching bounty hunter, matching his quick pace.

Orion glared at him as he slowed down. "Ceiling? The moon? The asteroid belt beyond the overshoot?"

"Funny guy."

"Don't you have an elsewhere to be?"

"Not really."

Orion blew out a breath. "Well, if you're going to simply annoy me by your presence, have you got any new leads?"

The answer was, of course, not yes but maybe. Balt couldn't tell Orion exactly what he suspected. The only lead he had made no sense. However, when smacked across the face with what was right in front of you, either you either eliminated it or came to believe it. Besela's name had come up one too many times from one too many people. How much did Orion suspect the pretty little waitress? That was a question that needed answering, but without revealing anything of what Balt himself suspected, it would be tricky. "No. How 'bout you?"

"No."

The man lied. Balt couldn't fault him. He'd lied, too. "Then where are you heading?"

"To the bar for a drink." Orion said it a bit too smoothly. That had not been where he'd been going when he'd started out. Another lie.

"I'll join you." Balt better keep Orion in his sights so Orion didn't move one step ahead of him in the game they always played. He couldn't help but smile in amusement. This would piss Orion off. Always a good way to spend some time.

An expression of irritation moved across Orion's face, but he didn't say anything, walking slower than ever. Even more evidence Orion had been headed somewhere different but changed direction when Balt had asked.

They walked to the bar.

Orion grabbed a table near the entrance. His eyes drifted to the bar.

Desire rolled through them both. Balt didn't have to look at Orion for his reaction.

Fuck, no one had ever affected Balt this way.

The woman bent to get something from the floor. Damn, but no one without a heartstone should make his heart beat like this.

A quick glimpse confirmed Orion had a hard-on as well.

That increased Balt's response, to know the Kurlan was turned on, too. He blew out a breath. That shouldn't be happening.

They both took their seats.

"So are we buds now? Sharing drinks together?" Orion broke the short silence as he arched a brow. "We going to get all chummy?"

"Hell, no. I'm just wondering what you're up to." He spoke a truth, which Orion wouldn't believe.

"Who says I'm up to anything?"

"Me."

"And you're the damn expert on me now?"

"Fuck, yeah. I am on everything. Haven't you learned that by now?"

They bantered back and forth until Besela wiggled her way over with two glasses. "One Tenaglian whisky and one tequila." She smiled as she set them down on the table with a soft clink.

"Thank you." Balt nodded in appreciation to Besela. "You're good." He'd like to know how good she tasted. He'd had a sip but he wanted a full appreciation of her. Only she might be the woman he'd come here to collect. He frowned. He still didn't see how that could be. But he'd find out. Then what? If she was, he'd have to deliver her to Ansel. Ansel didn't want the woman to come play a game of skill or for some fun. There had to be bad reasons why Ansel had put out the bounty on her head. Could he deliver her for that? No, one step at a time. He didn't know the beauty was anything but a simple Coronian yet.

"Goddess, she is, isn't she?" Orion took a drink from his glass. "She remembered mine after the second time."

"Remembered mine after the first time. I'm unforgettable." Balt's grin moved back on his face as he leaned back in his seat. "And irresistible."

Orion let out a loud snort. "No, she's got eyes. And a brain, which works, unlike most of your…conquests." The latter word was said with disdain. Did Balt detect a note of jealousy? No, he read too much into the comment.

"Beautiful eyes. Did I mention you have beautiful eyes?"

"That she does." Orion's gaze sought hers. "Eyes like diamonds that glow under a winter moon, love."

Balt rolled his eyes. Leave it to the faded out Union Alliance man to get all wordy. He could say in two words what it took Orion nine to say. He should use that mouth for better things than talking. Balt shifted in his seat, his heavy cock uncomfortable. He must be reacting this way to Besela. No way could any of his desire be for the Kurlan.

Besela didn't flush from any of the compliments. "You're not getting out of paying your bill by flattering me." Her mouth hooked up into a grin revealing her light brown teeth. Typical of a Coronian. And, not a Native. But, why did her name keep coming up? Nothing made any sense any more.

"Wouldn't think of it." Orion drank the rest of his whisky as he settled his bill. After he'd finished, he mouthed, "Keep the change, love."

Balt did the same, paying for the tequila and giving her a generous tip. She rewarded them both with an upturn of her lips.

As she walked back to the bar both sets of eyes followed her.

Damn. How could they both be interested in the same woman? That made even less sense than his investigations. Balt mulled it over as he looked down into his glass. They had such different tastes. What was it about this one that had them both in a knot?

Orion got to his feet.

Balt did, too.

"Leaving? You haven't even finished your drink yet." Orion's voice deepened as he shifted foot to foot.

Balt shrugged and tipped the entire glass back to drink it in one large swallow. The burn raced down his throat into his stomach to sit there.

"I'm heading for my quarters. I'm going to review some notes." Orion shrugged. "Try to figure out where Layla is. I have several leads." He scratched his chin where some fuzzy hair had grown. "Shave, too."

Not likely his quarters were his true destination. What was he up to? Balt had to find out. "I think I'll head for my bunk, too. Do the same."

Orion suspected something or someone.

After they parted, he planted himself near Orion's quarters to spy. So far, the man hadn't reappeared.

A tug at the back of his leather coat made him pause. Besela? His head swiveled around to look.

No, a boy stood there with a dirty face and wild hair.

Balt frowned in disappointment. "What?"

"You want lady with purple eyes? I take you to her. One ream of platinum. Up front."

Balt stared in the kid's greedy, piercing eyes. *Well, fuck me frankly.*

* * *

Orion slithered down the corridor toward Besela's quarters as he glanced furtively all around him, even into the dark corners of the long access hallway. No Balt anywhere that he could spot. The Amador couldn't exactly hide well or blend in. Good, his strategy had worked. Annoying son-of-a-bitch was out of the way for a spell.

The boy he'd hired should keep Balt busy long enough for Orion to do some snooping on his own. Having grown up a street urchin himself, Balt had a soft spot for boys trying to make platinum. Orion had never used the tactic before, but desperate times called for desperate measures.

A grin graced his face. How he loved to one-up the Amador.

Besela was still working at the bar. He'd checked on her from outside the establishment before he'd headed this way, being careful she didn't spot him. She'd be on another hour at least before her shift ended, or so he remembered of her schedule.

Arriving at her door, he pulled a lock pick from his pocket. He carefully clicked the lock open and slipped inside. The pick he used worked on most any door lock, even these. Zelda had put in good security measures for her settlers, more than most outposts did, but there were always ways around them.

Before closing the door softly behind him, he did one last check around. He didn't see anyone around, so no prying eyes to report back to Besela that she had an intruder. Especially if the suspicions he had could be proved wrong, she'd best not find out he'd been snooping around her things. Women didn't like that.

Turning around, he surveyed her small and tidy quarters. No clothing lay strewn on the floor. No remnants from any meals or plates lay around. Even her bed had been made before she'd left her quarters. *Aren't you a neat one?*

Her scent pervaded her space. He inhaled it. This was where she lived. Where she slept. Got undressed. Fire ran through his blood. May he come back there soon on a more pleasant treasure hunt.

He blew out a breath about what he might find there. What did he want to find? He wasn't sure.

He started looking through the few things she owned. He found nothing personal. Found nothing more interesting than her

underwear drawer in the small standard dresser, much the same as
the one in his own room. It did contain her intimate apparel and
nothing untoward. He kept his hands off of them, though he
wanted to finger and touch. Maybe soon, he'd get to touch while
they were on her, much more to his liking than the cool material
lying in her drawer.

Nothing in these quarters indicated she was more than
Besela, Coronian waitress in search of her heartstone.

He smiled as his gaze moved around the room. Relief
flooded him. He didn't want her to be Layla. He wanted her to be
the woman who'd find her heartstone, then screw him silly. Being
Layla would complicate his life a little too much.

He inhaled as he stood in the center of the small room,
taking in her scent again. He enjoyed filling his nostrils with it.
She smelled as if she were a succulent treat. One that he could eat
all day long and never grow tired of the taste. His heart beat faster
and his blood pumped as if it had caught on fire. Heat rushed
through him. She wasn't even there and look at the reactions she
could cause in him.

His eyes turned toward the bed as his thoughts went to
sharing it with Besela. A little small, so it would involve lots of
closeness. He could handle that.

Bloody hell.

He hadn't checked there in his search. Little could hide on
or in such a small piece of furniture, but he'd better be sure.

He took two steps and began patting the small bed down.
Nothing had been placed under or in the pillow. Nothing existed
under or in the covers that shouldn't be there. He got down on his
knees to peer under the bed-frame. Nothing but a slight coating of
dust covered the rock floor. *Good.*

Then, his fingers slipped under the side of the mattress as he hefted it up on its side to look underneath. A small, purple velvet box lay in the center between the mattress and support board.

He reached over to pick it up gingerly. He slid the mattress back into place. The box probably contained a piece of jewelry or a memento. Something special she didn't want stolen, which explained why it had been tucked away under the mattress. Theft could be widespread on the outposts. At Settler's Mine, Zelda kept crime to a minimum with her harsh laws and punishments. Still, it never paid to be too careful. Besela was all about that. He could tell from the way she kept her quarters..

He checked the time. He'd been in there a while so time was getting short on how much longer he could stay without getting caught. *Check this out, put it back, make the bed and get out.*

He flipped up the lid. And stared.

A heartstone on a silver chain rested in the center of the box.

He'd seen enough heartstones to know one when he saw it. She had her heartstone already. His eyes closed after a momentary view.

Bloody hell.

Why would she lie? This didn't gel with her story of being a Coronian in search of her heartstone. Hiding one's stone wasn't done. It was such an honor to find the piece of your heart, no one hid them from view.

This could mean she was Layla. What would he do if she was? Never had a woman intrigued him as she had. And, Ansel wanted her for dark things. Orion had no doubts about that. What would Orion do—what could he do—against that?

Warmth spread quickly across his chest.

He quickly opened his eyes. His gaze shifted downward. The first thing that caught his eye made his breath stop before blowing quickly from his nose.

The heartstone in the box had started a pulsing, green glow. He fingered the rock, warm to the touch. How could it be glowing?

His head came down to look at the stone in the center of the looped rope around his own neck.

A greenish glow emanated from it with a pulse in time with Besela's. The warmth he'd felt had been his own heartstone.

Once heartstones had claimed a person for their own, only one reason existed for them to glow again.

To claim another of Quatar descent as a mate.

Besela was his heartmate.

His mouth had dried out completely. He breathed deeply and slow. His heart pounded even more than before. He'd never believed he'd find his mate. Never. And now, in the most unlikely of places, he had. He'd found the one who completed him. His body flooded with emotion and lust. By Goddess, he'd found her, not even knowing he'd looked. Everything he'd ever thought about heartstones fell away when faced with the knowledge he had a mate to claim.

No wonder he'd lusted after her. First would come the desire and then would come the emotion to back it up. That was the way of the heartstone.

"What the hell are you doing in my quarters?"

He didn't jump at the voice. He hadn't heard the door open. He'd been so preoccupied staring down at the joined stones. Her approach had ignited the heartstones. Turning, he faced Besela, who had an angry look on her face.

The anger died, turning to an unknown emotion as he held up her heartstone next to his. "Apparently, I was finding my mate."

Chapter Five

Layla looked at the glowing stones Orion held in his hand. Tried to stay calm. "No. This can't be."

"It is, Besela. You're my mate. The stones don't lie." He moved closer to her. "They pulse in time to the other. Feel them." He offered his hand with her stone lying on the palm as if to touch her with the stone. The one around his neck matched its glow and pulse. Green. They both had green glowing heartstones.

"Don't touch me." She pulled away as he reached out to her. She moved further into the small quarters, hugging her middle. The mattress lay on the bed as if nothing had touched it. But he had, just as he'd touched her stone. Her breath came raggedly. He stood there now with heartstones that glowed. *Glowed.* How could this be? She couldn't have a mate now.

Her arms came around to fold across her chest. "What are you doing in here?"

"Why did you hide your heartstone?"

"I...had to. You were snooping! You went through my things." Her anger grew at the violation of her things. A good way not to focus on the mate standing before her. "How dare you."

"It doesn't matter." Orion shook his head as though he couldn't comprehend the news himself. "It doesn't matter what I did, love. We're mates."

Her anger faded. "I can't...no, this...I can't be mated to anyone." The danger would be too great. Orion had now been placed in her life, but at what cost to him? Dammit, he didn't even know what this meant. She tried to call back her anger at his breaking into her rooms. But all she could see was his warm eyes.

"Besela. You can and are. To me." His voice took on a hard line. "We can't deny what the stones say. What they've fated us to be. Mates. Goddess, whatever problems you have. They're now mine." He took a step closer, edging forward even more as she didn't walk away. "Or, should I call you Layla now?"

Her eyes met his. No surprise he'd figured out who she really was. She moistened her dry lips. Did he even know what her being Layla and his mate meant for him? Who she was would destroy him. No, she couldn't let that happen. "Yes. I'm Layla. And that's why we can never be." She laughed, the sound brittle to her own ears. "You know why. Ansel won't stop. He'll keep coming. And he hired you to bring me to him. He'll be after you for not doing your..."

His hand touched her bare arm.

Electrical currents raced up her flesh. She shuddered from the ratchet of desire. "We'll face it together."

The desperation grew. To be in his arms. To be held as no one else had ever held her because he was her mate. Why shouldn't she want this so badly it hurt? But, like everything else she'd ever wanted, she couldn't have the simple feat of his arms around her. "No."

"Yes."

And Orion did it. The unthinkable. He pulled her into his arms as she'd wanted. She couldn't resist. The warmth of his body enfolded her to seep its warmth into her bones. The strength of him captured her. His musky scent filled her nostrils. He smelled divine. The world slowed its spin and narrowed down to the man and woman in each other's arms. She snuggled her head into his warmth, breathing in his scent. Her hands clutched at his back.

His head dipped down. The first kiss he placed landed in the middle of her forehead. Then, he planted one on each eyelid, her nose, and each cheek. Feather light, they barely registered. Yet, the heat grew within her, magnified by a million slip streams of currents running through them both.

His head drew up, only to lower again. His lips met hers. Gently, he kissed her. His tongue traced the seam of her lips before parting it to gain entry. He explored her as if she was something he longed to eat. Some delicacy. She'd been kissed but never this way before. All she wanted was more. More of him. His touch. His mouth. His body. Everywhere and everything tingled with anticipation.

He maneuvered her back two steps, using his big body to guide her. Her back touched the cool stone wall.

The kisses grew more frantic. More frenzied.

Her thighs clenched together as moisture flowed.

His lips left hers to slowly nibble down her neck. It tickled, making her squirm. He put one hand on her hip, steadying her. The other hand directed her head up and to the side, giving him ample access to her neck.

She'd had no idea being with someone could tempt her, or that her throat could be so sensitive, only she had, hadn't she? With Balt. This was different, yet the same reactions bombarded her.

That scattered thought left her as Orion nibbled and laved his way to the hollow and back up again. She became lost in the sensations swamping her.

His hand left her throat to stroke down across her collar bone. When he cupped a breast, she gasped a little. He didn't move his hand, containing her firmly in his palm. His thumb passed across the top. She only felt pressure. The padding had a nipple so that if someone touched her, the breast felt real. But the covering didn't allow her to feel much. She longed to toss off her shirt and all the layers underneath to the floor, to have his hands on her bare skin.

His mouth moved away from her throat to whisper with a note of frustration, "You're wearing padding, aren't you, love?"

Her breath wouldn't come, but she nodded.

He moved further away, dropping contact with her. "Your hips? And a...butt? They are heavily padded, too."

She nodded again. "My whole pelvis and ass."

He sounded curious now. The bounty hunter had kicked in amid the desire. "Coloration?"

"Toner. It will wear off in a week or so if I don't reapply it."

"Contacts? To disguise your eyes?"

"Yeah."

"Your teeth?"

She put her thumb and pointer finger in her mouth behind her front teeth and popped off the prosthesis. She laid it on her palm and held it out for him to see.

He took a step back before he picked the mouth piece up from her hand to examine it closely. "How? How do you have all this stuff at your disposal? It's state of the art, or it wouldn't look real enough to fool anyone." He handed the mouthpiece back. "You don't even talk funny with this in."

She put it back in out of habit. He'd already busted her, but someone else could come barging in her door. "That's a long story. One you don't need to know now." Or ever. Tears pricked at her eyelids. Orion had no idea what he'd gotten himself mixed up in by the glowing of his whimsical stone. Her eyes sought out her heartstone. The necklace lay on the floor near their feet. She hadn't noticed he'd put it down. That he'd lost himself in her to put down the heartstone tugged at her emotions. Warmth filled her stomach. "Right now, just hold me."

It might be the only calm moment they had. Balt still pursued her, and Ansel was bound to send more looking for her. Not to mention, the Union Alliance would soon have its own skilled minions after her.

"I will. But I want to see you first, love." He swallowed. His throat worked up and down. "Without all the disguises."

"You want to see me?" She blinked.

He nodded. "The real you, Layla."

Did she even have a real her? That was a question to ponder later. "I can't do anything about the toner. That takes time to wear off." She had applied it everywhere in the rush to get away from Ansel. Why, she didn't know. She could have left the color off her middle. If anyone was close enough to see that, they'd see her padding so it didn't matter.

"I know. Take the rest of it off then."

"O.K." She moved to her dresser. After popping out the prosthesis again, she placed it in its container. She slowly took out her contacts, putting them in the solution to keep them stable. The long-wear lenses hadn't been out of her eyes since before Settler's Mine. There'd been no need. Until now.

Orion sat down on her bed.

She heard it creak. His eyes must be on her because she felt them as if they were burning a hole in her back. A shiver raced along her spine. He wanted to see her. She'd be naked for her mate for the first time. How would he react? Her heart pounded in nervousness.

Turning to face him, she pulled the tunic over her head. Her upper and lower body remained encased in the special padding.

His head shook back and forth as he examined her. "New technology."

She nodded and unfastened her pants. They'd been a prototype. Slowly, she lowered the pants down her legs. His eyes watched her the whole time. She shrugged off her boots and pants at the same time. Sucking in a breath, she unsnapped the padding. For it to conform to her body, the straps had to be cinched up tight. She peeled it from herself as if she were a bug or reptile shedding its skin before dropping it to the floor.

With it went all her disguise. She'd never felt more naked than she did at the moment she faced Orion. So few had seen her. She'd been disguised all her life. The heartstone meant she was supposed to strip everything bare before him. This was only the beginning.

Orion's nostrils flared. His eyes swept her up in some space gale that whirled and twirled her around.

"Except for the skin color and the short hair, this is me." Not that she'd ever get back the woman she'd been as the pale-skinned, long-haired Native. That woman, or girl, was already long gone. This one was so different. So jaded. But, he couldn't know that. Not yet. "I'm Layla."

"You're beautiful." His air rushed from his nose in one big exhale. "I never expected…this."

"You thought Besela was beautiful. I look very different than she did." How could he think both were beautiful? She ran a hand through her too short hair.

"Yes. Yes, I did think that Besela was beautiful." He got up and stalked to her side. "By the Goddess, Layla is exquisite."

Her throat burned with emotion that puttered down to her stomach and further below. "I…this…only because of the stones."

"No. It's not *only* because of them, love. I found you desirable as Besela because I liked your spirit. I still do, especially seeing how clever you are. That's the attraction, no matter how you look." He held a finger to her lips. "Don't talk. Let yourself feel. Me."

His hands lifted to run along her arms. The hairs on them set straight up as goose pimples erupted. One hand went the base of her neck to play in the shorn hair there. The other grasped her hip and brought her body close to him.

His hips thrust against her midsection. His erection pushed against her.

She could feel him so much more vividly than she had through all the padding. Her body tingled at how much he wanted her.

She wanted him, too.

Wanted him inside her.

This might be her only shot at experiencing him this way. Despite their new status as mates, she couldn't allow him to be brought into her life. But, she could be selfish, just this once. Let him love her with his body. Experience what it could be to have a mate. Then, she could leave him, secure in the knowledge she'd kept him safe. Ansel wouldn't kill him for not bringing her in, but he would for being Layla's mate.

"Orion." She brought up her hand to stroke his face. "I want to be with you."

"Be with me?" He stared down into her eyes. "Just so I don't misunderstand."

"I want you to have sex with me. Now."

* * *

Orion's blood boiled as if it were the fiery lava on the volcanic planets. "Yes." He attacked her mouth with a vengeance before pulling back to agree again. "Yes." He'd make Layla his with his body over and over again. Then, she'd accept and believe they were mated. He'd do anything in his power to protect her. The sentiment engulfing him shocked him. The stones' glow had opened up a part of him he hadn't known existed.

His lips plundered her sweet ones as one hand slid up the smooth skin of her stomach to cup a breast much as he had before. Only this time, when his thumb stroked across a nipple, her body shuddered. The uncontrolled reaction made his hand tremble with the enormous turn his life had taken.

His mate. He touched his living, breathing mate.

The being he'd never thought he'd find.

And he liked her, not only for her toned body, but because of the whole package. Such a thin but muscular woman hid under all those layers. He'd enjoyed her company long before the heartstones expressly fated them to be together. Soon he'd never be able to envision his life without her.

Even without looking, he knew the rocks that bound them together still glowed and pulsed, even separate as they were. He'd soon have her pulsing with need and want. He already did. His cock couldn't get any more turgid.

He flicked his thumb across her nipple again, before pressing down on it with the pad. He moved to ring circles around the super soft skin of the areola. She'd even used toner even here, so he didn't know their true color. But, one day, he'd find out. He'd bet a pale pink to go with the paleness of the rest of her.

He kissed her collarbone, nipping at the thin skin above it, before planting a string of kisses across the tops of her breasts. He moved his head down to barely touch one nipple with his tongue. Her body jerked in reaction. He eased the nipple into his mouth, slowly, pulling it in and out, tonguing her before slurping the tip completely in to suckle.

She moaned, her breath catching in her chest. "Orion."

He moved his head away and blew cool breath on it. She made wispy noises of abandon, which filled his ardor to the top.

As his mouth went to her other peak, the hand that had been on her breasts moved down to rest parallel against her stomach. What a flat tummy she had. The strong muscles tensed under her skin. Each little movement registered. All of her was toned and well defined.

His hand moved lower. Her stance widened as her legs moved apart. One finger moved into her slick wetness. His eyes closed briefly as she coated his fingers. He wanted to shove into her, to take her with his cock now, quick and furious. He'd grind down into her until they were one. Bloody hell, they were already one. They'd been mated.

No, this might be her first time with a man. And, it would be their first time together. She deserved more. She deserved it all. All the pleasure he could wring out of her body with his hands and mouth.

Orion gritted his teeth, searching for his control. For his mate, he would locate willpower and give her her due. He'd make it spectacular for Layla. Only then would he take his own pleasure. He couldn't wait to be fully encased inside the woman of his dreams.

His finger found her clit and slid it back and forth. Her body arched with more whimpering. He pinched it gently between two fingers, sliding it between them. After releasing it, his thumb pressed hard against the swollen flesh.

He looked behind her to the dresser. Looked sturdy enough. And it would put her pussy exactly where he wanted it. At face level. He wanted a taste of her so bad he could imagine the flavor.

He lifted her up to sit on the dresser's top.

Her purple eyes stared back at him curiously. They mesmerized him with their candor and depth. No wonder she'd needed contacts. Her eyes revealed everything inside and more. Knowing her would make reading her eyes easier. And that might take a lifetime. What a wonderful way to spend it.

"I'm putting you where I want you." He grinned at her, positioning her with her mound near to the front of the dresser.

"I want you inside of me." Her voice took on a plaintive note as did her whole entire face. She touched his jaw again. "Even you aren't that flexible or large enough to take me here. I'm too high up."

"I'll take you. Don't worry about that. But, all in good time, love."

"We don't have time. Do it now."

He pushed her thighs apart. "Sure we do." And he lowered his head to push into her pussy.

Her breathing hitched. "Orion."

Instead of answering, his tongue swept up to lick her before going all the way down. He found the little sensitive piece of flesh his fingers had located earlier. He worked it over and over with his tongue, moving it up and down by flicking it, before sucking it into his mouth.

Her slick folds captured his fingers as they entered her. Gently, he pushed one finger inside, into her molten depths. He wiggled it around while moving in and out as he would with his cock when the time came.

Orion set a furious pace with his tongue while keeping his finger at a much slower thrust. Layla's hips bucked.

He added a second finger to glide inside his willing woman. Her walls tightened around him. She was tight, but no virgin. This foreplay would make it easier to enjoy their first time together. He would still take her slowly. Wanted to give her everything and more.

Her swollen sex rubbed against him with each thrust of her hips. He could smell nothing but the sweet scent of her arousal, which now coated him completely.

The third finger entered her. She was much tighter around him. Did she want more? Another finger. His cock. His hand slipped in her wetness. She wanted it all. He'd give it to her. First, he'd seal their bond with sex. Then they'd learn to be together. It was the way of the stones.

His tongue and teeth continued their relentless assault on her clit. Her hips lifted even further off the dresser.

As the fourth finger entered her, she keened, her entire body tensing. She batted herself against him, trying to work out the sensations inside of her. Her channel almost tightened around his fingers to where he couldn't draw them out. She tried to milk them, drawing out every last throb of her climax.

As it swirled to an end, his assault turned furious again. He sped up the pace of his mouth, while being slow with the fingers contained in her. He varied the motions, keeping her on edge by not knowing what he'd do next.

She rewarded him with a second orgasm. A cry of his name and the tensing all over again told him.

"Dammit, Orion." Her throaty speech came from a panting mouth. "You're trying to kill me."

He pulled away his mouth from her glistening sex. "No. The opposite. I want to make you live." Making her feel more alive than she'd ever been would be the best thing he'd ever done.

He resumed his ministrations of both fingers and mouth, bringing her to a third peak of pleasure.

Her breath soughed through her open mouth. "Please. No more. Can't take...I want you. Your cock. Inside."

Now, she'd be ready for him. "Yes." He pulled out his fingers. He looked up into those wonderful expressive eyes of hers.

"My mate. I will do whatever you wish. I will please you over and over again."

She groaned.

Before he could move to take her off the dresser, his com went off. "Answer, you fucking, asshole worm." Balt's voice boomed into Layla's quarters.

Bloody hell.

Orion closed his eyes, lifting his head to place it against her chest. Balt had the worst timing ever. If Orion didn't answer, Balt would continue to yell at him. Not exactly a romantic setting for taking your mate for the first time. He could turn it off, but Balt would still come looking for him. Ten to one, the other bounty hunter could track his com's signal even with it off. He could break the communicator into bits, but then no one would be able to contact him until it had been fixed, and he didn't have a spare. Balt would still come looking for him, and Orion's interest in Besela hadn't been hidden. Once checking his room, Balt would head here. The Amador would barge in and interrupt them anyway. Orion was screwed instead of screwing.

Maybe he could talk the huge man down.

"Sorry, love, I have to take this, or he'll come here." He grabbed his com and put it near his ear. "What? I'm a little busy right now. Can't this wait?"

"You pissant. You sent me on a fool's chase all afternoon. I'm looking for you, and when I find ya, I'll show you what for."

Orion shook his head. "Balt, I really can't talk right now..."

"You'll fucking talk to me when I'm bashing your head in."

Orion shot a smile to Layla to reassure her. Balt talked trash this way a lot. He didn't mean half of it. Oh, he'd make Orion pay but wouldn't really hurt him.

"Oh, and by the way, I think I know who Layla is. You'd never guess her identity in a million parsecs. I think she's been right under our noses. You're going to flip your lid if I'm right."

Chapter Six

"Bloody hell." Orion pulled back from Layla as the com shut off. Balt had broken the connection.

Layla bit her lip. Her body and senses screamed at the interruption. Her body trembled from everything that happened. Her body missed his against it. She cursed herself. The relationship could never be, so this was for the best. She could have none of it, beyond this one little thing. The Fates laughed at her as usual. She'd never gotten anything she'd ever wanted. Why should now be any different?

Even as Balt had taken away her one time with Orion, he'd given her an avenue of escape. She'd have to content herself with this point of pleasure. Forever. Of all the things she regretted, the one she longed for the most was tasting him. She'd wanted her tongue to explore every centimeter and every crevice of his body, especially those hard parts, which had been against her. "What's wrong?"

"Balt has an idea who Layla is." Orion wiped off his mouth with one hand. His mouth, which had been covered with her essence only moments before. "And, he's pissed with me right now. Not that that's unusual, love."

"I could tell from his yelling." She hopped down from the dresser. No need to stay up there any longer. Sex had left Orion's mind. He had leapt into protective mode. She didn't bother dressing as she'd have to put back on her disguise and that might clue him in that she'd be running as soon as he left her quarters.

His eyes strayed to her for a second before he squared his shoulders and continued to talk. "He might suspect you. Balt's not dumb. I'm sure he'll come to the same conclusion I had. Besela keeps coming up in any discussion about who's new to the station."

"I guess this is over then." She pursed her lips together. Maybe later, when she'd gotten away, she'd mourn the loss. Emote something for once. But not now. Now she had to do what had to be done. She compartmentalized her priorities. Her arousal waned away as she put herself to the task of leaving him.

He leaned down to plant a toe-curling kiss on her lips. "It's delayed. That's all. I need to either find out what Balt knows. Or better yet...get him off Settler's Mine." He nodded to himself. "Yes, I need to get him away from you." He turned to the side to walk around as though he needed to move to think.

"How will you do that?" Their short mate time was over even if he didn't know it yet. Better he be alive without his mate than dead. All he'd lose then was a mate who wasn't good for him. She'd never forgive herself if she caused him harm. She'd done enough damage to people she cared for already.

"I...I know how. I'll tell him I have a lead." He snapped his fingers. "Not anything specific." He paced. "Oh, yes. I'll tell him I have to leave. He'll know it's a lead on you. He'll follow me. I'll lose him. And I'll come back here." He placed a quick kiss on her lips. "I'll be back as soon as I can, love."

It never occurred to him that she would leave. Mates didn't leave each other as she had to do for him so why would he? Her heart cried out at the pain of life without him even as she calmed her face and breathing. It had to be done. "Be careful."

"You'll stay here until I get back? You'll be safe here, love."

She nodded but didn't say anything. Hated the small lie, but it couldn't be helped.

He grasped her shoulder tightly. "I'll be back. I promise. Trust me."

Her skin tingled. She wanted to lean into him and trust his strength, though she couldn't. Her heart would break once he walked out that door. Or rather, once she got away from here and could mourn his loss to her dying day. But, for now, she had to let him go. Her one shot at love, and she couldn't even take it. How cruel were the Fates.

She'd leave him better off without her. She might be his one shot at love but it wasn't as if it would leave either of them an emotional cripple.

He released her with another quick kiss.

She watched him hurry out the door.

She trained her eyes on his broad back until the doors closed and she couldn't see it anymore. She still wanted his touch. Such a big, beautiful, intelligent man. He was all she could have asked for in a mate. As soon as he'd found out about their mating, he'd hadn't hesitated about being with her as so many would have. Hell, he'd been sent to collect her for a big sum of platinum, yet he'd thought they could work things out. But it wasn't possible.

No time to reflect. Time to go.

She quickly put her padding back on. Her skin remained sensitive from the loving his tongue had given her earlier, so the padding chafed her in all the wrong ways. She still ached for his big cock inside her.

Layla popped in her contacts and prosthetic from the secret compartments. The case hid them under makeup containers, which contained actual makeup.

How much freer she'd been for a few minutes, not having to hide her true self with Orion. Well, that wasn't exactly true. He still didn't know everything there was to know about her. Some things had stayed hidden and always would.

She grabbed the bag from beside the door to start the process of packing. Everything she owned would fit inside it. The single piece of luggage always reminded her of how little she had. She'd come from nothing to nothing and would always have nothing.

You can thank the Union Alliance for most of your life's path.

No, the responsibility didn't entirely lie with them. Others shared in the blame for her tattered life. Dr. Bennett had been the one to panic. He'd been the one to put her life in jeopardy.

If only...

Don't go there. Her head shook as she tossed clothes, too big for Layla but perfect for Besela into the open bag. Those thoughts got her nowhere. Best to think about where she was going rather than where she'd been.

Just where was she going?

She didn't have quite enough platinum yet to make it beyond Union Alliance territory. Making do would have to be her way until she did. Another heartstone mine lay on the fringes of the territory. Much rougher and without the reputation Setter's Mine had, it would have to be her destination. There, there would be work, and most wouldn't ask too many questions of a Coronian without her heartstone.

She'd have to mask her trail better, too, this time. Sloppy planning had put Balt and Orion on her trail to start with. She wouldn't make that mistake again.

One book lay on top of her dresser. It was one of her only holdovers from that old life. She flipped through it. A collection of poetry by different races, including Emily Dickinson, Lothario,

Sharon Oles, Meginnion, Robert Frost, Canton, Alice Walker, Noralu, and Maya Angelou.

She stopped to read a well phrased poem about the shortness of life. No one had long to live so one must make the most of their days.

She rubbed her hands up and down her arms as chills erupted on her. Passionate words had always made her feel real reading them, even when she'd had doubts about the sanity of her existence. She didn't read it often for that reason. But today seemed like a good day to take in the words.

Layla tossed it in with the clothes. Her eyes flew around the room, making sure she had all her clothes and makeup cases.

Should she leave Orion a note?

She owed him something at least. None of this had been done by him. He'd been caught in it all as she'd been. He didn't deserve to come back to empty quarters with no explanation left for him.

What would she say?

"Hi, I'm running away from Settler's Mine because I don't want you hurt. If I stay, you will be. Have a nice life, my mate."

"There are things I can't tell you about myself. To do so would endanger your life. So, I must run to the ends of the galaxies. I must stay alone, or others could get hurt. Don't follow me."

"I have to go."

She ran the possible words over and over in her mind. Nothing seemed adequate without being melodramatic. It would be worse in person so she'd best hurry. She had to get away while Orion stayed busy with Balt. Ironically, Orion would help her evade Balt's suspicions by his actions.

In the end, she settled on a few metered words and scribbled them down on a notepad from Settler's Mine with a pen also from the mine.

Orion,

I'm sorry I can't be the woman you deserve. I have to go or you'll be in danger. Don't come after me.

Layla

PS. You're the best time I've ever had. This isn't about you. It's all about me.

The words looked so mundane and trite, even though they were all she possessed. *Please let him understand.* He wouldn't, but at least she'd tried to explain, instead of leaving him hanging. She'd at least given him that, all she could.

Soon, everything had been packed.

Except her heartstone.

It lay as if it were a traitor on the floor against the wall where Orion had dropped it while she'd been in his arms.

She pulled on her shoes, looking at the stone. The stone would remain hidden inside the little box in her bag. Where it couldn't cause any more trouble for her or anyone else.

A rare few of Quatar descent never found their heartstone, which was considered a tragedy for them. For her, not finding it would have been lucky.

From what she'd read, one stone was the catalyst to ignite the other or others. Most of the time when a woman was involved, it took her stone to get the other or others glowing. A woman, by her stone, chose her mate or mates. So, her stone had started the glow within Orion's. She couldn't even blame one bit of the mating on him. It had all been her.

Odds were against the stone triggering another for her. Most never found their third bond. Some went through life without ever finding their second mate, so when one did, the discovery was celebrated. The three heartmate bonds were even more celebrated and heavily rewarded by the Union Alliance.

After standing, she headed for her stone to pack it away.

She'd just reached her stone, when the door flew open and a booming voice ensued. "Hello, Besela. Or should I call you Layla?"

* * *

The woman looked startled before her face calmed into that serene expression she always had. Must be a Coronian thing. "What...how...or...what are you doing here?" She hesitated, before saying, "Who's Layla?"

"Nice try. Orion tried to get me off the station by leaving himself. Let's just say he thinks I'm following him." He'd paid a local yokel to take off in his shuttle after Orion. What could Orion be up to? Trying to get him off the trail so Orion could make the capture? He didn't bother to ask her. Besela or Layla wouldn't give him a straight answer.

Warmth spread across his chest, but he ignored it.

"Look, I don't know what you want, but I'm busy right now." She looked down at her feet, not meeting his eyes. "I have things to get done. I don't know who or what you're talking about. So, if you'll excuse me."

"Getting ready to leave, I see." He waved a hand around the room indicating its emptiness and her packed bag. "All packed and ready to leave. Quick, aren't you? But not so fast. I got some things to talk to you about."

And that's when his gaze turned to the heartstone laying against the wall from where she'd been going to collect it. *The glowing heartstone.*

Balt's hand slapped at his own heartstone. Warmth played across his fingertips. He looked down, chin meeting his chest. The stone pulsed with a green light. He didn't have to look to see it pulsed in time with the stone on the floor. He blinked his eyes. The glow didn't go away.

Only one thing made a stone act this way.

A mate.

He staggered a little on his feet. "Is that your stone?" He pointed to where it lay.

Why didn't Layla have it on? Not wearing it must have been part of her disguise. Made sense, except that it exposed her desperation. No one hid their stone once they found it.

His breath caught, waiting for her answer. The answer had to be yes. Nothing else explained the glow. Unless someone else hid in her closet.

"What?" She raised her head to look toward it. Looking back at him, her eyes bulged. "Oh, my...." Her hand came up to cover her mouth. "It...no. You've got to be kidding me."

"No, it isn't your stone? Or are you denying what we are?" He moved toward her. She had to accept them as mates. Fate had decreed what would happen. "Don't be doing that. We are what we are, and the stones show whom we are mated to." Placing his hands on her shoulders, he looked her in the eye. "Is that your stone?" He spoke slowly and deliberately. His heart raced. His future lay in her next words.

"Yes." Her head shook back and forth as if she could deny the one little word. "But, this can't be."

His mate stood before him. His heart shook inside his chest. He'd never thought about finding her. Now, he had. He wanted to wrap her in his arms and safely tuck her away with him. Forever. "It can, and it is." He gently shook her to reinforce what he said. "You're my mate. But, are you Besela? Or Layla?" His eyes searched hers for any answers, but she lowered her lashes, shading them. "Who are you? I need to know your true identity. I need to know who I've been mated to."

"Who do you want me to be?" She pulled away from him to stalk a few meters away. "Besela? So you can fuck her without worry of repercussions? Or Layla? So you can turn her over and make the money you've been promised?" Running a hand through her hair, she pushed it back. "If I admit to either, what will you do?"

"I'd never turn in my mate." He would treasure her. For always. Now that he'd found her, something empty in himself would be filled. He could already sense it beginning. His mate was someone he already liked and was attracted to. He couldn't have asked for better. "Either identity, I'm going to love and protect with all of my might." And, Amadors had a fucking lot of might.

"Ansel will kill you if you stay with me and help me escape." Her lips glistened from moisture brought out by her tongue. "You know that, right?" She turned away from him. "He'll hunt us both down."

"No. He'd try and take me out. But I'm damn hard to kill." He came up behind her to wrap his arms around her. "You are Layla? Aren't you? That's why you're running away. Orion and I were getting too close to who you are."

Breath blew out of her mouth. "I am Layla."

Had Orion known for sure? Was that why he'd taken off as he had? To keep Balt from the capture? Poor pissant. Now there'd be none. He'd not let Orion take her in, either. "I knew it." He turned her to face him. "We'll deal with Ansel together. Whatever you must have done, we can work it out with him."

"I doubt it."

"I can help you. We'll face anything together from now on." He pulled her against him. His lips found hers and devoured them. Her taste made him moan. So delicious. Her lips opened under his probing ones. She seared him to the bone with her response.

His mate.

He could hardly believe it. Of all the times and places for him to find his mate—not to mention people. Fate had a sense of humor.

Balt's hands tangled in Layla's hair, stroking through the silken strands. Maybe she'd grow it long again, wrap it around herself one day. Maybe she'd rub the length all over his body. Natives didn't cut their hair. Being on the run had been the only thing motivating her to do such a thing. Once he took care of that, would she grow it out to its former state?

He touched her body, stroking gently up and down her back and ass. She pressed her body against him while he rubbed his erection against her. His need for her ballooned out of control. How much could she feel through her layers? He couldn't get enough of her or close enough to her bare skin. "How much padding are you wearing?"

"Quite a bit."

"How easy is it to get off?"

She blinked at him. "I have to unfasten it. That's all. It's tight against me to conform to my body, but it's easy enough to remove though. Why?"

"I want you. I want to love you." He wanted to stake the claim on her body that the heartstone had already claimed for him. Sexual bonds came first with heartstones, and then emotional ones. "I want to…show you pleasure in the way only I can. Let me."

Her eyes clouded over with unease, before a laugh burst from her in a short bark.

That hadn't been the reaction he'd expected from her. "What?" His mouth curled into a frown.

"Nothing." She pulled away from him. "Don't you need to watch out for Orion? When he comes back, he'll be looking for you."

"Yeah, he will. Probably pissed, too. Why all this concern about Orion?" Something that sounded as if it were a growl rose up, but he shoved it back down.

"He'll...interrupt us. Shouldn't we deal with him first?"

What did the woman have on her mind? He watched her face suspiciously. "I'd rather take pleasure with you first." Maybe even second, and third. And if there were time, fourth and fifth.

Layla tilted her head to the side as though thinking about what he proposed. "I know. But, I think dealing with Orion should come before we make love. We don't have a lot of time before he figures out you aren't in the shuttle and comes back." Her face grew wistful. "Much as I'd like to have time with you for pleasure, I don't want to be...interrupted by him."

"I suppose." He folded his arms up about his chest. The heartstone continued to put out a heating warmth. The light pulsated, too. "The cocksucker isn't taking you in."

"I know." A wan smile graced her face. "He won't be. He...might have a few surprises for you."

He arched a brow but her head ducked down so he couldn't scan her face for her emotions. Surprises? What the fuck did that mean?

"You should intercept him before he gets here."

"Maybe I should go watch for him." She had a point. He didn't want the man barging in on them. He needed to talk to Orion before Orion did anything else. An angry Orion would use a phaser or taser on him. Once Orion did that, he'd be down, as Amadors were susceptible to such weapons. If he couldn't talk or move, it would be hard to protect Layla. Best to confront Orion on Balt's terms rather than meeting him on Orion's. "I guess I should go deal with him first. But it won't take long."

"No. No, it won't."

He moved to the wall to pick up her heartstone. The thin chain looked delicate against his fingers. "Let's get this back on you."

"What?"

"Let's get your heartstone back around your neck. Where it should be. You don't have to play anymore, Layla. Or pretend. We will work this out. I can't wait to see you without your disguise. You'll do that for me? When I come back?"

A pulse worked in her throat. "Yes."

"Let me put this on now?" The symbolism of the gesture wouldn't be lost on her. She'd be wearing the thing that tied them together. Maybe it would help her believe they had a chance of escaping Ansel.

She turned around so he could help her put the chain around her neck.

"That's better." He turned her around to face him. He picked up the stone and held it against his, pulling her closer to him. "See how they glow the same color? See how the pulsations are in time to one another?"

She nodded, her head barely going up and down.

"We're mates, Layla. Joined now as one."

Balt released the stones and leaned down to catch Layla's lips in a sweet kiss. She opened for him again, letting in his delving tongue. The kiss deepened.

His cock throbbed painfully, reminding him of the want and need in his body.

He placed his forehead against hers. "I want you."

"I know." Her breath rushed out against his nose.

"I'll take care of this and come back as soon as I can."

"What the hell is going on here?" Orion's pissed voice shattered the passion haze around Balt, who hadn't heard the door open.

Fuck, he'd forgotten to lock the door after he'd busted it open earlier. He moved away from Layla. "Look, pissant..." And that's when he saw that Orion's heartstone possessed a green glow. A pulse in time with Balt's and Layla's. "Oh, fuck."

He, Orion, and Layla were all mates.

Chapter Seven

Orion looked around Layla's quarters. She'd been packing. All her stuff had been put into bags. "You were going to run? How could you run from me after...?"

He moved further into the room, still looking around. The door clicked softly shut behind him. "And, you, asshole. You pulled a fast one on me." Wasn't the first time that had happened. What got to him was finding his mate, ready to run, with Balt in her presence, so he reacted angrily. He shouldn't, but couldn't contain the emotions rattling around inside him without erupting in some way. "So, you could come back here and make moves on my mate. Goddess, I don't think so. I should take you out."

Balt's face still had the shocked look that it held when Orion had walked in.

Orion's gaze swept down to be captured by something. Something that glimmered and winked at him.

The stone on Balt's chest emitted a green glow.

Balt's chest. Not Layla's.

Orion's gaze darted to Layla. She'd put on her heartstone. It thrilled him to see it there, perched around her neck where it belonged. The stone pulsed in time with Balt's. A quick look down told him that his pulsed in time with both of them, which could mean only one thing.

It couldn't be, could it?

Orion's hand came up to grasp his stone. Warmth filled his palm. "What in the hell…"

"We're mates. All three of us." Balt folded his arms across his chest. "The Fates have joined us."

Mated to *Balt@* Layla, he could see being mate to, but Balt… This was hard to work through. Did the Fates know what they were doing? Orion opened his mouth to speak, but Balt spoke first.

"You already knew Orion was your mate, didn't you? You knew before I came into quarters."

Layla's gaze shifted between both of them and the door. The woman still wanted to run for it.

They both noticed at the same time. Balt and he both moved closer to one another to patch the hole between them, so she could not dart for the door.

She squared her shoulders. "Yes."

"Why didn't you tell me about that? You were going to run from me, too, weren't you? That's why you were so eager for me to leave you."

She didn't answer, which was all the answer they needed. At least she'd planned to run from Balt as well as from Orion. That made Orion feel better on some twisted level.

She'd better damn well answer Orion's questions. He moved toward the bed and Layla. A slip of paper torn from a notepad lying on the table caught his eye. He picked it up and read it quickly before balling it up. "Quite a note." How could his mate find being with him so distasteful, she'd needed to run as soon as he'd left her alone? Fate had willed them as mates. She should be helping him celebrate. Along with Balt.

He approached her with the scrunched-up paper.

"What do you want from me, Orion?" She ran her hand through her short hair, an obvious habit. "Whatever it is, I can't give it to you."

"Truth. Honesty." Orion waved the paper in her face. "Not going behind my back to leave me. How could you do that?" He crumpled the note more and dropped it at her feet. The ball made a soft plop when it hit the stone.

Her gaze followed it to the floor. Layla didn't shrink back from his threatening stance, which most would have done. She simply glared and met his gaze head on.

"Orion. Let her talk." Balt sounded concerned at Orion's temper showing. Balt was the hot-headed one. "We need to find out what's going on. Not scare her."

"Stay out of this, Amador." But he backed off a meter. Maybe Balt was right. She'd talk if he didn't get in her face.

"No. We're all mates. This concerns me and you. And Layla. So, don't tell me what to stay out of."

"If I stay with either of you...it's going to get you killed." Her eyes flashed wild and furious. Maybe getting out of her face wouldn't work.

He'd seen animals trapped before. They possessed the same look she did now. What had her so afraid? Only Ansel? Or more? If only he could hold her. Comfort her. First, they needed answers.

"I'm hard to kill, Layla." Balt spoke as quietly as Orion had ever heard him. "I think I told you that before." He kept his voice at a soothing level, but it was firm and commanding. He reached out to lay an arm across Orion's shoulder.

The weight of Balt's touch took some of Orion's pique away. He liked the arm there. "So am I." People had tried to kill Orion. Many times. He'd gotten used to it. Nothing she told them could take away what they were to each other. He'd risk danger for his mate. How could he make her understand she had to accept them? Fate hadn't given her a choice. Yet he wanted her to come to accept them on her own, not be forced into anything. That would be no way to start as a tri-mate pair. Orion's gaze shifted to both of them. They'd have enough problems adjusting to this as it was. "Good thing, too, thank Goddess."

"You two don't understand. At all."

"Then why don't you explain it to us and make us understand. Since we're now both your mates." Balt stood as an unmoving force beside Orion's closer position to Layla. Balt spoke in that reassuring voice. "Make us understand why you'd rather be running away than with us."

Orion nodded, backing up Balt's words as Balt backed him up with his body. "Tell us what's going on, love. Why you can't be with us to be what you are. We deserve that much from you."

"Ansel hired you two. To find me. Doesn't that tell you how bad he wants me?" Tears threatened in her voice, but she managed to keep it steady. "He set you up against each other as rivals so that he'd have me delivered by one of you."

Orion had had that same thought once. "Why does he want you so badly?" That part didn't make sense.

"Yeah, not as if you have a dick. Course…things change." Balt's eyes cut at Orion as he commented on Ansel's preferences.

Orion gritted his teeth but didn't say anything. Yes, he'd been with Ansel before Ansel mated. Up until now, few women had caught Orion's interest. He and Balt would need to argue some things out later. This being mates stuff wouldn't be easy for them, but Orion would try it for Layla's sake.

"I…it's a long story."

"And we've got nothing but time to listen." Balt widened his stance.

"Just suffice it to say, Ansel's not going to give up or in. And, with you two with me, you'll be in danger." She blew out a deep breath. "I can never give you two what you want. Even if I escape beyond Union Alliance reaches…yes, they want me, too…I'll always be looking over my shoulder and be in danger. Do you really want that kind of life with your mate? Do you really want to live the way I will be living?"

"Fate hasn't given us a choice."

Orion froze. Union Alliance wanted her, too? Bloody hell. What had the woman done to deserve all this attention? It had to have been big.

She saw Orion's reaction to her statement and turned away from him, but not before he saw the look in her eyes. He'd hurt her without meaning to. Despite her words, she wanted them to make her theirs. She wanted them to challenge her. To make her danger theirs. Her eyes betrayed much before she turned away even camouflaged brown as they were. How would they bring that out to the surface to get her to admit it?

"You don't believe you can be with us." Balt tucked his hands behind his back, watching Layla.

"It's not a matter of belief. It's what I know to be true."

Balt caught Orion's eye and stalked toward Layla. "I say Orion and I can show you what being together means. We can show you how good it can be between us. How it was meant to be."

Orion nodded. The salty man did have a brain above his body. Of course they could show her what was meant to be. Show her sexually how good it could be, and the other would fall in line.

Layla's eyes widened, and she backed up a step.

Balt stopped. "Don't. Don't ever fear me. You're ours, woman. The only mate we'll ever have. We're yours."

"But..."

Balt held up a hand. "I will never ever hurt you. I will kill anyone who does. You need to accept that, and what it will do to us if you leave."

"What do you mean? What it will do to you if I leave? The only thing my leaving will do is protect you. Better for me to leave you alive and wanting than dead." She banged her hand back against the wall. "All I want to do is protect you. Why can't you see that?"

Orion shook his head. "No. That's not true at all. It'll do something to us if you leave us. You're our mate. Our one and only. While we have each other, you're the tie which binds us. Leave us, and you condemn us to a life of unhappiness."

"That's...that's not true." Her voice wavered with uncertainty. For all her bravado, Orion could see she didn't want to hurt them. "It can't be true. They would have told us that... The bastards."

She hadn't known what being mates meant. What hole had she lived in not to know that?

"It is." Seeing how she'd almost run from him had given Orion heart palpitations that he'd covered with anger. To lose her forever would tear him up. That was the way of mates. If she left now, they'd mourn her forever. She'd mourn their loss, too. It would rip them all to shreds.

Balt moved in to stand beside him. "Give us a chance, Layla. We can be good together. Real good."

She turned her head but didn't deny them.

"We can help you."

"No one can help me."

Orion had never heard a more lost voice. His arms itched to enfold her in them, but before he could move, Balt did.

Balt did what Orion wanted to.

She stiffened, only to relax as his hands traveled in circles, running over her back.

"We can. But you have to let us. Say you'll let us try. First, let us show you the way of mates. The way it can be with mates. Right here. Right now."

* * *

Somehow being enfolded in Balt's strong arms, against his hard body, she could almost believe nothing could touch her. She could almost believe they could keep her from danger. When Orion joined them, pressed up against her back so that she was sandwiched between them, the feel of him increased that belief. For the first time in a long time, safety touched her being. Maybe a relationship with them was possible.

"What do you say?"

She heard the rumbles of Balt's deep voice against her ear. She buried her face into him even more, inhaling his scent. His wonderful musky smell filled her with wanting.

"Layla." His soft voice had such a commanding lilt to it. No one had ever sounded so authoritative with such a quiet voice. How they had liked to yell... No. She wouldn't think about it. Not now. She'd only think about the two in front of her. The two she'd be hurting greatly if she left. So much hadn't been told to her about mates. Yet another thing to be angry at Union Alliance for.

"What?"

"What do you say, love?" Orion's voice echoed behind her. His hands gently stroked along her sides.

Would it hurt anything to be loved for a few hours? To take what Fate had given her? But the real question remained. After indulging in them for any length of time, would she be able to let them go, especially knowing what she'd sentence them to? She liked them already. Possessed an attraction for them both. Knowing that they were all mates made it that much harder to distance herself from them. She steeled herself. If faced with a choice between their life and their emotions, she'd pick their lives. She could walk away if she had to. But maybe giving them a chance... They were the only mates she'd ever have.

"I say, yes." Her voice sounded so foreign. The out loud words surprised even her. And they filled her with eagerness.

She could hear Balt's grin in his voice. "Are you sure, Layla?"

No, she wasn't sure of anything. But she'd try once. For them. "Yes. I'm sure. What do...we do now?" Balt chuckled, followed by Orion. "O.K. I know what we're going to do...but..."

Balt leaned over to kiss the top of her head. "We take it slowly, one step at a time. This is new for us all." He leaned further over to kiss her on her lips. His mouth brushed across hers gently.

Her stomach fluttered. Their touching bodies had already made her tingly. Each press of his lips charged her as if he were an electric current against her wanting mouth.

Orion's hands stroked gently along her hips and side. "Why don't we move this to the bed?" Her skin burned wherever Orion touched. Arousal flowed deep within her veins. Her mates would incinerate her before it was all over.

Balt didn't break away kissing her, instead deepening the kiss to explore every nuance of her mouth.

She moaned under him. He knew what she enjoyed and didn't hesitate to give it to her. She responded frantically to each thrust of his tongue even as he gave it back to her threefold. She shivered under his assault

Orion's hand drifted up to cup to a breast. He massaged gently while Balt explored her at his leisure. Her hips thrust against Balt as she arched back against Orion. If only the padding had already come off. She wanted them to be skin to skin.

Orion repeated, "Why don't we go to the bed?"

Balt broke off, leaving her mouth wanting more of his. "Because the bunk's meant for one."

"So?"

"What are we going to do, take turns? It's not a big bed. I thought this was supposed to be about all of us together. The bed doesn't lend itself to that. I'm fine right here."

The sensual spell which had been weaving around her abruptly ended. She glanced back and forth between them. They hardly noticed. A sigh broke free from her. Disappointment filled her. This wasn't going to work. Not this way.

Orion stiffened against her back. "Who decided you'd be at the front? That's not all of us being together. That's you being able to kiss her at will while I'm stuck back here." He removed his hand from her breast.

"This isn't the Union Alliance. We don't have assigned positions."

"Goddess, I know that. But who put you up front?"

"No one put me here." Balt's hands tightened on her arms. "I'm here because you were spouting off, and she needs something gentle right now."

Orion growled. "I can be gentle. You're there because you always think you're the best for the job."

"Who thinks? I know."

She couldn't help it. She started laughing. It was either laugh or cry, and she refused to shed tears.

Both of them straightened up to look at her curiously.

She moved from the middle of them, breaking contact with their bodies. Even as amused as she was, the coolness settled within her at the loss of them against her. This one might be permanent. "I'm sorry." She waved her hand back in forth in front of her face. "I...just...can't..." She dissolved into another fit of giggles.

"What's so funny?" Orion's voice broke into her guffaws.

"I think we are. We've amused her." Balt moved to sit on the bed. "Haven't we, Layla?"

"What do you mean amused her?"

Layla fought back laughter enough to get out "You two will argue over anything." She'd never seen two men more competitive with each other. And now, they were her mates, meaning they were mates to each other. Life had put them in an ironic situation. Two rivals were now forced to become allies and lovers.

"Bloody hell." Orion's face lit up with realization. "We should be enjoying you together. Not sparring."

Balt nodded. "That we should. Layla has a point."

Layla sobered to look at them. "You wanted to show me how we could be together. How the relationship would be. This is how it's going to be? You two one-upping and arguing with each other all the time?"

"No." Both of them spoke at the same time. "We won't do that."

"You can't stop arguing long enough to take me as your mate together for the first time. How on earth could you protect me as you said you will when you can't even have sex with me without quarreling?" She moved to her bag. She put one hand on the rough material. "I think you two unfortunately gave me the answer I needed." Her voice became rough with tears, which threatened to spill. She liked it better when she'd been laughing at them. That had kept her from being overwhelmed with her disappointment that it wouldn't work after all. When had she become so hopeful a tri-mate pair would work out? She shouldn't have. Nothing in her life was ever meant to stabilize.

"Layla." Orion moved to grab her hands from the bag. "Don't. Look, this is new to all of us. Balt and I…we've got some things to work out so we can be mates. That's our problem. Don't walk away yet, love." She held on so he finally let go of her.

"No. This is a problem for all of us now. All three of us. Not just you two. How you two act to each other affects me."

"She's right." Balt scratched his chin. "Our rivalry does affect her and the whole mate relationship. But, Layla, you have to give us time. This is new to us."

"I don't have the time. I wish I did." Her gaze spun round the room at her two earnest mates. "But I don't have time for you to figure this out. I'm wanted by too many groups. Dangerous people will come after me. And, if I can't count on you to watch my back, then we're lost. All of us. I refuse to be the cause of you two getting hurt because you two won't help each other. I'll watch my own back before I let that happen."

"You're part of the problem."

Balt's bald statement struck her square in the face. She sputtered. "How am I part of it? That's bull. I'm not the one arguing about who was in front and who's gentler a few minutes ago."

"We're all mates, right?" Balt looked to both of them for acknowledgement. "Not just Orion and me, but you, too, with us?"

Orion held up his glowing heartstone. "Yes."

Layla fingered her own heartstone. "You already know the answer to that. We all are mates." But not for long.

"What does being a mate mean?" Balt shifted, the springs of the mattress creaking under his weight. "It means we are all joined, right? We're all together. There's no more one each of us, there's three. We're all a single unit now."

What was he going for? She didn't know, and time had been ticking too quickly away already. She gripped her bag so tightly it hurt. Didn't want to hear about them being joined. Because they weren't. And that hurt her. "And, we've established you two can't be together without fighting."

Orion shifted to rest back against the wall. His face looked thoughtful as though he knew where Balt traveled with this reasoning. "Mates have to trust each other. Completely."

"Exactly. And you two don't. You're viewing each other as adversaries, not as mates. That's our problem."

"Or, our problem is that *you* don't trust us completely."

She started to say something.

"Let me finish. That's something that's hanging between all of us. If you can't trust us with all of you, then Orion and I can't work through our rivalries. The secrets you keep rest right in between all of us as a barrier. How can Orion and I work through things when you've already got something put between us that shouldn't be there?"

Orion nodded. "Until all the barriers are down between us, we'll never be able to work together as mates. They all have to come down. I'm willing to work at this, love. I think Balt is, too. But are you?"

She swallowed deep tears. They were asking the impossible. To share all her secrets. She couldn't do it. At least leaving, there was still the hope they wanted her. After she finished, they wouldn't want her at all.

"I am, Layla. I want this more than anything. Even if it means being mated to him forever." He thumbed at Orion with a grin.

Orion shot him a sign meaning to "fuck off' but smiled as he did it.

This was good-natured teasing. The kind between mates, unlike what had happened earlier.

"The question is, are you? Until you are, we can never break down everything between us."

Her lashes shut, blocking out her view of them. They were right. Until all three of them completely let go, they'd never be true mates. Did she dare release the secrets she kept and tell them what she'd never told anyone else? Her hopes had been dashed once. Did she dare give this another chance?

Chapter Eight

"You'd better sit down, Orion." Layla paced in front of the bed. Her body felt as if it were a spring stretched out of place as tenseness invaded every muscle and nerve. Telling them this was the most difficult thing she'd ever done. "This could take a while." Would she have the bravery to tell them everything? She surveyed them. Yeah, she had to. They had every right to know what they were getting into before they made the commitment to her and her life. And if she had to leave them, maybe explaining her situation would help them understand.

Balt patted the stretch of mattress beside him. "Come sit your ass down by me, mate." He waggled his brows at Orion.

Orion hesitated a moment, looking into Layla's eyes, but stalked over to sit on the mattress by Balt.

That was progress at least. They were sitting on the same bed. And Balt had broken the seriousness of the moment for her. Her body relaxed a little as she took a deep breath, and her heartbeat slowed. "Did I mention you two are nuts?"

"We have nuts. There's a difference."

"O.K. You're crazy then." They were crazy to even be trying this with her. She didn't want to get started. Ironic how she always ended up doing things she didn't want to. When would she ever do something she wanted?

"Crazy about you. That much is for sure." Balt smiled gently at her. "Now tell us your story."

He'd eased her into it again. She licked her lips with trepidation. How should she begin? Best to start at the beginning. Maybe that would help them understand. If they could. She folded her hands. She wasn't even sure she understood it all. "My life changed at the age of seven." She looked at the men sitting on her bed. "My parents were very pro-government. They thought Union Alliance was the best thing ever. Most Natives are that way."

Orion made a sound of agreement. "I knew that. Quite a few Natives were in my classes."

Her eyes swept to Orion. Classes? What was he talking about? She hadn't heard anything about him involving a school.

"I went to the Academy, love."

"Oh." She hadn't known that. The knowledge deflated what little confidence she had.

Orion had been shocked by her revelation that the government was after her. How much did he support the Union Alliance? If he was a fanatic about it, as her parents had been, that could cause a rift between them. As it had with her parents. As if they didn't have enough problems to deal with. She tensed even more, not wanting to go on.

Orion's eyes scored her with intenseness, asking her to continue.

"Lots of Natives join the Union Alliance soldier ranks. It's expected to find some way to serve our government, be it that or some other way. Did you go all the way through the Academy?"

"No. Dropped out after second year...well, they asked me to go. I had trouble...with following the chain of command." He shrugged. "I don't take orders that well."

That was good to hear. Her body relaxed. He wouldn't be a fanatic about the government and support them blindly, as most did.

"Still doesn't." Balt's comment came under his breath, muttered loud enough for them to hear.

Orion glared at Balt, who looked unrepentant.

"Anyway, when I was seven—right after my birthday, in fact—my parents were approached by Union Alliance agents. I was...special, smart. I'd been selected through a lottery of gifted students to attend a special school." Her throat ached. She swallowed to clear it. "My parents were thrilled I'd been chosen." She'd never seen them so happy. So proud of her. How easily that had ended later. She refused to let the sadness get her. No looking back. "The luck of the draw selected me. It was completely random." A chance number had sealed her future. Had it been one more up or down, and her life would have been different on so many levels.

She started. Her hand went to her heartstone.

Would she have come to this place at this time if her life hadn't gone the way it had? Would she have met Orion and Balt, her mates? Maybe the life she'd led had put her on this path for a reason. Maybe it would all be for something besides disappointing her parents or getting herself killed. Maybe something good would come out of her past. For all of them. It was the first good thought she'd had in a long time. She held onto her suppositions tightly. Needed that goodness to offset the bad she was about to express.

"What kind of school had you been selected for?" Orion leaned forward on the bed as if to hear better.

"They had other names for it. Long names only known to higher-ups. But, the truth was, it was a spy school. They taught people to be agents for the Union Alliance."

She watched as they both digested what she'd said.

"What did they teach? Exactly?" Orion's eye twitched as if he knew but wanted confirmation.

"They taught us how to go in to a situation under deep cover. How to disguise ourselves and blend in." She rubbed a hand across her chin. She'd never said these words aloud. How disconcerting yet liberating it was to hear them. "How to use weapons. How to kill."

"You were only a child." Balt's face wrinkled with distaste. "How could they do that to children?"

"They wanted us young so that we'd grow up knowing all of these techniques, so that it was second nature to us. This way we wouldn't hesitate when something needed to be done." She clenched her hands, fingers biting into her palms. The pain steadied her from memories too painful to have. "You'd be amazed what children can do." Flashes came before her eyes. Sparring. Children down and bloodied. Begging for mercy. Being told to have none. She shook off the images. Had to focus on what to tell them.

"I've heard of those schools, but only things couched in rumor and speculation. No one knew for sure they even existed. Goddess." Orion's face drew up. "Didn't they shut them all down even as they denied their existence? After some outcry or something. That was in the rumor mill, too."

"When I was nineteen all the experiments with young children came to a halt." She blew out a tiny breath. Had to keep breathing even as she told them all her secrets. Would they turn away from her after she was done? She wouldn't blame them if they did. "Another life change. But, the damage had already been done."

"Damage?" Balt asked.

"I'm not normal. I could fight you both and take you out if I had to."

They looked skeptical.

"I went to school with an Amador. One lots bigger than you, Balt. I know your weak points. I know most races' weak points. We had to recite them over and over again. Get one wrong and punishments were severe." She met their eyes. "I could have taken down Chumsky if I had wanted to." Had she not been pretending to be a Coronian, she would have. Too many questions would have been raised by it. Coronians didn't fight. Not as she would have. She never would have let him hurt her, though. Or Balt or Orion.

"So, that's what this is about? You're a highly trained weapon?" Orion shook his head. "That's not horrible, love."

Something clanged in the distance.

But it was. They had no idea the things that went on in her head despite her attempts to stop them. "Isn't it? When I first meet people, I look for their weaknesses. I look for how to kill them." Her eyes sought out Orion's. "I didn't recognize your race as Kurlan, but I researched you." Hadn't even been aware she'd been doing it until the page had flashed up on the screen. Hated herself, but had been unable to stop it.

"You did what?" Orion shifted uncomfortably.

"I got on a computer in the bar, and I researched your species. I made sure I knew every weak point you have. Those gills. They show everything you feel when they are uncovered, and are vulnerable to attack."

His hand slipped up to cover them through his high-necked shirt.

"It's because that's what I was trained to do when I came into contact with a new species." Assess how to kill them. Before they killed her. One of the most troubling aspects besides lying— an anathema to Natives—of her training.

"How many are out there like you?" Balt asked.

"We had different training. I can't imagine how the others handle their...gifts." It wasn't a gift. It was a curse. She'd been cursed since she was seven. "Killing wasn't even my specialty. Not to mention..." She broke off. She couldn't go on, thinking about her comrades. Or about what she hadn't told them yet. The real reason behind everyone's interest in her.

"You weren't trained to be first and foremost a killer. That's something." Orion's eyes flickered with an emotion she couldn't name.

She bit her lip before plowing ahead. "Maybe. You can't imagine what it's like to live each day with training you can't control. Or that's not useful in everyday life." They hadn't trained her for the normal world. Only for their own games. She was so tired of playing the games.

"No," Balt said softly. "I don't think we can. That's how you were able to hide from us so well? Your training?"

"You are good. I've never seen anyone go to such lengths before." Orion saluted her.

Warmth crept up her face. No one had ever praised her efforts before. The instructors and scientists hadn't been big on positive feedback. Neither had Ansel. She sobered quickly. The big revelation was still to come. "There's more."

"What else?" Orion placed a hand on his leg.

She would have enjoyed that hand touching her, soothing her through this difficult revealing. She'd thought she'd been naked before him earlier. That was nothing compared to now. Every part of her would soon be showing. "There's a chip in my head. That's why I'm wanted by everyone." The damn thing had plagued her for so long, destroyed any normalcy she might have ever had. "The Armageddon chip."

Orion's voice came hushed and low. "It can't be. It's a myth."

"I don't mean to interrupt you both. But can you please tell those of us without government ties what in the hell you're talking about? So we're all in the know." Balt folded his arms across his chest. "What's an Armageddon chip?"

"They used us for experimentation. Cyber technology. They had used them on soldiers before, but not to the degree they pushed us."

"What kinds of cyber tech?" Balt drummed his thick fingers. If only they touched Layla instead.

"Some of them messed with emotions, either blocking them all or pumping up the aggression. Can you imagine a Sitron with even more aggressive tendencies?" She'd almost killed Layla once. She'd acted as though she were a viper throng, hanging on with her jaws and not letting go. Had the chip finally driven her over the edge of insanity? Layla had never heard once school had ended. "Be glad I don't have my aggression pumped up. With you two in my room after Orion came back, all I could think of was escaping. If I'd had one of those chips, I'd have attacked you. Instead of trying to get you out of my way, I would have killed you."

"Bloody hell." Orion rubbed his face with his hand. "Sitrons are bad asses all around without a computer in their head. Goddess, what were they thinking?"

"They were thinking of making people as weapons. We were to be their special forces. Their elite." She'd never felt as if she were an elite fighter. At seven, all she'd wanted had been her mommy and her stuffed Caflack, which she'd been forced to leave at home. How many times had she woken up crying? More than she could count. Self-reliance had become the only way she'd survived. Now she was being expected to depend on others. How ironic life could become.

At least she'd been blessed not to have a non-emotion chip as her reality. Although maybe it would have helped her leave Balt and Orion. Instead, she was sharing her danger with them, completely unsure if it was the right thing to do.

"And you were picked for the Armageddon chip. Did it do anything like the others?" Orion leaned forward, balancing elbows on his legs.

"It doesn't do much by itself."

"And again, the Armageddon chip is?" Balt's voice came edged with impatience. "For those of us without 'high-up friends'?"

"Union Alliance has enemies. Lots of them. There's another federation they've been engaged in war with for centuries. They're losing the fight."

"You're fucking with me." Balt shook his head, negating what he'd heard. "And, what does that have to do with anything?"

Another clang came from somewhere nearby. People mining for their futures, unaware a piece of everyone's future lay nearby, contained deep within her skull. Something she'd never wanted. Her hand tightened. It had caused her more trouble than anything else that had happened.

"She's right." Orion nodded. "They are losing. It was...one reason why I got kicked out of the Academy. I kept pointing that out from the little bit of intelligence we'd receive during our practices. I was told to desist. Union Alliance doesn't like anyone to keep reminding them of their failures."

"The powers that be decided that in case of widespread fighting or losses, a chip needed to be made with ultimate secrets of the Union Alliance. Just in case the leaders were all gone by assassination or other means, the government would have an out of information ready to help them regain control."

"And, they put that chip in your head." Balt moved, the springs clinking. "That's fucked up." They both had seemed to want to move around, but had stayed put, probably worried that would disrupt her. And it would have. It was lots easier to focus with them in one place.

"Yeah, it fucked me up. There was a plot to assassinate the entire government. Once the danger passed, the idea was to move it around from agent to agent. The agents themselves didn't always know who had gotten what chip or especially, which chip was embedded in their own head." Her own personal hell had come later. As it had for everyone who'd been chipped.

"Moving it around didn't happen?" Orion asked.

"No, the school had to shut down. I don't know all of why. Some of us were returned to our original way of life without any...debriefing or new training." They'd gotten nothing to help them deal with what they'd become.

Balt's lips thinned. "That's no way to treat people with that kind of intensive training. It must have been hard for you to rejoin your society."

"You have no idea." She'd gone from star student to a young woman with no skills that mattered in the "real world." In the world she'd been dropped back into, the abilities she possessed didn't matter to anyone. To find a place where they would have mattered would have meant her accepting that part of herself. Something she hadn't been ready to do when she'd first been released. So she'd tried to fit into the normal world she'd left behind as a child. That and the inability to reveal where she'd been had been hard and caused her lots of grief. "I couldn't tell anyone about the school under point of death. Nor could I tell them why I'd been returned home."

"How did your parents react? Did they..."

She put her arms behind her back. "They...didn't react well. They thought I must have been sent home for a reason, most likely, not a good one. They thought I had disgraced them in the eyes of their government. Natives do not tolerate such things."

Her family had lost the perks associated with her status with Union Alliance. Her parents had been pissed over the whole situation. The only one there to bear the brunt of their anger was her.

Her back still bore minute traces of the beatings they'd administered when she'd returned, unable to talk about why she'd been sent back. Until the last time, when instinct had taken over with the fear for her life... Her father had survived, and she'd run away from both parents before she had done something she couldn't take back. She'd never wanted to hurt them but because of Union Alliance, she had, with her mere presence in their lives. It was better on them that she'd run away. This had strengthened her belief that it would be better on Orion and Balt if she left. Now she didn't know what to think. New ground had been breached. What would it create?

Orion patted the bed beside him and Balt. "Come sit, love. You've been standing the whole time." He looked concerned. Her emotions must have shown on her face.

She'd hurt her father when she'd fought back. Would she ever hurt them? She pressed nails into her palm. *Never.* She had control of her abilities more now than back when she'd returned. "I'd rather stand."

"But I want to touch you. I need to touch you." The plaintive longing in his voice made her toes curl.

Balt agreed. "Come sit with us."

"Please."

Sighing, she moved toward the bed and sat down in between them. She closed her eyes briefly, her body rigid. Balt tugged her legs on his lap, and Orion pulled her back to lean against him. "Better?"

Slowly relaxing, she started again. "Yes." It was. More than she wanted to think about or admit. Touch had never been for the sake of touch before. There had always been a purpose behind it.

But Orion and Balt had no hidden agenda, except learning about her.

Both of their hands and bodies against her made her relax, making her feel safe and warm. More than she'd experienced in a long time. Since before age seven. Even when she'd returned home, it had never felt safe. And now the time had come to destroy it. She took a deep breath, summoning the courage. "Before we talk about Ansel, I need to tell you. The way I understand it, Union Alliance wants..."

"What do they want?"

She turned her head. "They want me dead. If I'm taken out, so is the chip. My brain processes keep it alive. Kill me and it dies. They'll kill me before they let it fall into anyone else's hands."

* * *

"Before we finish talking, I need to do something." Orion hopped up from the bed to his feet.

"Where are you going?" Layla looked at him from her place on the bed by Balt.

"I need to go to my shuttle."

Layla's breath sucked in, but only slightly. Had he not been watching he wouldn't have seen it. Bloody hell, she thought he would run after hearing what she was.

He rushed to reassure her. He had no intentions of running. But he had no intentions of letting Union Alliance kill his mate either. "I have people I can contact, love." He walked back over to the bed to caress her cheek. "People who can tell me what's going on with Union Alliance. And who else Ansel has hired." He lowered his mouth to hers to explore. His tongue glided across her seam before rushing back in. He found it hard to pull away from her, but he did. "I'll be back for you to finish. Promise. But, for us to make our next move, we need to know some things. This means I need to contact people."

"Need me?" Balt didn't move from his perch on the bed.

"No. No need for you to come." He met Balt's eyes. "Be on guard."

"Always am."

Orion strode for his shuttle on purposeful legs. He'd find out something that would help them.

He'd just finished talking to his old Commander from the Academy when a knock sounded on the shuttle door. Drawing his phaser, he walked to the door, hit the button to open it with his gun pointed. At Balt's chest.

Balt shot him a droll look. "Jumpy?"

Orion lowered the gun but didn't reholster it. "What the hell are you doing here? And where's Layla?"

Balt stepped into the shuttle, shutting the door behind him. They made a swishing sound as they closed. He leaned back to flip the switch that locked them. "Working."

"You're kidding me."

Balt could barely straighten up to his full height in the small shuttle. He took two steps, his feet clanging on the metal floor. No, Balt wasn't known for his stealth abilities. In the little bay of the shuttle with the two of them, the small space was cramped as hell.

Awareness pinged along Orion's senses. They didn't usually interact in such crowded conditions. Orion's cock hardened.

"Nope. Clyde called and asked her to cover another waitress's shift. She's a couple of hours into a four-hour shift. I decided to come see what you'd uncovered before her shift ended."

"Goddess, she'll run." Orion's heart raced, thinking of Layla taking off for parts unknown without them. He couldn't lose her now.

"Nah. She won't. She promised."

"And people's words are so trustworthy." Orion snorted.

"We have to trust her. She'd told us enough. She won't run again unless we give her reason to."

Sometimes Balt would spout out a gem showing how much he understood about people. He was right. She'd stopped running from them the instant she'd started her tale of the past.

Orion's hands clenched on the phaser in irritation. Balt should have stayed with her. Maybe he should put the weapon on stun and use it on the big lug. Might make him feel better. "You left her alone." Goddess, the man could bring out the most irritation in him.

"Clyde's looking after her."

"*That* makes it better." Orion stuck his phaser into the holster at his side. He didn't turn his back to Balt but faced him.

"It should. Clyde likes Layla. He'll protect her because of that, not because I asked." Balt took another step, frowning at the sound it made. "He's a Wolfton. He could bite through me if he wanted to. And, the bar is public. No one Ansel sends will want to take her down with so many people around."

"Union Alliance..."

"Won't either. They don't want her to be public knowledge any more than Ansel does. Layla knows to stay in Clyde's sight until one of us comes back."

"I told you to stay with Layla." Orion gritted the words through clenched teeth. He glared at the Amador through lowered lids. Didn't the man ever listen?

"You told me to stay 'on guard,' which I am." Balt folded his arms across his massive chest. "Besides, I don't take orders from you. Or anyone."

"You should." Orion's face pinched up. "From someone with a brain."

A smile crossed Balt's face. A feral smile as if he'd been waiting on something, and it had just been delivered. "Ain't you, that's for sure."

Orion clenched his fists. Bloody hell, the man would frustrate a cleric monk. "Is."

Balt took several steps closer, getting into Orion's face. "Ain't."

Orion's mouth dried at the proximity of Balt's body. His musky scent pervaded the shuttle. Orion didn't move back but stood his ground. "Why are you here anyway? Did you come down here simply to annoy me?"

"Tempting but no. I'm here to plot our next move. Have you found out anything?"

"Nothing vital. Looks as if everyone is at least a few days behind us. Ansel did hire someone else, but they're in search mode according to my contacts." He wiped a hand across his face.

"Good." Balt's glittering copper eyes swept across Orion's face. Had they ever been so red before? "I also came down here to hash some things out. In private."

Something charged in the air. It rushed between them. Some type of current rent the atmosphere in the shuttle. His skin prickled with an awareness he hadn't had before.

"Oh?" Orion lifted his chin defiantly. He prepared himself for a blow from Balt. They'd come to blows a time or two before. Seemed logical they might now. "What things do we need to hash out?"

"This." Balt dropped his head and his lips met Orion's head on. Before Orion could pull back, Balt's hands had gone around his head, holding him in place while Balt's mouth plundered Orion's at his leisure.

Chapter Nine

Orion's senses swam at the invasion of a mouth instead of fists. A blow he'd expected, not this melding of mouths in a passionate frenzy. He didn't pull away at first—he couldn't—allowing Balt to deepen the kiss. The man tasted of finely hued spirits. Orion finally nipped at Balt's lips, breaking the embrace by sheer force. He couldn't breath, needed a moment to get some air. Was it the kiss or his panting depriving him?

Balt held him tightly with hands clenched. He ran one hand through Orion's hair. It tickled, sending running sensations down Orion's spine. Balt played, letting the hair swirl through his fingertips.

Orion's neck prickled. His skin had never been so sensitive before.

This shouldn't have caught him so off guard. He'd had no idea Balt was even attracted to other men. Most of Quatar descent were bisexual, but Orion had never seen Balt display interest in anything but women. "Have you even been with a man before?" The words burst out of him before he thought them through. Why he had to know, he wasn't sure.

"Yes."

"When?" Orion heard the disbelief in his own voice. Why so much tension on that point? Because he'd wanted to be Balt's first male? Shivers raced down him at that. He had. Goddess, when had this all become so important. When they'd become mates?

Balt grimaced as the question finished. "It doesn't matter when. What matters is that we work this out between *us*. Now. Here." He moved his face closer to Orion's. He wore a serious look on his face.

Orion stared behind Balt at the grey metal facing of the shuttle. "There's nothing between us." Until now there hadn't been. Balt was laying open the line between them. And Orion wasn't sure he liked it.

Balt's lips curved into a sneer. "You're lying." He pulled on Orion's hair. He yanked just harshly enough to be painful against the pleasure as his head dipped in to allow his lips to reclaim Orion's. Not a deep kiss, until Balt's body moved completely against Orion with one step.

His hard body.

Big muscles touched Orion in every place possible. Balt rubbed his cock against Orion's thigh.

The kiss became so deep, Orion's senses swam. He came close to climaxing right there.

A moan escaped Orion's lips to be fielded by Balt's mouth. Orion managed to cram back the second one. Goddess, he wanted this. Had he always?

Balt's tongue pierced his lips, giving him no quarter, nowhere to run. No denial could be made as lust roared to life between them.

Orion's heart pounded as his breath came in spasms. Air didn't want to move through his lungs or his gills.

Balt pulled his head away. He tipped Orion's chin up with two fingers so that Orion's eyes met his. His eyes said more than his mouth ever could.

Something did lie between them.

Attraction.

Had it—this heat—always been there, simmering below the surface? Yes. It had always been there. Desire flared to life as if it were a rocket, igniting anything in its path. Volcanoes erupted inside Orion, heating him from his core outward.

Balt's eyes bore into his as if they could see into his very soul. Never had his eyes seemed as intuitive as they did at that moment. His hands tangled more into Orion's hair. "Say it." He shook Orion gently.

The importance of acquiescing aloud wasn't lost on Orion. "Yes." If it had been a current there before between them, with Orion's admission, it snapped with electricity. Orion shivered with the snarl of it.

Balt trembled. Did the flare go off inside him with Orion's single word? Balt wiggled back and forth, grinding his cock into Orion's leg, showing his desire. It had.

Orion's own cock pulsed. He wanted to rub it against Balt. Wanted hands and mouth on it at one time. So many things he wanted. Balt would give them all to him.

Balt let loose a grin, which twisted Orion's insides almost as much as the following words. "Good. May not have to punish you yet."

Orion moved quickly away, slipping out of Balt's hands. He turned before pinning Balt up against his body and a bulkhead. The muscular body against him turned up Orion's fires even hotter. He rubbed his own cock against Balt's thigh. *Take that.* "Maybe I'll punish *you.*"

Balt wanted control over this encounter. Orion didn't intend to make it easy for him to have it. He'd concede control eventually, he always did, but Balt would have to work for it. His cock strained against the confines. That work would be fun for both of them. How long could he hold out? Probably not long. Damn, he'd almost spilled during the kiss.

Balt's chuckle was low and without humor. "Try it." He didn't fight Orion's capture, tolerating it.

Orion continued to rub himself against Balt. His lips slid down to press kisses along the side of Balt's large throat. The skin tasted like a mix of salty and sweet. He pressed his tongue in tight to lave along a vein.

Balt twisted his head to give Orion better access. A pulse flicked in his throat. Sweat coated his body. He might look disinterested, but something raged inside that big man.

Just as it raged inside Orion.

Their lips met in a frenzied mating of flesh.

Balt's muscles tensed under Orion's hands.

Orion groaned at the play of them under his fingertips. He wanted to taste Balt everywhere. To twirl his tongue around every crevice and orifice. His hips shimmied, shoving his cock back up against Balt. He couldn't get close enough. Wanted inside at the same moment he himself wanted to be breached. Any control he had had ebbed away.

After a moment, Balt broke free from the kiss and turned around quickly, pushing himself away only to come back around with Orion pressed into the side of the shuttle where Balt had been a second ago. He placed a muscular arm around the middle of Orion's back, pulling him back against his hard body. His hand crept under Orion's high-necked tunic to graze against the bare skin of his chest.

Orion's muscles sucked in as the hair stood up all along his abdomen. He shuddered as Balt's teeth nipped along his throat. Not quite pain, but a definite amount of pleasure.

Balt blew against Orion's gills, causing them to rise slightly. His hand came down between their bodies to grasp Orion's balls.

Orion lifted his body up, widening his stance, as Balt rolled them around.

Releasing Orion's balls, Balt slid his hand up the base of Orion's cock before he squeezed and pumped it through the leathers, showing that his hand had been around a cock before. He knew what to do with it and deftly showed it, even through pants. Goddess, did he ever know what to do with a cock.

Balt's hands slipped up to the base, as far as they could go before shimmying back down.

Orion's blood pumped in time to the rhythm of his heart. Time to acquiesce or should he fight Balt's control some more?

*　*　*

Balt shuddered at the man under him. So good. *Fuck.* He wanted to fuck Orion's ass more than he'd ever wanted anything. He ripped the snap open on Orion's leathers, almost taking off the metal clasp with his fingers fumbling.

Orion sucked in a deep breath. It whistled in the air.

Orion wanted this as much as Balt did. How much would Orion challenge him? Could be fun if he did. Balt yanked the pants down Orion's lean hips.

Orion's thick cock sprang free with a bob.

At the sight, desire engulfed Balt as he forgot to breathe. Balt twitched his hips back and forth in a thrust. Not where he wanted to be. Slamming into Orion was all he could think of.

No, first he had to make Orion want it. Worse than he already did. He wanted Orion asking for him to take him.

His fingers grasped around Orion's cock, playing in a drop of moisture on the tip. The drop told him as much as Orion's other reactions had about what he wanted.

He played his hands around Orion's cock, dipping down to the base of it then back up to the top.

Orion's breath hitched.

Balt pulled one hand off Orion's cock and spat in it. Not his usual way, but it would do for this. He wasn't stopping here, was he? He paused. No fucking way was he stopping. He had lube. But it was in his quarters or on his shuttle. Surely a man with desires such as Orion had some. "Where's your lube? Here?" His voice sounded so rough. Could he pull away if the lube wasn't here? He took a deep breath. He'd have to. He'd never hurt anyone, especially Orion.

"On...near my chair." Orion blew out the words from his heaving chest. He waved a hand, making his cock move side to side.

Balt spat again in his hands and rubbed up and down Orion's thick length. "Good."

Orion's head threw back as a moan escaped his reddened lips.

Balt created a funnel with his hands and ran Orion's cock between them. Such an electric shock to the system.

Orion strained against him, trying to make the touch last for as long as he could.

No. You don't. Balt minimized the touch, trying to drive Orion crazy but not give him all that he wanted. Orion would have to work for it. Balt's hands fired alive with the friction as they stroked around the hardness covered by soft skin.

Orion's hips had begun to twitch when Balt pulled his hands away. He let loose a curse.

"Problems?" Balt arched a brow at him.

"No. Should there be?" Orion returned the arched brow but his breath came in pulsating gasps.

Balt's mouth twitched. So that's the way he wanted to play it, eh? His voice took on a more commanding tone. "On your knees."

"Not likely."

Balt pushed on his shoulder. "On your knees, or we won't be needing that lube."

"You always have to be in charge?" Orion hesitated and then went down on one knee.

"Yeah."

Orion dropped down to the other knee. "Not doing what you tell me." But he was. To get what he wanted.

Smiling, Balt reached down to undo the front of his pants. He pulled them down just enough to expose the tip of his cock.

Orion tried to look anywhere but there.

Balt grabbed Orion's chin to make his eyes look straight ahead.

As he released Orion's chin, Orion licked his lips. "Bastard."

Balt watched as Orion couldn't take his eyes away. He slowly lowered his pants until his cock sprang free. He dangled it in front of Orion's face.

Orion's eyes shuttered closed as though he couldn't take seeing what he was seeing.

No, Balt needed him to look. Needed to see the desire in those Kurlan's eyes. "Open your eyes."

Orion's eyes sprang open.

Balt rubbed his cock against Orion's lips.

"Basta..."

Balt bumped his cock into Orion's mouth. "Established."

With a shudder, Orion sucked Balt's cock into his mouth. Warmth and wetness enfolded the tip as Balt widened his stance.

Orion moved his mouth up and down Balt's length several times.

As Balt's hips shifted, Orion broke free, letting Balt go with a *pop* sound of his lips.

Balt had to clench his hands against the bulkhead to keep from cramming his cock back into Orion's mouth. The loss of sensation hurt, and it was fucking cold.

Orion didn't stay away long. His talented mouth went up and down Balt's cock a few more turns as if Balt was a stick of exotic candy. He sucked in a breath around Balt's cock, using suction to draw Balt's length in deep. He deep-throated Balt, going all the way down almost to his balls.

Balt's head fell back to the cool metal of the shuttle now behind him. His fingers tightly gripped the roof where an open pocket met the side of the shuttle. Fuck, would the little man have him spilling as if he were a youth, before he'd even breached the man's ass?

He clenched around the metal edge until it was painful, giving him some strength to regain his control.

Orion broke free of Balt's cock. Wiping his mouth, he said, "Problems?"

"No." Balt answered as Orion had a few minutes earlier. He shrugged off boots and pants at the same time. He hurried, needing to be as close to Orion as he could get.

Orion stood up and did the same.

"We need that lube now."

Orion dashed to the front of the shuttle and came back with a little tube clutched in his hand. His face lit with a light flush, a sign of his arousal.

Balt couldn't wait to see him flushed and sated afterwards. His gills would vibrate. Fuck it. He'd never attributed his interest in Kurlans to Orion, but when he'd taken male lovers, he'd tended to go for that species. He'd hidden his attraction behind barbs and insults just as Orion had.

Orion's voice drew him out of his thoughts. "You know I'm not always the one who takes it up the ass, right?"

Orion still wanted to assert some dominance. A usual thing among Kurlan lovers.

Balt reached out to pull Orion against him. He shrugged off the man's tunic and let his hands roam Orion's chest. Small hairs prickled up over the hardened muscle. Balt enjoyed Orion under his hands. His finger tweaked a flat nipple. It peaked between his fingers into a hard little nub. "I know." He never made it to the other side. Balt pushed Orion's hair back, threading his fingers through the dark locks. "Turn around."

Orion's gills flapped, with lighter colors on the inside. He turned around quickly, but not before Balt noted his obvious signs of desire. Not that he'd ever revealed to Orion how much he knew about Kurlans. Orion's arousal had been upped, that much Balt could see, but by what?

Only one thing made sense.

Orion liked being ordered around.

Not anything Balt would have suspected. Orion would have to dominate him at some point, but with this experience, Orion wanted to be the bottom. And Balt was only too happy to oblige him. "Spread your legs."

Orion complied without a protest. Then, he bent over a small containment pod, leaning his torso over it, thrusting his back end in the air. Not what he'd been ordered to do, but Balt would overlook the disobedience this time. Orion's breaths came in tortured gasps, audible in the enclosed space.

Balt reached down to secure the lube from Orion's clenched hand. Balt rolled it back and forth across his palm, warming it up. Couldn't have his lover cold. His eyes were drawn to the curve of Orion's ass. He wanted a taste of it. A taste of the man splayed before him. The only sight that would thrill him more was to have Layla there with them. Soon. It would be soon.

He popped open the lube.

Orion's muscles tensed at the sound of the top coming off.

Those muscles would soon clench under Balt as he breached his ass and took him. Balt swallowed, mouth working to make it less dry.

Balt liberally drizzled a generous amount of lube on the crack of Orion's ass. His hand reached out to press fingers in and make sure the lube dripped down. One finger slipped inside, probing to play.

Orion's muscles relaxed around him.

So a second finger joined the first.

Orion's chest heaved. "Screw me."

Balt couldn't conceal his smile. He'd planned to have Orion asking for it and here it was. Orion was tight around his fingers but not too tight. More play wasn't needed.

He pulled out his fingers and drizzled more lube onto his cock. His other hand swiped quickly down his cock to coat it with the lube.

He pressed forward and the tip of his cock slid against Orion's opening. He slid in a tiny bit.

Orion gasped. His fingers bore down on the pod until they were white.

Balt slowly pressed forward. He'd go in a little more and stop, allowing Orion to adjust. Soon he was fully seated within Orion's depths.

He wanted to slam. Wanted to pick up the pace. Gods, this slow going was killing him. "You ready?"

"More than ready."

Orion moved back against Balt, and he lost it. All control left him. He needed this. His face and body broke out into a sweat as his hips pressed back then forward. In and out, he slapped against Orion.

Orion's hips bucked back against him.

Balt's hand slid around to the front of Orion to find his hard cock. His fingers still had the lube on it from coating his own cock. He grasped Orion in his slick hands, sliding up and down his length at a rapid pace. His cock was so thick, so engorged.

Orion let out a frenzied groan, moving back against him even harder.

Balt must be balls deep inside of him, or at least, it felt that way.

The little grunts that Orion made from each slap of flesh made Balt crazy. So vocal and so expressive. He'd never had such a lover. They should have done this long ago.

Orion let out a howl. Warm goo coated Balt's fingers as Orion exploded.

What Balt had been waiting for.

His own orgasm close, Balt worked back and forth until he could contain himself no longer. His orgasm made his eyes see the heavens. He'd never come so hard and so much.

Orion lay under him as their senses came back.

Balt pulled out of Orion. He planted a quick kiss on his lips, enjoying the satisfied look he saw on Orion's face, knowing that he'd put it there.

Orion's gills moved back and forth in cool down mode.

"Now that that's settled between us, let's go find our mate. We can take her while we still have the time."

Chapter Ten

Layla saw Balt and Orion arrive together as she set a drink down in front of another patron. They walked in step together and looked united. That gave her pause even as her heart sped up at their presence.

Seeing both her mates together got her juices and libido going. Could she be any luckier than with the two of them?

Something was different about them. Balt's arm had drifted around Orion's back. Her eyes blinked. Just what had they been doing while she'd been working? Her sex clenched. If they had been having sex, oh, now that was a sight she would have bought a ticket for. Who'd been the one to penetrate the other? Her heart pounded. If only she could have watched. Just their hands on one another turned her on. More than that would drive her crazy. Had they worked things out between them? It would mean a lot to her if they had.

Balt stalked over to her with Orion right behind. His smile made her heart beat faster. "Is your shift over?"

"Not yet."

Clyde's growly voice came from behind her. "You can go."

She turned to face the burly man. "You sure?"

"We're slow." He shrugged. "I can handle it until Drewel gets here." Drewel was the waitress for the next shift. His nose twitched. Was that a grin trying to creep up on his face? So she was aroused. Wasn't as if Balt and Orion could smell it. And they'd had their round of loving. She was still waiting for hers. Had their encounter helped them? What was the question that needed to be answered?

Balt's arm crept up her back to her shoulder. His touch made her shiver. His fingers were hot through the material of her shirt. "Come on, Besela."

For a moment, she didn't recognize the name. Somehow it made her stomach do a flop that Balt had remembered to play the game. He hadn't slipped and called her Layla. "Let me get my bag." She grabbed a small bag that she brought to work when Orion had dropped her off. "See you later, Clyde."

"Later." He turned to a man at the bar and nodded.

"So, what were you two up to?" She glanced back and forth from face to face. From their reactions, she could tell. They'd been having sex.

Orion grasped her hand in his to hold it. "I think you already know, love."

"Yeah. I think I do."

"And now it's time for us all. To make this arrangement work." Balt grasped the other hand in his. They ushered her between them through the bar door and out into the corridor.

She slowed them almost to a stop as they rounded the next corner. "Are you two sure? You want to be with me?" How did she want them to answer? Parts of her were so conflicted. The part that wanted to be with them was steadily gaining ground. It was just so hard to let go with all the things from her past. She almost reached up to touch her nonexistent heartstone, pulling Orion's hand with hers. She'd left it in her quarters to keep up her disguise.

Balt squeezed her hand. "You know the answer."

Orion gripped her other hand tightly. "You do know what we think." He gently drew her hand to his mouth to kiss. His mouth fluttered warm on the back of her hand. "Your quarters, mine, or his?"

"Mine."

They both turned their head to look at Balt.

Out of the corner of her eye, she saw that Orion had to tilt his head far forward to see Balt.

"It's the biggest."

She looked to see Orion bite down as if he had to hold back a comment.

Balt shot him a withering glance with humor sparking in his eyes. "It is. I've seen hers and yours. Mine's the biggest."

She couldn't bite back the laughter.

Orion started with her and after a moment, Balt joined in.

"Your quarters are fine. They probably are...bigger." She tried to withdraw her hand but Balt held on. She rearranged her fingers with his. "I would like to get some things from my quarters."

"I can think of one thing you need." Orion made a swipe of his hand around his neck to indicate what he meant.

Yes, she needed to retrieve her heartstone. Especially now, having met her mates, she felt almost naked without her stone. That he wanted it, too, made her heart pump faster. "Yes. Yes, I do. That and a few other things."

Orion's hand slid from hers. "Do I need to retrieve anything from my..." He coughed. "...quarters?"

She looked over at Orion. Why the cough?

"If you're talking lube, yes, that would be good. Otherwise, get something for that cough." Balt tugged her in his direction. "I'll go with Besela." Several people were milling around so he used her disguise name.

The care they took with her made her feel cherished. Only little things but they meant so much to her because no one had ever shown her any care. Holding her hand. Keeping her disguise. Wanting her to get her heartstone.

"I'll be there soon." Orion left, muttering about things trying to be kept quiet instead of being broadcast in front of the whole damn mine.

She and Balt reached her quarters. She stepped over the threshold and entered. Balt followed closely behind her. "Just be a second."

He'd already picked up her heartstone and stuck it in his pocket. "There's that."

She pulled some clothes out. "Did Orion find out anything?"

"There are people after you, but they are way behind you." He winked at her. "We have more than enough time to have a little fun."

And then what would they do?

Her head swam. Just what were they going to do?

Ansel would never stop. Union Alliance would never stop.

They might be screwed before they'd ever get the hang of screwing.

* * *

Orion grabbed a small bag and stuffed a couple of things into it. He found his regular lube and the kind that warmed to the touch. He reached down to adjust his hard cock. Nothing would bring down that hard-on but being with his mates.

Taking two steps, he decided to grab some weapons, too. It should still be a day or so before anyone after them arrived to Settler's Mine, but he might not make it back to his room before then. If he were lucky.

His cock twinged. *Here's to a few hours of time with my mates.* He still had trouble processing that he was mated to the big lug and the lithe waif.

After dumping a couple of phasers into his bag, he dashed out of the door. He'd never wanted anything more in his life than what he was about to do.

Reaching Balt's quarters, he knocked on the door.

"Who is it?" Balt's voice sounded as if it were nails pounding on metal.

"Me." That would annoy the other man.

Balt opened the door. "Who the fuck is me?"

"As if you wouldn't know my voice." Orion pushed into the room.

Balt locked the door behind him. His quarters were carved out of the rock of mine, just as all the rooms were. Incandescent lights hung out of the stone ceiling. Balt's quarters were deeper within the mine and chillier as a result.

Balt reached over to pat his ass. "True. I'd know it anywhere." He patted Orion's right cheek.

The cheek clenched under Balt's hand. Things seemed slick between the cheeks from the earlier screwing. Good sensations spiraled through Orion as he remembered. Now their encounter would be with Layla. They had time and would show her they could be together. Anticipation rolled through him.

"If I didn't, all I'd have to do is ask to see your cock. I'd know that anywhere." Balt waggled his brows at Orion, who turned as if he were going to pull his cock out.

Orion stopped when his gaze turned to Layla.

She sat on the bed, her legs folded up under her. Her padding had disappeared. She held her head in a regal arc as though she were royalty.

Damn if the bed wasn't bigger than his or Layla's.

"Goddess. You look pleased with yourself." He couldn't take his eyes from her.

She did, looking as though shadows had lifted from her face.

And her eyes met his.

Purple eyes.

Captivating eyes, which held both men in their stead. The slight hint of sadness, which had never seemed to leave them, had diminished.

They'd banished her sorrow for a little while. Good. It might return but at least they had this time together.

She'd taken off all the vestiges of Besela to become Layla. The Layla who was their mate. The only thing that remained of her disguise was the make-up she'd used, which would last a few weeks more. He still couldn't get over the elaborateness of the Coronian look she'd possessed.

His gaze swept across her, taking in the beauty who would soon be his banquet. She would be a delicacy to Balt and he would savor. She wore a tunic dress, which matched her eyes and must be one of her own instead of Besela's because it fit her though she wasn't wearing padding anymore. Her stance grew more prideful as she noticed his admiration.

"I like you without the padding."

"I like me, too. Just myself. Without any disguises. I'm hardly used to it, though." A shy smile graced her lips. "I'm glad you do, too."

Had she still worried he wouldn't like her looks because he'd been attracted to her as Besela? It was the woman under the looks he wanted. They were the trimmings on such a wonderful package. He admired her strength and fire. He'd reassured her once. Time to do it again. "I do."

She brushed a hand lightly through her hair. "What now?"

Orion moved to her side. "Whatever you want, love." He took her hand and kissed it, lingering over her sweet taste and scent. His tongue grazed the pad between her thumb and forefinger. He nipped it. His tongue licked across the spot. Her hand jerked with a shiver, but she didn't pull it back. He released it as his tongue reached back where it had started. That was only the beginning. He'd taste all of her before he was through. He couldn't wait.

"Well…" She bit her lip, scraping her teeth across it. "I think both of you are wearing way too many clothes."

That they were. All of them. And getting naked seemed as if it were a fine idea.

"I like the way she thinks." Balt reached up to the top of his shirt.

"Ah, but I think you two should undress each other. Since you've worked out all the kinks."

Orion heard the bedspread rustle as she moved around on the mattress. He chanced to look and saw her kick her legs out from under her to recline on her side. He wanted to run his tongue down her side. She looked delectable.

Balt's arms dropped away from his shirt. "You don't want all my kinks out. They're way too much fun."

Orion moved over toward Balt. "I'd have to agree on his kink. Let's keep those. For fun." He couldn't wait to see Balt unveiled. Hard to believe it hadn't been that long since the shuttle.

Orion wanted him again, along with his desires for Layla. And this time, they'd all get what they wanted.

"Whatever. Just get undressed." Her voice lilted upward as if in expectation.

It was a test. A test to see if they could actually work together to be with her.

Orion would pass it.

Balt spread his arms wide and down by his side, directing his gaze toward Orion. "I'm waiting on you."

"I'm not one to disappoint anyone." Orion moved closer and put his hands on Balt's waist to pull his shirt up over his head. "I'll never disappoint the two of you."

Balt allowed him to take off his shirt. His mouth curved up into a moon of a grin.

Orion heard Layla's intake of breath as the shirt came off. So, she liked seeing Balt's naked torso as much as Orion did.

Balt flexed his arm muscles, his eyes spitting fire. A fire that threatened to consume Orion within a flaming passion.

Orion was close enough to touch the Amador. He splayed his hands across Balt's muscular pecs.

Balt shifted his weight, his breath exhaling from his mouth.

Seeing Balt's reactions made his own that much more potent. Orion had to touch more, found a nipple and rolled it between his fingertips. Palms down, he ran his hands down across Balt's abdomen. A big man. And all his.

He reached for Balt's pants to unsnap them, but Balt laid one hand on top of his. It covered his hand and more. Big hands. Yet they could be gentle. Sparks flew along the touch, too. Balt's hands heated him up. They were much better for this than the fighting they'd always done. Who would have known his biggest rival would wind up being his mate?

"Your shirt needs to come off first." Balt squeezed his hand. "Only fair you be as undressed as me."

Orion dropped his hands to show his agreement with what Balt said. "There you go." He'd still get to finish undressing. And get pleasured in the process.

Balt reached toward his middle to pull the shirt over his head.

Orion shivered as the colder air chilled his skin.

Balt's finger came up to run across his chest and then pull on a nipple. "I didn't notice that before."

Orion had a pierced nipple. "You were a little more focused elsewhere." He caught his breath as Balt continued to tug on the piercing. His cock engorged more than it already had, to the point his head twirled around. Or maybe it was just the pleasure of the sensations.

Balt never let it get painful, only tugged enough to make Orion shudder. "Maybe I was."

Orion moved closer to reach for Balt's pants. "Your turn."

Layla made a strangled noise from the bed. "I'm glad you two have worked out your differences." Her breath hitched.

Did she enjoy watching them as much as they were turned on undressing? A voyeur. That could be fun.

"Me, too." Balt dropped his hands from Orion's chest.

Orion reached over to unsnap Balt's leather pants. He unzipped them before sliding them down Balt's hips. Balt's cock immediately sprang free. The man must not ever wear underwear. Not that Orion minded.

Orion shoved the clothing down to Balt's ankles. What a beautiful sight that heavy cock was. It tempted him to take it in his mouth and never let it go.

Balt quickly took off his boots and got the pants off the rest of the way. He grinned lazily at Orion. "Now I get to do you."

"Thought you did that earlier."

"So, who..." Layla's voice sounded breathless and embarrassed at the same time. "...who..."

Orion figured out what she wanted to ask. His skin heated at her interest. Yes, she did want to be a voyeur. One day they'd indulge that fantasy. But not today. She'd spent a lot of her life watching it go by from her disguises. Today, she'd be a participant.

"Who took who earlier?" Balt stopped Orion with a hand to his stomach, which sucked in at the heat of Balt's hands on his bare skin. "I took him. By his choice."

Orion's heart pumped at Balt's words. Kurlan men were known both for aggression and submission. He shared those traits with many of his race. They all seemed to be built that way.

Interesting that Balt had seemed to know a lot about the Kurlan sexual practices. He'd have to ask him one day where he'd gotten that information.

"Ohhh." Layla's voice grew hoarser with the answer.

Orion looked up into Balt's serious gaze.

Balt didn't look down but kept his eyes even with Orion's as he unsnapped Orion's pants. The sound clicked followed by the whir of the zipper. Balt slid Orion's pants down, inching them down his legs. Orion's cock freed itself from the pants and jumped for joy at not being confined.

Balt stood back and looked his fill. "Oh, yeah, I'd know that cock anywhere." He reached down and palmed Orion's cock in his hand.

Orion ground himself against Balt's palm. Nothing could be better than this. Of course, something could, and he was about to experience his greatest adventure. A *ménage a trois* with his mates.

Balt released him as Orion reached down to shrug off his boots before kicking off his pants.

Both of them turned to face Layla as a single unit.

"Now we're naked." Orion grinned at her. That they'd all enjoyed getting that way was evident from their erections and from Layla's flushed face.

She couldn't keep her eyes from going back and forth between them both. "So you are."

Balt took two steps to the bed. "And now, you're wearing too many clothes."

Orion shivered inside. This was going to happen. He was about to make love to his mates. It would be a bond sealer for all of them.

* * *

Balt watched as Layla stretched out on the bed. She flexed her legs out, the muscles stretching and pulling. He fought the drool back. Fuck, what a fine looking woman. And she was his.

She knew he watched. She liked that he watched.

So he kept on watching.

Her hands ran down to her legs, stroking, smoothing down her dress and running across skin.

His gaze shifted to Orion, who watched just as he did. Their eyes met briefly before coming back to Layla.

"I guess I need to get undressed then."

Balt shook his head. "We'll undress you." No greater present had he ever unwrapped than this.

"Oh?" Her eyebrow quirked up. It had been dyed to match her hair. He'd not noticed that before. "I get personal service?"

Orion moved to help tug her from the bed with Balt's help.

She stepped away from them after reaching her feet.

"Love, you can have personal service anytime you like." Orion stepped forward. "Balt, why don't you unbutton the back of the dress?"

Balt moved to her rear. He cupped her firm asscheek in his hand. "Sure." His hands moved slowly up her back to the top button. He swiftly undid it. His mouth descended to taste the newly exposed skin. Sweet and salty flavors meshed with his tongue. She shivered.

Second button came loose. His mouth shifted down to take advantage. She moved back against him. The contact fueled the inferno raging within him. He wanted to grab her, take her to the floor. He clenched his butt muscles, trying to keep control. He would take this slowly. Would make this perfect for both his mates. Even if he died from pleasure. But what a way to go.

Third and final button came loose. His mouth swept in to caress her tasty flesh. At the same time, his hands went onto her shoulders. He raised his head, resting it on top of her shoulder. Gently, he pushed the dress down her arms, exposing more of her front. The material fell completely off her arms.

Orion moved in to ease it completely down. The dress had gone far enough to expose her breasts. It stopped at her hips, hanging on by a pelvic bone.

Balt saw her breasts bounce from his position over her shoulder. He'd expected rosy nipples to go with her naturally pale skin. But, of course, her coloration would be off for another few weeks. Such a brave woman to take off the way she had. She hadn't rolled over or given up for Ansel. That took courage. His heart jumped. So much to love about this woman.

She shifted, and the dress fell off.

His gaze wandered further down to see dark hair at her pussy. She had colored everywhere. The sight of her naked, even from his restricted view, left him speechless for a moment.

"Beautiful." Orion's voice came hushed. Almost reverent.

"Gorgeous."

She shivered against Balt's body.

A delicious shake from her told Balt of her desire. "Enjoy yourself, little one."

His hands slid around to palm the bottoms of her breasts. They hung heavy in his hands. He liked the weight of them. One thumb came up to brush across a nipple. It rolled hard against his fingertip. He steeled himself to go slow, though he wanted to plunge himself into her. He had to make this as pleasurable as he could for Layla. She hadn't had a lot of pleasure in her life. It was their job to give it to her. No matter how slow they had to go.

Orion caught his eye. His gaze flicked down to Layla's chest, telling Balt what he wanted to do.

Balt nodded. Not permission, but awareness. After moving both hands to one side, he tightened his hold around Layla's left breast. Cupping her in the center of his hands, he enjoyed the shape of her, resting within his palms. Such a soft mound, fitting completely within his hands.

Orion lowered his head and placed his mouth over Layla's nipple.

The sight of Orion's mouth going down on Layla made Balt moan. He'd never seen anything sexier.

She gasped. Her body relaxed against his. But not completely.

Balt straightened up. "Lean back. Rest your weight on me." He wanted her to do this for him. Trust him enough with her body weight. Needed her to relax into this moment and keep nothing back.

Sucking noises erupted from Layla's front. After a second, she flopped back on him, resting all her weight.

Thrills raced through him at her trust. A small step. But huge for her. Balt couldn't see what Orion was doing, but from Layla's whimpers and the noises, it must be good.

Balt squeezed her breast in between his hands as Orion took his time, pleasuring her flesh.

When Orion pulled away, her breath came in raspy pants.

Balt looked over to see Orion trying to catch his own breath. His gills flapped with the color of desire evident.

Balt moved his hands to her other breast.

With a smile on his face, Orion lowered his head to take her other nipple into his mouth.

Balt peeked over to watch as it disappeared against Orion's tongue. Want and need coursed through his veins as much as blood. His world had narrowed down to these two people. Their pleasure had become his.

Balt lowered his head and kissed the side of her neck. Slowly, he laved his way across the smooth skin. He found the sensitive soft spot under her ear and kissed.

She made a whimpering noise. Her body went boneless against his.

He nipped at her earlobe before driving his tongue into her ear as he had earlier, before they'd been mated. Her body shook as he spiraled his tongue around the outer shell of it, before plunging in again.

Soon, he'd drive himself home into her warm depths. His cock jerked as his hips spasmed against her.

She let out another moan. "So good."

She was letting herself go. And that upped everything. Every emotion. Every desire.

Balt whispered against her ear. "Enjoy it. Enjoy us."

Chapter Eleven

Layla was drowning in sensations. They'd barely scratched the surface of being together, and everything they did made her want more.

Balt whispered something else against her ear before his tongue swept in again to explore.

Her skin burned wherever his tongue trailed. How many times had she let them at her throat? Both of them. Vulnerability existed there. She'd been taught that over and over. Maybe what they had together would overwrite her training. Warmth of hope filled her from that one little inaction on her part. The small things would lead to more normalcy. Or at least, she prayed they would.

He thrust in and out, much as one of them would do later.

Or maybe even both of them.

Her whole body became one big shudder at that. When would they take her together? Her hips moved forward as need filled her.

Orion's tongue rasped against her nipple, drawing it in again and again into a mouth boiling hot as if his lips were a furnace.

Her knees nearly buckled.

Her sex pulsed in time with her racing heart. So swollen. So needy. So wet. Yet, what they were doing wasn't enough. She wanted it all. Both of them together with her.

She rolled her head away from Balt's questing tongue. "Bed." She could only manage one word.

Balt pulled his head back.

Orion continued to suckle until Balt wrapped an arm around her to tap on his shoulder. "Bed, Orion."

Orion's head came up.

They moved to the bed together as though they couldn't bear for the touch to be broken.

That was true for her. She didn't want to lose the contact, even for a moment.

Balt slid onto the bed first, going up against the far wall. She slipped in next to him. Orion followed them, lying on the outside corner of the bed.

"Your bed is bigger, you big bastard." Orion's hand came in to stroke her cheek. She nuzzled into the touch. His other hand rubbed across Balt's arm.

"I paid extra." Balt turned her head slightly to him to claim her lips. His kiss was gentle at first. But as her response to him grew, so did his ferocity. He took claim of her lips as if he were a master musician.

Orion's hands caressed her back, gently kneading her muscles.

Her hand rubbed along Balt's side, before hesitantly drifting down along his hip. His breath hitched, but he didn't let go of her lips.

Did she dare?

She did.

Her hand rolled down his hip to touch his heavy cock. His thickness rolled against her hand.

A strangled moan sounded against her lips.

She'd seen male's penises before. But she'd never touched one this way, nor of her own free will, with time to explore. Before, she'd been made to touch. Made to do. It had been a part of the job. This was completely different. This was for her own pleasure. Hers and her men. And her curiosity and desire would be sated along with Balt and Orion's.

She took advantage and ran her fingers all over Balt's cock. He widened his legs before finally breaking the kiss to roll over a centimeter. The soft skin stretched taut over him as down would over flint metal, the hardest metal in the galaxy. She'd never noticed how a man was so hard and so soft at the same time. Touching him filled her with wonder.

Her fingers reached his tip. She looked at the small hole covered by a glistening pearl of moisture. She swirled her pointer finger in the drop. Brought it up to her nose. The drop smelled little. No detectable scent. Then, she put it up to her mouth to lick it off. Saltiness coated the tip of her tongue. It tasted as if his come were an apple, an old fruit from another planet, coated in salt. She sucked the finger into her mouth to get the entire flavor from it. Such a delicacy. She'd never tasted anything sweeter, because it came from him.

A strangled sound came from behind her.

Orion.

His hands withdrew from where he'd been stroking her back the whole time.

She hadn't forgotten him, but he'd been neglected back there with no one to play with him. Time to rectify that.

Putting her hand back on Balt to a sound of muttered delight, she turned her body so her free hand's attention went to Orion's long cock.

His cock felt much the same as Balt's. Silky, yet unyielding. She liked them both under her hands. Better yet, she enjoyed both their reactions. Both of them seemed to enjoy her touch there immensely.

Balt's head had been thrown back against the wall. His expression was one of pure bliss.

Orion looked much the same. His panting lips became tense with desire.

Her hands went down to cup the sac up under Orion. Cool skin met her hands. She scrunched her hand up around the taut skin, squeezing him.

"Goddess." His voice sounded broken.

She released Balt. "I'll be back." She'd always come back. And he'd be there. That surety rocketed her desires into the stratosphere. Now it was time to pleasure Orion the way she had a second ago earlier with Balt. With her mouth.

He chuckled weakly. His eyes sparkled, shining in the lights.

How she always wanted to see him this way. Lost in abandon. Maybe if this worked out between them, she could.

Her other hand went to Orion's cock as the first hand stroked his balls.

His hips bucked, growing wilder with each touch of her hand. His eyes closed. His chest rose and fell with great heaves.

To be the cause of the reactions in both strong men humbled her. Who knew mere touching could do this much? She hadn't.

Layla released his cock and dropped her head down to just above his stomach with her feet tossed up to the head of the bed. She wanted to see his face when she took him in her mouth. What would he taste like? Salty? Sweet?

She opened her mouth to an O and engulfed the head of his cock. His eyes shot open as she watched his face, while taking him deeper into her mouth.

A medley of emotions crossed his face as he panted. His face tensed as his hips bucked.

He tasted sweet. Almost as if his come were flavored with caramel, a treat she'd had once. She sucked as much of him as she could in, reveling in his taste and reactions.

He tasted better than the caramel. Just as the quick sip of Balt had tasted much better than a salted apple.

They tasted better because of her emotions for the men. Her men. She needed to start thinking of them as such.

Orion grasped her head with one hand to pull her mouth in tighter against him. "Love, don't stop."

She pulled back deliberately to tease him. "Stop what?"

He groaned.

Instead of taking him into her mouth, her tongue swirled all the way up and down him a few times. Then, she sucked him all back in, taking him down until she almost choked. She backed off and suckled him up to the tip before going back down to his base.

Her lover's cock in her mouth and all she wanted was more.

The hand sliding between her legs caught her off guard at first. She popped Orion out of her mouth. He made a sound of protest.

A holdout from her training. She needed to see who'd touched her, though it had to be Balt. She winced. Would it ever leave her?

Balt's hand withdrew to run along her side. He'd moved without her noticing. "I'm playing. That's all."

Orion's breath came noisily through his nose as he repeated, "Don't stop. Love, please."

She couldn't resist the tremor in that strong voice. Her desire cranked back up to give him pleasures. She wouldn't stop again. No matter what her training told her.

Her mouth returned to Orion's cock, taking it all in, then out. More come had leaked to sweeten the taste of him even more than his own unique flavor. Oh, how she liked him in her mouth. He beat every dessert she'd ever had.

Balt's hand slipped in between her legs again to part them. Her sex, already more sensitive than usual, jumped at his touch. She couldn't help the reaction, though she desperately wanted his finger to go there.

"Shhhh, little one." His hand slipped up her thigh before covering her. "So hot. So wet." He let out a growl.

So hard to concentrate on her mission with Balt's hands touching her, but she continued her assault on Orion's cock. As Balt's finger slid into her slick heat, her mouth sped up on Orion.

Her muscles clenched then released, awaiting Balt's touch. One finger slid in to swirl around her swollen nub. He pressed on it, as more moisture gushed.

No one had ever touched her there because of their own needs. Chills erupted from deep within.

A second finger joined the first. They twiddled her clit between them.

Her whole body arched even as she didn't stop what she did to Orion, only sped up the pace.

Balt patted her butt before pressing her legs further apart.

She didn't glance to see what he was doing.

Something warm and wet trailed up one thigh. She jerked. The muscles to her privates jerked in wanting.

Balt's tongue rasped across her slit. "You taste like honey." He smacked his lips together.

She bore down on Orion, sucking him in deeply while rubbing her tongue along the bottom of his cock.

The sensations from Balt's tongue sliding across her made it so hard to concentrate on what she was doing to Orion. She couldn't breath. Her breath came in struggling spurts through her nose. Nothing had prepared her for this.

Balt located her clit, circling it with his tongue.

She sped up the pace on Orion, frantically taking him in and out of her mouth, being careful to keep her teeth away from him.

The orgasm popped inside her without warning. The whole galaxy shifted to the spot between her legs and wrung her inside out. She released Orion, crying out with the force of her pleasure.

Swirling back down to herself, she glanced at both men to see Balt had a self-satisfied smirk on his face, and Orion looked...deadly.

"Bloody hell..." Orion's voice was forced out of his mouth.

Balt reached over to run a hand gently over her cheek. "Have you ever..."

Her tongue came out to moisten her bottom lip. "I've had sex before."

"But have you ever..." Orion hesitated. "Have you have ever had..."

"Been fucked up your ass?"

Orion glared at Balt. "I was getting to that."

"Too slowly." Balt shrugged before looking at Layla. "Have you?"

She shook her head with a gulp. She'd heard it could be painful. "No. Haven't done that before." All in the school she'd attended had found their heartstones as young teenagers so they could have sex. It had been required when entering the stringent curriculum. Sometimes the job called for sex, especially with infiltration, but they hadn't made them do everything in the sexual realm.

Getting one's mate had eliminated one from the program permanently. Having sex with others wasn't permitted in Union Alliance rules once mates were found. Some did it, but most were happy enough with the mates they were fated with.

She'd lain awake some nights, wishing for her mate so she could leave the school, yet scared her mate wouldn't like what she'd become.

Her gaze swept across Balt and Orion. Now, she had them. And they wanted to accept her. How lucky could she get?

"We'll take it slow." Balt moved in to kiss her.

"Very slow." Orion rubbed against her side.

They would. She'd never had so much faith in anyone before. Not the way she had in the two of them.

When Balt pulled away, he sat up slightly to kiss Orion.

Her sex pinged, especially when she saw the kiss deepen further. Oh yeah, she wanted to watch the two together one day.

Orion pulled back, panting. "Bloody hell. I could explode."

"I know what you mean." Balt looked at Orion, and he looked back. The connection that had grown there was obvious.

It warmed her to see it. She was the link that had brought them together. It made her insides gooey when thinking about it.

"You or me?"

Orion's neck cords stood out as he stretched. "You."

"You sure?"

Orion nodded. "Yeah." A smile broke across his face. "You'd crush us on top."

Balt pulled Orion's head to his again for another all out kiss. "I wouldn't."

"I know. You. This time."

Something about what was to come had been decided. Her heart sped up. They'd worked it out together, instead of arguing, without any prodding from her. A definite improvement. There would still be trials to face but this made things better. Maybe they could make this work.

She reached up to touch her heartstone. They all glowed but it had intensified at that moment. She'd seen the pulse of light. Her emotions had done it.

Balt released Orion and lowered his head to kiss her. His tongue swirled in to play with hers. He tasted of Orion.

A shiver rocked across her from kissing one lover and tasting the other on his breath.

Balt's hand skimmed across her middle before going up to her breast. His tongue continued to dance with hers, gently probing her mouth. He left nothing unexplored.

Her body fired up as if it were a kiln under his expert touch and kiss.

He rolled her over more on top of him.

Orion's hand centered on her back, steadying her on top of Balt.

Balt's cock rolled against her. The hardness rubbed her. It would soon be inside her, a delicious thought. She couldn't be sure where. Another delicious focus. It was going to be so good.

Balt continued to kiss her mouth while stroking her breasts. She lifted up her chest slightly to give him better access. Each caress made her purr as if she were a Sendalian kitten.

Orion's hands left her back.

Their loss was noticeable. Her flesh cooled from the disappearance of his heat.

Balt distracted her enough. She lost the focus to what Orion was doing.

Something warm and gooey dribbled into her back hole. It ran to the edges, coating her. One drip ran down her backside.

She broke off the kiss.

Orion's hand centered on her back again, pressing in. The touch centered her. "Going to play, love."

Balt pulled her more up against him with a soothing murmur.

As much as she tried not to be nervous, anal sex made her so. She'd had enough pain in life to know she could take it. But, from her mates, it would be harsher. She'd do it for them, despite her anxiety.

Orion's finger pressed into the middle of her back into her spine.

The touch radiated out along her back in waves of pleasure. Her slickened sex clenched as if it had been touched. She arched with a slight whimper. Her mind left her worries behind with the touch of a man who knew where all her pressure points were.

Balt reclaimed her mouth, doing wicked things to her tongue with his.

Orion slowly moved down her back, pressing into each part of her spine individually. He reached the last knob before her butt and paid it special attention. He pushed his pointer finger into it, rolling it around for long seconds.

Her whole body went boneless. Her eyes rolled back up into her head. It felt as though he touched everywhere instead of only that one spot. Sensations roped through her. She'd had no idea a back could be so sensitive.

Balt wrapped an arm around her to sift through her hair. He slowly dragged his fingers through each strand. Then, his hand crept in to massage her scalp.

Curls of pleasure radiated through her neck.

They'd taken their time with this. They'd loved her body and weren't finished with her yet. They hadn't even breached her, which they could have done. Instead, they'd taken time to swell her passion. She wasn't used to foreplay. Their needs were mighty, yet they took their time. For the first time, she was cherished. Loved. And she wanted them more now than ever.

A finger pressed into her butt hole.

Orion's.

Caught by surprise, she tensed her butt cheeks as he wiggled the tip of his finger around the opening.

Balt nipped at her lips. "Relax, little one."

"Relax, love." The finger ringed the hole.

The sensations weren't painful yet. Just different.

Did she want him in or out? Definitely in. She didn't want to lose the wicked heat romping through her.

Slowly, she let each muscle unclench and relax.

The finger remained exactly where it was, rimming only slightly.

Finally, every part of her let go the tension.

"There we go." Orion's voice came softly behind her. He patted her back gently with his other hand.

More warmth oozed down past Orion's finger.

Her center grew delectably moister. It throbbed, so swollen and needy. She needed more. More from them.

Balt was happy to oblige. His long finger slid down between their bodies. He strummed her clit.

Her dry mouth opened with a groan. The sensations were intense as the tensing of her walls made sensations on her back end that much more pleasurable.

Orion's finger pressed into her butt hole, but only further a tiny bit. He wiggled it around again, allowing her time to adjust to his finger before pushing in even further.

Nerve endings fired off back there.

She'd never thought of her hole as an erogenous zone. But damn if it wasn't blowing air on the fires they'd already started to fan the flames. Not to mention Balt's fingers on her clit.

Balt shifted his weight, removed his fingers, and reached down between their bodies.

Before she realized what was happening, he'd lined himself up so that he knocked at her entrance. The tip of his cock stroked against her open channel.

She sucked in a deep breath, hardly able to wait for him inside of her. She arched her hips to hurry him along inside her. Needed it now. Needed him to complete her.

Balt's tip dipped into her entrance.

The movement electrified her skin. Her whole body pulsed with an enchanting hum. Yet, it wasn't enough. "More."

Balt's body tensed as he let out a loud groan. "So wet."

She parted her legs more. Needed him to drive himself home then and there. Couldn't wait any longer for his possession.

His cock drilled more into her depths, going about halfway inside her channel. She sucked him in, opening up for his penetration.

And, it still wasn't enough.

He surged his hips forward to grind against her. He slipped more inside her. Almost filling her. Almost all the way in.

Orion's finger continued the motion inside of her, probing millimeter by millimeter.

And even that wasn't enough.

She looked up to see him under her as if he were some great canopy of man. His face pinched with his mouth contorted. Had to be the strain of holding himself back. She didn't want him to hold back.

Orion's finger probed more into her butt hole as Balt slowly lifted himself to her to plant further inside her. He lodged all the way in, stretching her to her capacity.

Not painful, entirely pleasant and earth shattering. Her back arched from the sensations.

By pressing himself down into the mattress, Balt withdrew a little, using slow careful movements.

Not what she wanted from him right now. What she needed right now. On top and seeking control, she didn't want careful and slow. She wanted him frantic. "Harder."

His eyes blinked down at her in rapid fire movements. "Don't want to hurt you." The words gritted out between clenched teeth. Sweat beaded on his forehead and nose. His skin had reddened.

She looked down to see his hands had turned almost white from clenching into fists. "You won't. Harder."

She went down to fully meet his thrust. She ground her hips against him, deepening the penetration from her position on top.

His eyes rolled back along with his head in his state of pleasure.

Orion's finger pushed more down into her. He had to be a joint into her at least now. He probed down further. More pressure. His finger grew fatter. He must've added a second one. His pressing in became rhythmic with the thrusting in and out that Balt's cock did. Orion matched them pace for pace.

His doing so heightened her sensations, making them almost unbearable in their intensity of desire.

Everything swirled around her. Her vision clouded. She moaned. Flames licked at her whole body. Split from above and penetrated from below. Nothing could send her in the stratosphere faster.

The heartstone hung low from her body, almost touching Balt's. She didn't have to look to see their glow.

Her body broke out into a sweat as goose pimples erupted everywhere. A second orgasm hovered just out of reach.

Things in her back hole grew even more pressurized. A third finger had been added.

Too much pressure. It bordered on pain. Too far stretched out.

She tensed up, which meant she bore down on Balt.

The orgasm, which lay just before her, faded away with the offering of pain instead of pleasure.

Balt groaned at the tension around his cock. Her muscles clenched at him, stilling his movements just as they did with Orion's fingers.

The fingers yanked away from her ass. Despite the intense pressure being released from her hole, she winced at them going away. She didn't have too long to think about their withdrawal though.

Breath returned to her body as Balt lifted upward again to press into her. His cock lurched up, filling her most delightfully. He took away the memory of the pain. Pleasure began to build again, taking her along the winding track of it.

Orion lifted himself on top of her back. He held himself up by his arms and legs, so his front only just nudged her back.

"Orion?" She stilled again. Anxiety filtered through her. She hadn't taken that much of his fingers. He hadn't probed all the way inside her hole. His cock was bigger than that. It would hurt.

"Shhh." He pressed his sticky cock down into the small of her back. The moisture-covered hardness rubbed against her.

The sensations reset her senses aflame.

"Don't let me distract you."

Ha. As if that were possible.

She bore down again on Balt, taking him in fully and then withdrawing him from her up to his tip. The arousal slowly blossomed from Balt lodged within her. Several thrusts against him took her back up the plateau.

The act of arching upward brought her into contact with Orion's body and cock with her back.

With a sound she couldn't identify, he slid his cock into the cleft of her butt, twisting it around against her. He wasn't entering her hole, not even close. But in the tight space, his cock rammed up against her.

She relaxed.

He wouldn't enter her back there without warning.

How much she already trusted these two men.

Her mates.

Her focus shifted back to the sensations of one man above her and one below her. Heat built forth and billowed around her again.

The next thrust of her hips, he followed her down, keeping his cock close to her to maintain the contact of their bodies. He ground down a little pressing it into her skin as Balt's cock became fully seated inside her walls.

Sandwiched between her mates, the contact of their body inflamed her senses, which were already on overload.

Each move downward, Orion followed her with his body, slickening her back with the lube on his cock and pressing that hardness as much against her as he could. Each move downward brought Balt further up into her.

She'd never been so close to anyone. So personal. So intimate.

It was almost as if they moved as one. As if they were one.

When she thrust up, it brought her rump against Orion's cock even more. And Balt moved through her with a slide. She edged on the brink of some mountain, about to jump off and loving every minute.

Balt grasped her hips, steadying her, trying to control the movement and bring them down with a faster motion.

She wouldn't let him take control, instead making each movement her own, keeping the pace according to what she set. Never had she been in control of something before. It was good to be in charge.

The pace quickened as Layla took Balt in and out over and over again. Her walls tightened around him as an orgasm burst forth from her body. She coated him in a fresh spurt of her cream, unable to hold anything back. Tears wrung from her eyes.

Orion's body shuddered over hers. His thrusts were jackknife quick against her. His body jerked once, twice, three times. A hoarse cry broke free from his lips. Hot liquid poured into the skin of her lower back.

She pounded herself against Balt with frenzied cries of pleasure. She milked him in her throes of bliss.

Balt's body went slack as his hips jerked. His hot seed spurted up into her, coating her. He shouted her name as his orgasm finished.

How she liked to hear her name in such a voice. Her heart clenched at the sound. More tears leaked from her eyes. Not of sadness. But of bliss.

She collapsed into a panting heap on top of Balt, who lay still against the mattress. Orion followed her down to lay upon her back, still resting some weight on his arms so he didn't crush her.

Balt's heartstone touched hers as Orion's singed her back.

They all breathed in time with each other.

As she panted, so did Orion and Balt. As her breathing slowed, so did theirs. She'd heard of mates whose hearts regularly beat together, who came together. The closeness and sanctity of the heartmate bond could be reflected in the physical actions of the mates in the bond. She changed her breathing, listening closely to them.

They changed theirs, too.

It had been the most beautiful, honest thing she'd ever done. Not much in her life had been either. Nothing like this.

Orion moved beside them, but she remained on top of Balt.

She drifted off to sleep, with Balt still inside her, Orion's seed drying on her back. In her whole life, she'd never gone to sleep so easily. So warm.

If only it would last.

Chapter Twelve

Orion woke to a chime going off. He blinked, wrapped under bodies and arms and limbs.

His mates.

His cock swelled to life. He palmed the length in his hand. What a great way to start the day.

His communicator pealed again.

Layla opened her eyes. "What's that?"

He disengaged her leg from between his. Her soft skin glided across him. Such a muscular calf. And to nibble up and reach those silken thighs...heaven. Tasting the space between those thighs, as if he were eating pure honey.

Yet another chime sounded.

Balt erupted in a soft snore, smacking his lips.

Orion shook his head, resisting an impulse to ruffle his hands through Balt's hair. And follow his hand down to stroke his mammoth cock.

Yes, this was the way to wake up.

The sound came again.

Orion's mouth thinned as he frowned. Someone had their spacesuit in a bunch trying to get him.

"What's that?" Layla repeated with a small yawn. She snuggled into Balt's chest, emitting a soft sigh.

"It's my communicator, love. Someone's trying to contact me. They've marked the communication urgent." He stumbled out of bed. Scratching his chest with one hand, his fingers made rasping sounds against the hair. He picked up his com with his other hand.

Orion looked at the message identifier. "Bloody hell."

Layla's head lifted, her eyes going wide in alarm. "What's wrong?"

There was no point in lying. No matter how much he wanted to. They all needed to be upfront with each other at all times, or this would never work out. "It's Ansel."

Her eyes drew open wider, and she shifted to sitting. "He's trying to contact you? Does he know?" She pushed her hair back.

"No. He doesn't know. I bet he wants to know status of my hunt..." If Ansel knew, then he would have called down a contract on Orion's life. If that happened, Orion had contacts that would let him know. They made it a point to know all and see all. Good thing. It would help to keep them all safe.

He hadn't been prepared for this confrontation just yet. What would he tell the maniac? Layla would never be turned over to the cruel man. How would he put Ansel off their trail? His mind searched for a plan.

Orion pushed a button, putting the com on standby, letting Ansel know he'd be picking it up momentarily before setting it back down.

He approached the bed to kneel on it in front of Layla. "Don't worry. We'll get through this." His hand reached out to caress her cheek. "I promise I won't let anything happen to you."

She pressed a soft kiss to the knuckle of his thumb. "You can't promise that. But thank you."

His chest constricted. It was a promise he wanted to keep. Somehow, he'd find the way to make sure she was safe. No matter what it required.

He slapped Balt's leg. "Wake up."

Balt shimmied away from him. "I'm awake." His voice was thick with sleep but coherent.

Orion slapped Balt's ass, making a smacking sound through the blanket. Had Ansel not been on hold, he would have followed it up by a nuts grab and squeeze. But that would lead to other activities in the bed, which they didn't have time for, though it would be more fun than talking to Ansel.

Balt didn't open his eyes, growling softly. "I can't believe you just did that."

"Ansel's on the com. For me."

"I heard that. So?"

"I'm in your quarters." Where had his pants gone last night? He searched. Though Ansel had seen his goods before, he didn't want to face the man without pants. "You two better keep low."

"We'll stay in the bed." Balt turned over to face Orion. "As I was before you smacked my ass. Which you will pay for later."

There they are. Orion yanked up his pants from the floor. He pulled them over one foot. He'd have one chance at this and one chance only. He called up the army officer he'd been. *Reporting in to a superior with nothing.* That's all he was doing.

"Hurry up. Ansell will click it over to view before you're ready if you keep him waiting too long."

As if Ansel had heard the words, the com chimed again. Balt had spoken correctly. Ansel could switch it over to view before Orion gave him permission. It wasn't done often because of protocols. But Ansel wasn't a patient man.

"See?" Balt pulled Layla down with him before pulling the covers up over them. "No matter what Ansel says, don't make a sound."

Orion finished pulling up his pants and picked up the com. He positioned it so the broadcast was away from the bed.

He pushed a button, switching the com on.

The connection took a second before popping in. A fuzzy picture, about the size of a monitor screen, appeared on the far rock wall.

The sound crackled. A scream rang out.

No sound came from Balt or Layla.

"Ansel." Orion spoke into the mic. He kept his mouth in a flat line without expression. The best look for reporting no news.

Ansel appeared in front of the screen, golden hair gleaming in the lights. Unlike Orion, Ansel was well illuminated. "I was waiting so long, I got distracted." He took a cloth and wiped red from his long hands. Blood. His youthful, feminine face took on a pout. "Took you a while to answer my call, Orion."

"Sorry. Was busy." He heard whimpers from somewhere behind Ansel. Orion swallowed. What sort of things was Ansel doing over there? Playing? Or working? Or a combination of both? Best not to think about that. Because then he'd wouldn't try to picture Layla in one of Ansel's torture devices. He couldn't afford the distraction of the thought that he'd make sure would never become reality.

Ansel peered over Orion's shoulder, his thin body stretching. "I bet you've picked up another muscular whore. You and your...appetites." His lip curled up in what Ansel must consider a grin. "You should come let me satisfy you once and a while."

Orion moved toward the screen. "You're mated. Broke my heart the day your stone started glowing."

It hadn't. They'd screwed a time or two until Ansel had been mated the first time. Ansel wasn't Orion's type. He didn't get turned on by cruelty and platinum. Not to mention, Orion's tastes ran to beefy men, leaving Ansel and his soft looks quite out of the pickings.

Balt. Now there was a man who Orion could sink his teeth into and not worry about. But never for pain. All this time, and he'd never admitted the attraction. Now, however, everything was out in the open. He resisted the urge to look at the bed as his cock rehardened. Orion shifted. Had Ansel noticed? Good thing he had put on pants.

Another scream sounded from somewhere behind Ansel.

Ansel clucked his tongue. "Quiet down." He shook his head. "Sorry for all the noise. You know how work gets."

"Yeah. Yeah, I know how your work gets." Orion managed to get down the lump in his throat. It would never be Layla. Or Balt. Orion would take a place there before he ever let Ansel get his hands on them.

Ansel bared his teeth. "Yes. I'm sure you do." He waved a hand in the air as if he fanned himself. "I had some men who betrayed me. Didn't get the job done. Now they have my...anger to deal with."

"Bad for them."

"Deadly, I'd say."

Orion heard another whimper but much softer than the others.

"Hang on a minute." Ansel moved out of screen range. A popping sound came with a curdling scream. Ansel moved back so Orion could see him, wiping his hands again. "Sorry. Had to take care of that."

Orion nodded. The less he said the better right now. Especially with Balt and Layla hearing this whole transaction. He needed to find out what Ansel knew and that meant talk to him. No matter how distasteful he found it.

"So, I haven't heard from you in a day or so. Unlike you. I wondered how your job was going."

"Going O.K. No real new leads since I updated you last." Orion kept himself looking directly into the screen. Ansel couldn't catch him in a lie, or they'd lose whatever maneuvering room they had.

"Hmmmm." Ansel tugged on his chin with one hand. "You didn't have anything last time. Neither did Baltazar."

"That big monkey couldn't catch Swellerin sickness if it went up his nostril." Orion couldn't keep back the smile. Balt would probably make him pay for that later, too. He couldn't wait. Ansel would take the smile in other ways so the expression worked.

Ansel chuckled. "You two boys and rivalries." He clucked his tongue. "I'm not seeing a lot of progress in finding me Layla. I like progress."

"I know. I'm working on it."

"I thought sending Baltazar would speed things up. I thought you two would motivate each other to get me what I want. I must have been wrong." Ansel's eyes bored into his. "Was I wrong, Orion?"

"I'm working on it." Orion put his hands behind his back. A sign of supplication from his Alliance days. They clenched together so he wouldn't turn off the damn monitor. *Let me get through this call.* He had to, if they were going to make it out of the predicament they were in. If Ansel found out Balt and Orion were hiding Layla, he'd try to make them pay. It wouldn't matter to him that Layla was their mate. All he'd care about was they'd helped her escape. They had one chance to play this out correctly.

"Not fast enough." Ansel shrugged one shoulder, then the other. "So, I made a decision."

"What's that?"

"Mercurior. He's now on the job as of twenty minutes ago. He's headed your way as fast as he can."

Merc was sadist dressed in bounty hunter gear. His captures got damaged in shipping. And he hung close to Settler's Mine. Much closer than the other yokels that Ansel had hired. He'd be there much sooner than anyone else. Even Orion had to admit, he was also better than the others Ansel had hired. He was just crazier than shit. "I see." How he kept his emotions from barking that out, Orion didn't know.

"Maybe you three can get somewhere on finding what I want." Ansel played games because he didn't mention the two other hunters Orion knew he'd hired. "To getting me what's mine. Instead of playing with meaty little whores"

Orion's teeth gritted together. He let out a growl. Good thing too, because a growl erupted from the bed. Orion's covered it. Layla better calm Balt down. Of course, there was no one to calm Orion down right now. His heart thumped in his chest. Maybe later. Maybe later, he'd find a way to kill the smug bastard on the other side of the screen

Funny, but Ansel had hired him a dozen times to retrieve people. Having a mate made Orion see things in a whole different way. If that were Layla in the back, screaming, whimpering, it would kill Orion with Ansel never having to raise a weapon to him.

He managed to spit out, "Maybe."

Ansel's eyes narrowed, looking from side to side. "Are your quarters bigger? They seem bigger than last time?" He continued to bob around, as if trying to get a look around Orion's body.

Bloody hell. Orion needed the call to end. "Yeah. I had myself moved. I gotta go, Ansel. Follow up some leads. Before I get scooped on the bounty." He clicked off before Ansel could say anything else. Something Ansel would berate him about later. But he could only keep his tongue civil so long, and Balt had to be already on borrowed time for keeping silent.

"That little pissant." Balt shot off the bed as soon as the com was down. "Merc's a crazy bastard." He paced back and forth, his big feet clumping on the stone. His face contorted in angry lines.

"Who's he?" Layla sat up, rubbing her hand across her face. "I haven't heard that name before."

"A bounty hunter."

"Like you?"

"Not exactly." Orion put down his com. "He's...not nice." That was an understatement. He grabbed his shirt. "I'd hoped we'd have more time. But Merc's going to be here within a day. We have to get the hell off of Settler's Mine."

Before anyone could say anything in response, Balt's com went off with a dinging chime. "Fuck."

Orion cursed, too. It didn't take smarts to know who was on the other end. "It's Ansel to tell you the exact thing he told me."

"I know. I'm not in the mood for him." Balt moved away from the bed. "You two hunker down on the bed as we did." He went to the same corner where Orion had opened the link.

"Are your quarters bigger? They seem bigger than last time?"

Orion froze before he'd moved a step toward Layla, who'd already lain back down under the covers, trying to ball herself up as much as possible. They'd just gotten her to relax with them. Now she was back to the tenseness and fear. Damn Ansel.

Her face remained set in a grim line of resolve.

"Balt. Don't answer it yet."

"Why not?" Balt paused with his hand already on his com button. He hadn't hit it yet, waiting for them to get ready, but had readied himself to.

"He saw this room. They do look alike at Settler's Mine but he'll notice too much of the same stuff. He'll see too much. You have to go...out in the hall." Orion gestured with his hands.

Goddess, they had to hurry if they were going to pull this off. He didn't want them all to end up in Ansel's chambers. Definitely not his first plan. "Pretend you're on a fact-finding expedition out there to find Layla."

Balt looked down at his state of undress. His cock hung heavy between his legs. "Like this?"

"Bloody hell, no. Get dressed." Orion found Balt's clothes and tossed them at him. He tried to ignore Balt's cock bouncing. But it was difficult. The damn thing was so big. Goddess, he wanted to take both his mates to bed instead of this crazy charade.

Balt caught them with a sweeping motion of his hands.

He shotgunned the words out to Balt. "Hurry up. Go." Adrenaline pumped through Orion. They couldn't get caught now. *Come on, man, hurry.*

Balt quickly pulled on his clothes, yanking them up and tucking things in. "Going." The com chimed again. "Shut up."

As soon as he'd gotten his pants up, Orion opened the door. "Go. Go."

"I am. Don't shove." Balt strolled out the door as though he were going for a stroll instead of to speak to a dangerous man. "Shut it behind me. He's about the open the link himself, the bastard."

Orion pushed the doors shut to make them go faster. They'd made it. One more small step in their favor.

He wouldn't hear what Ansel said to Balt. But, it didn't matter. He'd already heard the spiel, and not liked a word. Neither of them would hand over Layla willingly. But how would they evade Ansel and his far-reaching network?

"We're not going to make it, are we?" Layla blew out a breath. "I should turn myself in. Or run myself. All I'm doing is endangering you and Balt."

"Bloody hell, no. As much trouble as you went to to escape, you can't give up now." Orion watched as her whole body slumped. He'd never seen her so defeated, even when she'd caught him snooping around her quarters. He didn't like it. Wanted to beat anything and everything for her to never see this look again.

"Before, I didn't have anything to lose." Her voice steadied. "Nothing mattered. Now, I do have something to lose."

What Orion wouldn't give to make her fears go away. He wanted to promise her safety. The world. Hell, even the galaxies. He'd die trying for her. He went to her and took her in his arms, pressing her face into his chest. "Shhhhhhh." His hands traveled up and down her back. She shivered under his hand. Somehow he took as much strength from the embrace as he tried to give her. They stayed that way a minute or two before the doors swooshed open.

"That was fast." Orion watched as Balt threw down his com on the nightstand with a look of disgust.

"That's because I don't schmooze. I talk and get done what's to be done." Balt plopped down on the bed, his hand instinctively reaching out to Layla to stroke her leg. His thick fingers ran along Layla's colored skin. His face softened as he looked at Layla.

"Anything new?"

"Same thing he told you. With screams in the background." Balt's tone stayed neutral. "He had a new plaything to punish."

She moved her leg closer to Balt's touch.

Orion had never imagined seeing another's man's hand on a woman's leg would do things inside him. But it did. His throat worked. Something filled up his heart at seeing one mate comfort another.

Balt met his eyes. A flicker ran through them at whatever he saw in Orion's. A flicker of pleasure.

Orion didn't miss the way Balt's pants swelled in front either. Balt liked what he saw in Orion as much as Orion did in Balt. Bloody hell, they'd been rivals a long time. This becoming allies was coming easier than Orion had thought it would.

Balt broke his gaze away from Orion's. "How did Ansel find you anyway?"

"He approached me…after a falling out with my parents. He knew…somehow, he knew everything about me. Where I'd been all that time. What I'd done for my government. He offered me a job working for him."

She glossed over the time with her parents. But Natives were big on family. It had to sting, leaving them behind again. She leaned further back into Orion, seeking the warmth and comfort of his body. He stroked along the side of her hips. Her silken skin electrified him.

"So you worked for Ansel before he came after you."

"Only a little while. Ansel… One of his lovers, his mates, was in the school. He lucked out, didn't have a chip implanted. Ansel become obsessed with finding out everything."

"Why?" Balt clasped her foot in one big hand. He stroked along the arch.

Her foot moved more into his soft touch.

She was relaxing again with them.

Orion let her go on talking about Ansel. She needed to purge all this to them before they could make it work. He'd worry about Merc later.

"He wants to take over the government. A lot of those working directly for him are former agents trained where I was. He plans to locate them all and use them."

Orion hadn't known that. Union Alliance with Ansel in charge was a scary thought. With the chip in Layla's head, he might accomplish what he'd set out to do. Yet another reason, not that he needed one, to keep Layla away from Ansel.

"Did you suspect you had one before Ansel found out for sure?" Orion pulled her hair to one side. His hand caressed her neck and down her side.

Her voice dripped with malice as she tried to draw away. Orion had never heard that tone in her voice with anything else she'd told them. "A scientist. He sold the information about who had what chip implanted. Though Ansel wants them all, he was most intrigued by the Armageddon chip."

"One thing I don't understand." Balt yanked her foot back over to start stroking it. "Why did they let you go with it still there?"

Her eyes rolled back before she could answer. "Bureaucracy."

Orion's breath sucked in. She was so beautiful. That look on her face would make even a stoic burn to be the one to put the expression there.

"Now, everyone wants you for the chip. Not you...per se...but the chip." Orion saw the opportunity to talk to them about his plan. Much as he'd like to let Layla talk about more, they had a finite amount of time. Orion would have to find out when Merc would arrive.

"Yes. I'm incidental." She laughed, a little hollowly.

"We want you for you, love." Orion rushed to reassure her. "And only you."

She put her hand on his and squeezed.

"I have an idea." The best one he'd come up with. It was dangerous and he wasn't sure the idea would work. But it was something. He couldn't lose her.

"What is it?"

"They don't want you, right? They want the chip up here." Orion pointed to Layla's pretty head. Her shorn hair drifted through his fingers though he'd meant to only point. What a halo it would be once it got long again. He couldn't keep his fingers out of her locks now, it would be impossible to then. Of course, with what he was about to propose, her hair might be even shorter for a while.

"That's right." Layla nodded. "They want what's in my head, not necessarily with my head attached to my body."

"Why don't we get the chip out of your brain? Then they'd no longer want or need you."

* * *

Layla's face wrinkled as she considered Orion's words. It was something she'd mulled over before but hadn't had a good enough reason or enough money to attempt. "It's…"

Balt interrupted. "What would they have to do to her?"

Orion looked to Layla. "Surely you've considered taking out the chip? And know what the operation entails."

She nodded. "It's dangerous. Implanting is easy. You stick a needle in while viewing a brain on a screen, and the chip is inserted." She rubbed the side of her head. Was there a lump there? She couldn't be sure but always tried to find the point of origin where her life had changed for good. Where had they stuck the needle to bring the misery into her life?

"But what do they do to take it out?" Balt flexed one of his arms, as if shaking it out. "Can they draw it out with a needle?"

"They can. But it's a little trickier to find something embedded than to merely stick something in. The procedure's specialized. Expensive. And if they can't find the exact location by scanning—the thing does move around sometimes—they would have to open up my head."

"What are the chances they'd have to operate?" Orion's face pinched. He didn't like the idea of her going under a knife.

Neither did she. "Unfortunately, good. The thing in my head moves around without damaging any of the brain cells. From minute to minute even. And the chip camouflages itself. It's easier to get a fix on the general locale than it is to tell exactly where it's located. Once they're in they can find it."

"So more than likely, they'd have to cut you open?" Balt flexed out the other arm. "That's what you are saying."

"Yes."

"Then, fuck no."

Orion shifted closer to them on the bed so that he could touch them both at the same time. "Balt…"

"Fuck no."

"It would get them off of her. There'd no longer be a reason to pursue her. They don't want *her.* Only that chip. Get it out and no one will be after her."

"No." Balt shrugged off Orion's touch as though he couldn't bear it.

The ruin of their union had started. Coldness swept through Layla. She always caused discord. *Look at your parents.*

"You're being unreasonable. We have to consider all the possibilities. We can't dismiss anything."

"That's one idea I won't consider."

"Why?" Orion blew out a breath of frustration.

"I won't risk her life. *Our mate's life.*"

"Long as the chip is in her head, she's in danger already. Her life's already at risk."

"That's different." Balt moved off the bed away from them. "You know it's different."

"Not."

"Is." Balt punched a wall. The crunch sound echoed. He rubbed his knuckles. "I can't believe you'd consider this."

"I can't believe you won't."

"Guys." Layla had watched their argument escalate while she sat, resting with her head on a pillow. She'd been thinking while they talked. But their fight didn't need to go any higher in tension. Her mouth turned up at her mates fighting. She didn't like this turn. Her insides were eaten up with the guilt. Things between them been going so well. Nothing good was ever meant to stay in her life. "Both of you stop."

"Layla…" Balt smirked at her. "Tell him he's being foolish."

"No, she'll tell you you are."

"Stop." She tapped Orion on the head.

Balt snickered.

"Don't laugh. If you were closer, I'd rap you, too."

Orion shot Balt a triumphant grin. Then, he sobered. "The important thing is what you think, Layla. It's your head."

Balt came over to perch himself on the floor on his knees in front of Layla. He grasped her hands in his. One of them had bluish knuckles from the hit against the stone. "And it's not something you'll do. We'll find another way to keep you safe."

She rifled her hands through his hair, gently stroking along his scalp. Such a big man, yet so gentle with her and Orion. He felt things most deeply. That endeared him to her. She gently leaned down to kiss his battered hand. "I'm not convinced yet it's not the way to go."

Balt's face took on alarming concern. "But…" He fell silent as she held her finger to her lips.

She turned to Orion, who didn't look smug, only resigned. He knew it wouldn't be a win if he did that but only a play out of a situation he couldn't control. "Nor am I convinced yet it is the way to go."

"Fair enough." Orion stroked a hand along her calf. The fingers toyed along the place where her knee joined her leg bones. "What do you want to do?"

"I think we need to find surgeons who are skilled enough to do this type of operation, and will do it behind Union Alliance's back."

"That can't be an easy list to obtain." Balt ran a hand along the arch of her ankle. "They'd hide."

"I think I know who I can ask to find names." Layla leaned over to kiss Balt gently on the lips. She kissed Orion next.

"Who?" Orion looked intrigued.

"Don't worry about it. We need to go. And neither of your shuttles is safe for us to use anymore. We need transport."

Both of them jumped up. "I can arrange it." They looked at the other. "No, I can."

This mate bond wasn't going to be easy. Old habits wouldn't stand down overnight. The argument they'd had had brought out some of their old tendencies. They'd better get their rivalry resolved soon. Or she'd do more than rap their heads. She didn't have time for this squabbling over who was on top. "Both of you can."

"Fine." Balt's clipped speech spoke volumes. He didn't like this idea. How would he react if she decided to do the surgery?

"One of us should go with you. Keep an eye on you."

"I can take care of myself, remember? Transport's important. And I need to see this person on my own."

She also had a decision to make. She'd brought this down on her mates' heads. Leaving them would ease some of the danger on them. Could she do it? Could she stay with them, knowing how much peril she put them in? Running would be easier for one rather than three. She could find them again when the chip had been removed. If it could be.

"Are you sure?" Balt frowned.

"Don't make me show you I can take care of myself. Shoo. I need to do this on my own."

Orion quirked a brow. "Not going to tell us who you're going to see?"

She shook her head. "The only important thing is that they'll help me." *And talk more freely to me than you.*

She kissed each of them again, reveling in each of their unique flavors. They tasted scrumptious. If only they had time for one more round... But they needed to get things moving. She had a shift later and things to do before it. It would probably arouse less suspicion if she worked her normal hours and left after that. Might butt her up against Merc's arrival, but as long they weren't on the station together long, he wouldn't figure it out before she left with them or without them. "You two get going. Get us a way off."

Orion sauntered to the door and out, followed by Balt, who cast a look back, full of love and tenderness.

She swallowed. Her throat constricted as she watched the door close.

If she left them, she'd be saving them. She'd heard what Ansel had done to those people. It was all too easy to hear Balt and Orion in the screams. She couldn't allow that to happen to her mates. Time to think had run out. No matter what they'd shared, it all came down to one point. She couldn't let them be hurt.

This was why she had to go this alone.

Too much lay at stake for the three of them. Better a galaxy with an unhappy Orion and Balt in it than without them. They had each other now and had worked out enough to continue, until she came back to them. If she came back to them.

Her decision made, she strolled over to put on her Besela suit. She shut down her emotions. Couldn't feel too much, or she'd go nuts.

Six words kept ringing through her ears.

No one will be after me.

That had always been a dream, but now, she had a reason to stop running and take the risk. A reason to undertake the dangers of the operation, including that the doctor might just turn her in for a reward.

To make it back to Balt and Orion.

If she didn't die.

She hadn't mentioned one thing to them.

One person she'd been in school with had attempted the operation to rid themselves of the cursed chip.

And passed away on the surgical table.

That won't be me.

She'd make it. There was too much in her life to live for. Balt and Orion's faces passed before her eyes. For her mates, she'd explore this option and go through it alone.

She tugged on the last of the padding before putting in her prosthesis.

For them, she'd take off and not look back until they met again. Not if...until.

Now it was time to see Zelda and find a doctor she could talk to.

Chapter Thirteen

Layla rapped on the door with purposeful hands.

"Come in."

The door opened to Zelda's office. The buxom woman sat a desk, looking at a monitor. "Hello, Besela."

Layla shut the door behind her and walked carefully into the room. "I think we both know that's not my real name."

A hint of a smile graced Zelda's full lips as she leaned back in the chair. "Oh." The springs squeaked as if it were a mouse in danger. "I don't usually talk to customers in here."

"I can go…" Layla half turned. Maybe she had made a mistake in coming to Zelda. Butterflies raced across her stomach.

"No. Go on." Zelda put down the stylus she'd had in her hand. "What do you need to see me about? Are Orion and Balt bothering you?"

Layla scanned the small office. Like everything else at Settler's Mine, it had been carved out of the rock. The walls looked rougher here than the boarding rooms and the bar. No polishing had been done. The floor had more dips. The electrical wires hung as if they were wispy snakes on the ceilings, instead of being camouflaged. Zelda's wooden desk had some age to it as did her chair, unlike the rest of the mine where everything looked new and fresh. Zelda took better care of the mine than she did her own space. Somehow that relaxed Layla. It made it easier to do what she needed to do.

It was a hard thing for her to ask for help. Her training and time away had dictated self-reliance. She took a deep breath and plowed ahead before she could think anymore about it. "I need to talk to you. I need some help."

"What kind of help?" Zelda pulled her chair closer to her desk, sitting up straighter. She waved a hand at a rattan chair in front of the desk. "Sit."

"I…It's a long story, and I don't have time to explain everything." She pushed a hand through her hair. "I need an underground surgeon. Specializing in…chip implantation and removal."

Zelda didn't bat an eye. "Those names are hard to come by."

Layla met her steady gaze as though she asked about such things all the time. "Not for someone with your reputation." What would she do if Zelda had no names? She crossed her legs. No, this woman had to have a name.

"It will cost you."

"Doesn't everything." Layla's eyes shut briefly. Platinum made the galaxy turn. And there was never enough of it. Getting off the planet would cost. The surgeon would charge an exorbitant amount. She couldn't be sure she had enough now, much less if she paid out some of the platinum before she even met the scalpel wielder. She reopened her eyes. "I don't have much…"

"I don't want money. But, you'll owe me." Zelda nodded her head forward. Hair slid forward for her to push back with red-painted nails on long fingers. "I'll collect one day. When I need it."

The scent of jasmine hung heavy in the air. Layla breathed through it. "I agree to your terms."

"Be sure, Besela."

Layla opened her mouth.

Before she could speak, Zelda continued, "No other name. I don't want to slip where it counts. Keep in mind, my collection may come at a time you don't want to fulfill it. Think about it before you agree."

That it would. Layla had that kind of luck. But, when offered a deal by the devil to escape death, you took the devil up on the offer. Layla would do what had to be done. At least Zelda wasn't asking for her short supply of platinum. "I agree to it, Zelda. I'm sure." Her hands trembled as they rubbed up her arms. The mine was always so chilled but that wasn't why she shivered. She needed this name. Maybe if she survived, she'd have some kind of life. With her mates. This was the first step toward that.

"I'll get a list of names for you. When do you need them by?"

"I need them...now." Layla folded her hands in front of her. What would the future hold? She looked up to see Zelda watching her closely. Layla's whole world had bubbled down to the names of those would cut into her head and free her from the demon contained there.

"Now. Hmmm." Zelda tapped a finger on the desk. "Then there's really only one name you need. He's a friend. You give him this." Zelda reached in her desk, then handed Layla a stone. "His name is McTavish."

Layla took the cold metal in her hands. A mismatch of colors, it glimmered softly in the low lighting. "This?"

"He'll know you came from me. He'll treat you well."

Layla pocketed the rock. It bulged in her pocket, digging into her skin with blunt edges. The stone's weight and coolness would remind her of the things to come. "Where is he?"

Zelda punched a few things into a small triangle-shaped computer. She handed the flat screen to Layla. "The coordinates to him are here. Interface this with…whatever craft you use to get off the station."

"Got it." Layla surveyed the small computer. The cool plastic warmed to her touch. It had a small socket in the back for interfacing. Must have universal plugs so it would fit most anything. The little thing had been expensive. Not many had this type of technology.

Layla's throat constricted. And Zelda trusted her with it. A stranger. More than that, she trusted her with the name. Of a friend. Why would Zelda help her? True, Zelda said she'd call in a favor. But nothing Layla could ever give her was worth the market price of this information. Another would have taken all her platinum and an IOU. Before she could stop herself, she blurted out the question. "Why are you helping me? Doing all this?" In ways, it didn't make sense.

"Because I can."

"What if I die before I pay you?" There was a good chance that might happen. Asking the question brought up Layla's tension. No. Dying wasn't a choice.

"You won't. If you do, it settles our account." Zelda pointed to a small grey indention, remaining businesslike. "Push that completely in, and the whole thing will break apart. Nothing will remain of the machine, or the coordinates in its memory."

A protection switch. In case she was caught. "I understand." She straightened. There it was. Again. Reiterated by Zelda's use of a protection switch. Having mates gave her so much more to lose. Her heart thudded as if it were running boots on the stone floor before she showed the emotions playing out inside. She would be responsible if they were caught. She couldn't take them with her. It was impossible.

Zelda tapped her finger on her chin. "Do you need help arranging transport? I can arrange something for you." Her voice stayed low. Calm. Soothing.

Layla poked up her lip in a soft smile, despite her insides clenching up into a ball. How often had she hid her turbulent inside from the world? Too many times to count. As an infiltration operative, even involuntary reactions had to be curtailed. *Smile while you are dying.* One instructor's mantra came to mind. "And I'd owe you more, right?" She put the computer into her pocket. Its rounded corners pushed into her skin. Her pockets balanced with an item on each side.

Zelda chuckled. "That wouldn't cost nearly as much as that name. Hardly a durken or shallot."

She'd named old pieces of money. From before Union Alliance. Perhaps someone had rebel tendencies, and that's why she'd help Layla at such a low cost. Layla would probably never know the real reason, and it didn't matter. Zelda would help her. "I'll find a way off the station. Myself."

"Are you sure?"

A knock sounded on the door.

"I should…" Layla started to stand.

"Stay. Another minute." Zelda pointed for Layla to sit down again. "I have another question for you. Let me get rid of…" The knock came again, louder this time. Impatient. "Come in."

Bren sauntered in. He wore tight leathers, which clung to his body like snakeskin. His eyes gleamed brightly, looking at his mate. He noticed Layla and quirked a brow. "Should I come back later?"

The huge man had the looks that would turn any woman's head and most men's, even with his being mated to Zelda. But somehow he didn't catch Layla's eye. She noticed his looks and moved on without being led to lust. He was nice to look at. But not as fine as her two guys. The two guys she needed to leave. She'd leave here and go find McTavish on her own. They didn't need to be mixed up in the mess that was her life. Zelda would never tell them where she'd gone. She'd be doing this for their own good.

Yes, that's the plan.

"Yes." Zelda didn't hesitate in her answer shooing her mate away. She folded her arms in front of her chest.

"No." Layla stood. "I...I can go... I got what I came here for." She sighed. They'd be waiting for her to find them one day. If she survived. And angry with her. But, if the future all worked out, they'd at least be safe while she did what had to be done.

Zelda shot her a look.

Layla sat back down quickly. The woman had perfected a look, which said, "Defy me only if you dare." If the instructors in her school had perfected that look, there never would have been discipline problems. Best to keep Zelda happy with her.

Bren scratched his chest. His expression had a quizzical cast, but he didn't comment. He went behind the desk by Zelda. "Can I run one thing by you?"

"No." Zelda tugged her arms in tighter around her. "Well..." She huffed a breath. "Is it important, Bren? To the running of the mine?" She shot an apologetic look to Layla.

Layla murmured, "Don't worry about it."

"You said to alert you if Orion and Balt had..."

"Are they fighting? On my mine?" Zelda grimaced. Her hand went to her side where she probably had a weapon. "I'll kill 'em."

Layla tensed. Orion and Balt hadn't been on the best of terms when she'd left them, but surely they weren't doing anything stupid.

"No. They aren't fighting." Bren shook his head as though he couldn't quite believe it. "But they are...looking to leave the station. Quietly. And not the way they both came onboard. They want to abandon their shuttles here. I thought you'd want to know as you'd had..." His mouth drew up more. "Well, you know. And I think they're leaving together. With one other person, who they aren't identifying."

Zelda's gaze shifted to Layla with a speculative glow.

Layla shrugged. She didn't deny or confirm it, but it was enough of a non-answer that Zelda nodded as though Layla had answered.

"If they'd captured you to take to the asshole, you'd be in irons." Zelda tossed back her hair again. "Not walking around freely."

If only the announcement could come with more flair and celebration. Instead, it made her suck in her stomach to keep it from churning. This information couldn't get out. Not if Balt and Orion were to be safe. "They captured me, all right." Layla's voice lowered. "As their mate. Nobody else can know."

Bren's eyes widened more than she'd thought possible. Then, they narrowed as his shoulders started to shake. He tried to hold it in by putting a hand to his mouth, but deep laughs escaped his broad chest. "They are both mated to you?"

Layla nodded.

More laughs shot free from his lips. "This means they are mated to each other." He tried to stop but more laughter ensued. "I bet that went over well."

Zelda shook her head at him. Her mouth thinned, but twitched. "Shut it, baby."

"They're doing pretty well with the whole mating thing." At least they were trying for her sake. She'd never been so important to anyone before. Layla put her hand on the stone in her pocket, fiddling with it in agitation and to remind her of everything to come. Her other hand dipped to touch the computer in her pocket.

"Go somewhere else, mate." Zelda ran her hand swiftly over Bren's ass as he turned.

"Don't do that unless you plan to..." He stopped to grin at Layla. "...do something about it."

"Later. Let me talk to Besela a few minutes more." Her dark eyes sought out Layla's. "Help Balt and Orion find their transport and help them keep it quiet."

"O.K., Z."

Layla's voice cracked. "No one can know we're mates. Please." She had to be sure they understood the importance.

"You have my word, Besela. It will not leave this room. Right, Bren?"

Bren bowed to Layla. "You have my word as well."

"Thank you."

Bren straightened only to bow his head to Layla again. "Good luck, Besela." He grinned. It softened his hard face into something almost boyish. "You're going to need it." He left the office. The sound of his snickering carried back into the room.

Zelda leaned her body back in the chair. She pulled up her sleeves to display mocha colored skin. "Mates, huh?"

"Yeah. They're something."

Zelda's appraising eyes surveyed her until Layla shifted, uncomfortable with the scrutiny. "Balt and Orion aren't going to be easy to live with."

Layla's lips perked up into a smile. "I know." They would always keep her guessing. When she returned to them. However long that would take. If she could.

"They're bastards. Men without mercy. Money-hungry assholes."

"They're not that bad." Layla's head came up as her hackles rose at the words chosen. Her mates weren't. There were plenty of men who were assholes. Like Ansel. Those words didn't describe Orion and Balt at all.

"Aren't they? I think they are. They're bounty hunters. Delivering people to the highest bidder. And, even worse, they want to gyp the other out of a score no matter who deserved it." Zelda canted her head to the right.

"It was their job." She defended them. They weren't crass like that. They were...wonderful. How dare Zelda say otherwise?

"Yeah, their job. Delivering people to the asshole. Innocent people. Guilty people. So the asshole could do what he wanted to them. Anything. He has torture chambers. For anyone who defies him, it's worse."

"I know."

"You barely know them. Yet you'd trust them to take you off this station and not deliver you? Unlikely from where I sit. And not get into a fight over which one gets the bounty? They don't share well. At all."

"They have shared me. Already." Even tried against the rivalry they had shared.

"They still could turn you over to Ansel. You know what he'll do if they don't. Balt and Orion like to live."

Orion and Balt had defied Ansel.

For anyone who defies him, it's worse.

Once Ansel found out they hadn't turned her in, he'd have them on the run. And even with the secrecy they'd kept about the whole encounter, someone would find out—someone who would carry the news back to Ansel.

Unless Layla could stop things by taking out the chip.

They'd be in danger even *if* she left them. For not delivering her. Her leaving them wouldn't save them much grief. They could wind up in Ansel's torture chambers as easily with her as without her.

"It is their *job* to bring you in. How do you know they aren't going to turn you in at the first opportunity?" Zelda's face tightened. "How do you know they aren't going to get you on that shuttle and take you back to asshole?"

"They're my mates." They'd told her when they'd become mates, everything had changed for them. And she believed it. They would not let her down. She started. She believed in them more than she'd ever believed in anything else.

"So? You're worth a lot of platinum. Mates have turned over their mates for less."

"They wouldn't do that. They aren't like that." Layla's face wrinkled up into a frown. How dare this woman talk about them that way? They were honorable. Men who respected their mates. They'd never leave her.

The way she planned to leave them.

Her stomach curled. She couldn't leave them. Not this way. "You don't know jack shit about this situation. Thanks for the help. Whatever that's worth." Layla stood up quickly. Time to leave before she called Zelda something she'd regret. "Another thing. You're not involved in my life. The rest of it, I got."

A smile spread up Zelda's face. "Good to know the rest of your life you got under control. I'd hate to see you go it alone. Mess up you and your mates' chance for happiness." She reached in her desk to toss a small bag to Layla, who caught it with her hand outstretched. "Give that to McTavish, too."

Layla crinkled the heavy bag in her hand. It was full of coin.

She'd been had. By a master.

She'd defended her mates and in doing so, she'd been made to see she had to stay with them. They were already in danger. She wouldn't remove that by leaving. And they'd never do that to her. So why leave them?

Zelda waved a hand. "Go on. Get going. I have a lot of work to do."

"Thank you, Zelda." Taking a deep breath, she took two steps to the door.

"Good luck...Layla."

Layla didn't turn, but pushed open the door into the hallway. Just where were her mates? When she found them, they'd both get heavy kisses before her shift started.

* * *

Orion looked around the new shuttle they'd acquired with Bren's help. He'd come over and acted as go-between.

Layla had greeted them with kisses and gone to work at the bar. She'd work her final shift so as not to arouse suspicion. She had Clyde and Bren looking after her. And a communicator to contact them if things went wrong.

Soon as her work was over, she'd join them. And off into space they'd go.

Their adventure as mates was beginning. Nothing thrilled Orion more.

Sources said Merc would arrive right before her shift was over.

Timing would be everything.

Balt and Orion both had already made contact with him. He had no intention of seeking them out when he arrived. He'd told them to stay out of his way, which was what they wanted all along.

If they could take off as soon as Layla reached them, leaving both their shuttles there, it would take old Merc some time to figure out what had gone on. Besela wouldn't have missed her shift. Would have gone to her locked quarters after it was over to sleep. And, no one would have seen Balt and Orion get into this small carrier or know where they'd gone.

The plan was perfect.

"I don't like this." Balt paced the shuttle.

Except for one cranky Amador.

"I know. You've mentioned that before." About a million times at last count.

"Someone should be keeping an eye on Layla."

"We've been through this. Clyde will. Bren will."

"We could do it better. I should go to her." Balt placed his hand on the door to the shuttle as if to open it.

"Stop."

Balt's hand remained on the latch but he didn't open it.

"Staying hidden and Besela working her shift are the best ways to avoid causing suspicion. It's the plan."

Balt removed his hand to slam it against a bulkhead. He barely winced but it was the same hand he'd hit against the stone wall. There'd be a bigger bruise now.

Orion winced.

"I know. You've told me a million times."

So, they were even, then. "Merc won't know we're gone for several hours. We'll have a head start."

"Suppose he gets to her before she comes here." Balt paced again as if he were a caged liger.

"He won't."

"You're so damn positive. How can you be sure?"

Orion blew out a breath.

Balt's rant wasn't just about this. Balt wasn't happy with Layla's decision to see the surgeon. He was scared for her. Hell, Orion was too. Their mate would go under the *knife,* for Goddess' sake. But if it worked, it would mean the difference between them having a life or not.

"This is going to work out." Orion moved to Balt's side. He reached up to put his hands on either side of Balt's face. "For us." So weird saying that to Balt.

"It doesn't always work out." Balt let his face remain against Orion's hands. But his tense stance told Orion he wasn't calming. "Look at how many it hasn't worked out for. We're taking big risks."

Orion lowered his voice in contrast to Balt's booming words, but let his amazement show through. "I never thought I'd see the day."

"What day?"

"When you were scared of something." Orion met Balt's eyes. "I always thought you were fearless."

Balt's mouth tightened. "You take that..." His mouth drooped, and his chest heaved as though he'd changed course. "No man is without fear, Orion."

"You always seemed to be. So cocksure."

Balt chuckled. "My cock is always sure." His mouth closed. "Even when the rest of me isn't."

Orion stroked his hand along Balt's long jaw line. Such a strong face. Such a proud brow. He leaned forward to press a kiss on Balt's chin. "Layla will make it here. And she'll make it through the surgery."

"You can't guarantee that."

"No. I can't. But we'll face things...together."

"I don't want her to have the surgery."

"It's her decision." Orion would never push her into it. But it was the best option they had. Survival would be the outcome.

"If you backed me up, she wouldn't do it." Balt's serious eyes appraised him. "But you won't support me, will you?"

"No." Orion dropped his hands. It was Layla's decision. It was her taking the risk. Orion would support her, whatever she decided. He'd rather they take a risk now than live with it for the rest of their lives.

"Fair enough. But I will try and talk her out of it."

Orion nodded. "I wouldn't expect anything less."

Balt moved closer to Orion. "You know, we still have time to kill before Layla gets off work. And we can't leave here."

Orion's lips curved into a suggestive smile. "True." Did the big man have in mind what Orion thought he did? His cock swelled out generously. Yes, a little screwing in the shuttle would pass the time and take Balt's mind off the problems they faced. Would take both of their minds off the problems they faced. He moved even closer, absorbing the heat from Balt's body.

Orion couldn't wait to see that big body again. If only Layla were there to complete their threesome. No matter, there would ample time with her later. He kept saying that, to make sure he believed it. They would have a future. He'd see to it the best way he could.

"There's a game on the shuttle computer. First one to two hundred points wins." Balt started for the front of the shuttle.

Orion rolled his eyes. "Damn man." His cock didn't get the change of plans and remained engorged. Where was Balt's notorious libido? Maybe it was a bad idea, screwing with danger around, but sometimes the adrenaline pumping made for spectacular sex.

"What was that?" Balt stopped near the front, looking around.

"Nothing." With a sigh, Orion followed. He'd make it a point to kick Balt's ass in the first game and rub his nose in it, before he started any sex.

As soon as he was at the front of the shuttle, Balt pounced on him. "Gotcha. You really believe I'd choose a game over fucking? Not likely." His lips swooped down to crush Orion's under his and take Orion to floor. His hands rubbed against Orion, shimmying around his body as much as he could reach.

"Bastard." Orion shivered under the onslaught of Balt's questing tongue and hands. Balt knew where to touch him. How to touch him. Rough. Hard. Same with the kisses. "I'm going to get you for that."

"I already have things to owe you for…"

After those words, Balt couldn't get out any more words or even a moan because Orion's lips wouldn't let him. He kept Balt's lips and tongue busy. So busy that Balt didn't notice Orion wiggling under him. Or if he noticed, he couldn't comment.

Orion managed to snag a seatbelt on the right, pulling it over to him.

Balt pulled his head up, breaking off the kiss completely. "What the fuck?"

Orion took the tan belt and looped it around Balt's arm to tie it. It had to be loose enough Balt could break it, but secure enough to make him feel captured. Luckily, Orion had done this before. He grasped the seatbelt from the other side. Eagerness made him hurry.

Balt flexed the arm, which had already been restrained, as though testing it. "I've never been tied before."

"Good. It will be a first." Orion finished tying down Balt's arm with the belt. He'd never thought he'd find a first for Balt.

Warmth spread throughout his body at the knowledge. He slid out from under the man.

Balt went down on his hands and knees on the shuttle floor. "You want to top me."

Orion grinned, walking over the seat to behind Balt.

Balt's ass wiggled suggestively in the air. Encased in leather pants, it was quite a sight.

Once Orion had that ass naked, he'd nibble it along to his balls.

Balt cleared his throat.

Oh, yeah. Balt had said something, needing a response. What had it been? "What was the question?"

"It wasn't a question." Balt faced forward so Orion couldn't see his face. "You want to top me."

"Yeah." Orion couldn't wait to drive his hard cock into the sweet ass before him. It took him closer to the edge thinking about filling Balt. He'd have to keep his willpower up and take the larger man to orgasm first. How he enjoyed his work.

Balt tilted his head back to look over his shoulder. His chin jutted out below a full blown smile. "You have to earn topping me."

"Do I?"

"Yeah. And so far, I'm…" Balt tsked his tongue. "I'm not seeing it. I can break these when I want. And, if you don't earn it, I will."

Not a better challenge had ever been issued. And Orion was certainly up for the task.

Chapter Fourteen

Balt blew out a large breath, taking in as much air as he could. The bonds would come loose easily enough when he wanted. Orion's taking control had turned him on more than he thought possible. His engorged cock had become almost painful. Orion's touch made him about ready to blow. He steeled himself. *Not yet.*

Orion moved behind him.

Balt could hear the sounds Orion's feet made on the floorboards. Could hear his labored breathing. Smell his particular musky scent.

A hand moved around the front of his leathers before sliding down over his cock. A front came up against his back. Even through his leathers, he could tell a bared cock nudged him from behind.

Orion had been taking off his clothes. A naked Orion stood behind him.

Heat took over Balt's body. He roasted in the flames of his desire.

His cock lunged forth into the hand.

Orion cupped him, squeezing gently.

Yessss.

But Balt wanted more. Much more.

Orion's other hand slid around Balt's waist. He popped the snap at the top of his waistband. Then, his fingers eased down the zipper.

Balt couldn't hear the zipper over the blood rushing around in his ears, though he sensed the hand move down.

Orion's body briefly pressed in. Then, his hands slid up to urge Balt up to his feet.

"First, you want me to kneel. Now, you want me to stand?" He faked indignation.

"Only if you want the pants off." Orion slid around to Balt's front. "And, you do want them off, right?" He waggled his brows at Balt.

Balt shrugged as though he didn't care. The truth was, he did care. He cared a lot.

Orion slid down to his own knees in front of Balt. He placed his teeth carefully on the waistband of Balt's pants. Slowly, he edged them down with his teeth.

Balt had been stripped by mouth before. But it had never been this sexy. He clenched his hands around the bonds.

When the right side had slid down almost freeing Balt's cock, Orion leaned over to inch down the other side to match, again with his teeth. This time, he scraped a little skin.

A deliberate action that sent Balt's desire escalating.

Orion drew the pants down until Balt's cock popped free. His head canted to the side as he stared at Balt's cock. His mouth pressed in to lap at the pre-come gathered at the tip.

Balt's ass muscles clenched up as the warm tongue eased along his length. It worked a circle around him, drawing Balt deeper into his mouth with each pass. All Balt could concentrate on was the mouth around him. The pull of it. The strength of suction. The pleasure.

Balt's hands remained contained in the seatbelts. He had nothing to lean back against. And the rockets of sensations rushed through him, hard and strong in their depth. His knees knocked.

Orion pulled his mouth away. "So, am I there yet?"

Balt gritted his teeth together before answering. "No." Hard to get the word out.

Orion's grin looked wet. "I was hoping you'd say that." He dipped his mouth but not back to Balt's cock. Instead, he went back to Balt's pants, edging them down more. His mouth brushed Balt's thighs. The slight contact sizzled.

Once the pants were down around Balt's ankles, Orion sat back up.

Balt managed more words through a desire hazed brain. "I don't know; I liked that you'd bowed in front of me. As if you worshipped me." Orion needed shit given to him, or he'd think he had an imposter.

"Oh?" Orion dipped back down again, his head going to the floor by Balt's feet. "Like this?"

Balt didn't answer as he watched.

Orion lifted up his head to calf level. He ran his tongue up from Balt's calf to the top of his thigh.

Balt spread his legs more. His cock ached. So close to an orgasm. One touch, he might lose the load. No. He thought of some boring shit to ward it off. He'd hold his climax back.

Orion lowered his head and did the same to the other leg. Only this time, he didn't stop at Balt's thigh. Instead, he went almost under Balt to plaster his mouth at Balt's balls.

Balt widened his stance as much as his pants would allow. Torture. Trying to keep upright and not fall down.

Orion's tongue lapped at his balls with warm wetness.

Balt's head went back. His hips pressed inward, trying to maintain his stance.

Orion pulled in one ball with suction. One of his hands went around Balt to press against his ass. After a second, the hand wasn't pressing. Fingers probed into the hole. One finger rimmed it slowly before pressing in.

Balt pulled up on his arms. Only they wouldn't come but so far up. He wasn't used to being restrained. "Fuck."

The finger pressed in again, circling as if it were a whirlpool as it went down. The warm mouth continued to take in Balt's balls as far into it as they would go. Orion alternated sucking and licking.

Balt didn't pull anymore on the bonds, but closed his eyes, letting the pleasure eat at him.

And eat at him the desire did.

Orion's other hand clutched at his cock. It moved along from tip to base and back out again.

Eyes shooting open, Balt couldn't stand it. "I can't keep standing."

Orion's mouth moved away from his balls. "So, I'm doing enough, aye?"

"No. Not yet." Balt's breath flew through his lungs as if it were a bunch of Marsupial bats.

"I'll have to work harder then."

Without letting him down, Orion went back to his actions, mouth firmly sucking his mate's balls. Fingers, now multiple, fucking his ass. And, another hand running up and down his cock.

Balt moaned. The man could multi-task. His hips pumped back and forth. So many sensations at all his pleasure points.

Three fingers drove into his ass. No lube so the fit was tight and almost painful. He moved back against them, driving them deeper.

Balt poised on the verge of exploding. When the hand squeezed his cock, he did just that.

Consumed by the heat, his climax wrung everything out of him, leaving him breathless and still on his feet.

Orion moved his sticky hand, moving his face out from under Balt's legs. "Get on your knees."

Balt arched an eyebrow at the order. Orion liked to dominate and be dominated. How interesting. "Who says you've earned the right yet?"

Orion grinned at him, holding up a hand covered in Balt's semen. "You did." The smile dropped off his face. "Now get on your knees."

Unable to argue with the logic, Balt stooped down. His heart began to race again after calming. Few had ever taken him this way. And no one with Orion's finesse. No one had made him spill that way. Usually, he was the last to come.

Orion urged him forward, ass up in the air.

Balt heard rustling around behind him.

Warmth and liquid drizzled down his ass.

Orion's fingers splayed him, getting a bigger hole. One finger delved in to probe Balt.

Balt relaxed even as his muscles tried to clench and kick Orion out. He cursed his own tenseness. Nothing he wanted more right now than Orion's cock. Inside him.

Orion ringed further in. He kept his fingers going in a circular in and out motion, stretching Balt out even as they pleasured him. The lube made things slick and eased the unfamiliar tightness.

Balt groaned as the fingers worked their way into him. He'd stretched out so tight around Orion. Pleasure built and buckled inside him.

Withdrawing the fingers, Orion leaned forward.

Something bigger probed at Balt's hole.

Balt gritted his teeth together as Orion's cock slowly pushed inside him. So right. The desire banked and built inside him.

Orion would take it forward a little, then stop and let Balt adjust. Take it a little further and let Balt adjust.

Balt had never been taken so slowly. But, the minute pain was akin to pleasure, more of a stretching. Only he wanted Orion to...move. Faster. Harder. Take him fully. Balt had never experienced the raw desire humming through his veins this way before.

Orion had penetrated him.

Not only his ass either.

He'd penetrated his emotions. Long ago. Before Balt had realized it.

Orion picked up the pace.

Finally.

Balt rocked back into him as much as he could. His hands clutched at the bonds that held him in place. He wanted his freedom, but didn't want Orion to stop. Wanted him to keep going until he'd spilled his seed. Balt would take every last drop up his ass.

"Hurting?" Orion sounded winded.

Balt heard the slight sound of Orion's gills flapping. They were probably red and open. Good that he was affected as Balt himself was. "No."

"Not even your hurt hand?"

Hurt hand? Oh, the hand he'd slammed into the wall twice. Balt hadn't even thought of it, used to dealing with injuries, but Orion had. Even in the throes of his own passion. Balt wasn't much for sentiment, but his chest constricted. "No. It's fine." Everything was fine. He had his mate inside of him.

Orion surged forward, coming further against him.

Balt arched his back against Orion. "Fuck me, mate."

Whatever edge Orion had walked on, keeping tight control over himself, crossed over with those words. Orion's body slammed against Balt's with a slap. His hands clamped around Balt's body, holding him in place for Orion to ram him at a furious pace.

Balt's cock stirred, still not erect, but the desire roused high inside of him from the roughness after the care.

Orion's body went rigid, his breath canting out Balt's name. His hips rocked against Balt one final time. The orgasm gripped him motionless for several seconds before releasing his last spurt of semen.

Balt tugged his arms free and lay down to wrap them around Orion. They collapsed on the floor of the shuttle in a heap, sated and spent. Orion in his arms was almost too much after the sex they'd shared.

"Well..." Orion panted over the word so it was almost incoherent. He took a deep breath and got control of himself. "That was one way to pass the time."

"The second best way."

Orion pushed up to look at him.

They both said at the same time, "The best way would be with Layla."

And with those words, she appeared, opening the door to the shuttle, which had been locked to her hand print only. She tumbled in, shutting the door behind her.

Her gaze shifted to Balt and Orion on the floor. "Dammit, I missed it again. You two need to tell me when you're doing this."

They both jumped up to grab or pull up clothes. The time to bolt had come.

"Your shift's over?" Relief swamped Balt. She'd made it back to them. He almost fell getting into his pants. He stepped back to lean against a bulkhead. After standing through Orion's pleasuring him, his knees still jumbled together. He had some things to pay Orion back for. He'd have to take care of that next time. The fun would be in the execution.

"Yeah."

"Did you see Merc?" Orion pulled up his own pants, not bothering to snap them. He put on his shirt, but didn't bother buttoning it.

Balt looked at the little patch of skin showing above Orion's pants. He wanted to rake his tongue across the flesh. Wanted to unwrap Layla from the mounds of padding. He shook his head. No time. They had to leave. But there would be a later. For all of them.

She smiled before popping out her dingy teeth. "Served him a drink. He gave Besela a big tip." After setting down the prosthesis, she displayed a ream of platinum. Plunking it down, she started to unwrap herself from the Besela disguise.

Orion shook his head. "You do have balls, woman."

"No. I don't. But I'm glad you two let me play with yours." She winked before sobering. "I think it's time for us to blow the joint."

"Agreed." Orion hopped in the pilot's seat. "Where to?"

Balt settled in the copilot's chair. He didn't say anything about their destination. Didn't want to think about what lay ahead. Or that leaving under Merc's radar seemed a little too easy. Orion and Layla probably sensed that.

What could he say?

He didn't want Layla to do this surgery, but he'd have a long ride to try and talk her out of it. His hands clenched. If only he could put those hands around Ansel's skinny neck. That would solve all their problems. After being threesome, most twosomes had problems adjusting to a loss.

Only it wouldn't - even he knew that. Others would come. They'd keep coming. Removing the chip would eliminate the threat. But it was too dangerous.

I can't lose Layla. Not after I just found her.

Not to mention it might destroy whatever he and Orion had found.

She handed Orion a computer. "Plug it in. The coordinates to where we're going are in there. We're off to see a man named McTavish."

Orion interfaced the computers.

Fuck, she was really going to attempt the surgery. Balt would have his work cut out for him on the long ride there. But he'd find a way. He had to.

Orion pulled out of space dock. "Hold on."

* * *

The com sounded, jarring Layla from her thoughts. They'd gone several parsecs from Settler's Mine.

Only two people would be trying to contact them. Layla sat up from where she'd been reclining in the chair.

Balt switched over to answer the com. "Here."

Bren's voice came over the line. "Union Alliance operatives arrived after you took off. They're monitoring official lines of communication. Merc took off not long after they got here. Over and out."

Balt switched off the com.

Bren hadn't wanted to be detected. The quicker the transmission, the less likely that would be.

Zelda wouldn't like the government on her piece of property. Layla would almost want to be a bug on the wall to hear her objections. Not that Union Alliance would listen. They didn't listen to anyone.

The news filled her with alarm.

Orion blew out a breath. "That was close. We got off the station just in time."

Too close. Usually, they ran far behind her. They were catching up to her. Even more reason for her to try and get what they wanted out of her head.

"Why'd Merc leave?" Balt drummed his fingers on a console. The *tink tink* noise echoed in the shuttle.

That was Orion's habit. Looked as if Balt was picking it up.

She couldn't suppress a grin. It would aggravate him if she pointed that out.

"He's probably wanted by Union Alliance." Orion shrugged his shoulders. "He doesn't play well with others."

"What if he made us?" Balt stopped drumming. The sudden silence overwhelmed Layla. "Somehow he figured it out."

"Nah, we were too careful."

Careful.

Layla's head came up. She stared at the ream of platinum lying near her seat.

How carefully Merc had pulled the platinum out. His light blue eyes had stared into hers.

She'd met them dead on, not shrinking or blinking. Attempting to exude the Coronian calm she should have possessed.

"A little something to take with you." He'd handed her the ream. Fingers cold and pale. Lifeless. "On your travels."

She rubbed her forehead as the oddness of the encounter made her wary. It had struck her at the time, but she'd been too relieved at getting away from him.

Merc had been too…sane from what the guys had said about him. Too careful.

"Damn."

"What?" Balt turned to face her.

Orion's head perked up but he kept a close eye on the controls.

"He did make us." She ran her hand through her hair. They'd been close. After leaving her hair, her hand slapped the seat

"How?" Balt's tone sharpened.

"I don't know. But, ten to one, there's a homing device in this platinum." She grabbed the offensive piece of money and held it out. He couldn't have made who she was so fast, after five seconds on the settlement, could he?

"Let me see it." Balt reached out his hand for the ream. "I'll find the fucking tracker if its there."

"No." Orion shifted the several controls. "Don't destroy it. Love, are you sure about this?"

"Yeah. I'm pretty sure." *Let me be wrong.* For all their sakes.

Orion did some more shifting. "Bloody hell. There's a ship tailing us. I can pick it up on long range sensors, but it's coming up fast."

It had to be Merc. Things could never be easy for her. This was no exception. If only she'd realized what the damn thing was before she'd brought it onboard. Damn. Everything always ended up being her fault. Her training was slipping, caused by the presence of mates in her life. She'd be happy for that except that it had cost them now.

"How close are we to our destination?" Balt leaned forward again, looking at the blue screen.

"Not close enough."

"Besides." Layla slipped the ream in and out of her fingers. "We don't want to lead Merc to McTavish."

Balt nodded his head but didn't look back. "Can we outrun him?"

"Not as long as the tracker is on board. His ship is more powerful than this one." Orion blew out a breath before turning. He quickly turned back, looking as if he did some calculations. "He's still far enough away. And we are close enough."

"For what?" Layla leaned forward eagerly. Orion always came up with a plan. Strategy must have been his focus at the Academy.

"The shuttle has an escape pod. The pod has enough power to make it to McTavish. Merc is far enough away, he won't track it before it gets out of his range."

Layla unbuckled her seatbelt. "Let's go." They had a way out. Thank Orion's Goddess Layla hadn't killed them with her mistake.

Balt undid his belt and started for the back.

Orion undid the map and handed it to Layla. "It'll interface the directions to the pod. Get you to McTavish." He pressed several buttons. More than likely deleting any coordinates from the system.

Layla took it, clutching it so tightly in her hand the smooth edges bit into her palm. "You're not coming with us." He wouldn't have handed her the map otherwise.

Orion looked back at the controls without meeting her in the eye. "Merc won't know who's on the ship, but he'll be able to scan for life forms. If there's no one here, he won't stay with it. He might pick up the pod if he gets close enough. Someone has to keep him interested in the shuttle."

Dammit. Layla saw the logic of his argument. But she didn't want to leave her mate. She cursed the Fates for putting them together only to put them in a situation where they had to be ripped apart. "There has to be another way."

Orion shook his head.

There wasn't.

Orion was banking on the two of them making it to safety.

"I don't want to leave you." How could she leave her precious mate? She'd been prepared to earlier. But not like this. Never like this.

"You have to. Go. For me. Be safe." He reached around his neck to hand her his heartstone. "Take this. Keep it safe for me. Just in case."

Tears pricked her eyes but she blinked them away. "We will find you again." She meant it. No one would keep her from Orion for long. Determination set in the thin line of her mouth. "And return this to you." She held it tightly in her grasp, the way she wanted to hold him.

"I know."

Balt called from the back. "If he can't find Layla, he'll take you to Ansel. He'll figure you helped her."

And they all knew what that meant. Torture. All kinds. Ansel knew ways to bring out pain in ways none of them could comprehend.

"I know." Same words with the same meaning. Orion pushed another button. "I won't let him catch me."

Orion understood that better than any of them. And yet, he'd sacrifice himself to the asshole to keep them safe. More tears escaped as she blinked them away.

"I could stay." Balt's voice got nearer but neither of them turned at his approach.

Orion stayed focused on the screen.

She kept her gaze on Orion, memorizing every atom of his person. It might be a while before she saw him again. She inhaled, taking in a deep breath of his musky scent, which she loved so much.

He let out a slight smile as if he knew what she was doing, but answered Balt. "No. You go with Layla. Keep her safe. Make sure she gets to McTavish. Help her decide on the surgery." Orion knew Balt didn't want her to have surgery. Balt would make sure there were no unknowns and try and talk her out of it. That way Orion could be sure the procedure was what she wanted. He was looking out for both his mates as best he could.

Layla looked back and forth at the two men. Her two men. Her heart thundered in her chest. Somehow over the course of being mated, emotions had evolved in her for them both. She loved them. For the men they were. So different, yet both so good for her.

Orion glanced back at Balt, and a heated look passed between them.

Balt's eyes simmered fiercely for a moment before Orion dropped his head.

They hadn't said anything out loud, but they'd said goodbye in their own way.

"Go. There's not much time now. If he realizes something jettisons he may figure it out. I'll find you."

So little time to say everything in her heart, which felt as though it might break into a million pieces at leaving him.

Balt tugged on her arm. "Come on, little one."

Layla took a step before turning around. She leaned over to press a kiss on Orion's lips. She played her tongue at the seam before pulling away. Such a beautiful face. She'd keep the image of it in her mind until they met again. "Please be safe." She laid the platinum on the seat beside him. "We'll be back together soon."

Orion smiled. "Good."

Balt looked back to Orion as he shuffled Layla to the back of the shuttle. He pressed her into the small pod in front of him before ramming his bulk in. "Plug in the map when we're clear. Hold on. It's going to be a bumpy ride."

Chapter Fifteen

After what seemed like hours in the tiny escape pod, they finally landed. Balt held Layla's hand as they departed the small pod. It had had enough juice to get them to McTavish. There had been a few seconds where he'd had doubts, but here they were. A place he might lose his other mate. "Are you sure about this?" Not that they had much choice now. They didn't have any way off the rock.

"Yeah." She exited the pod and looked around the disheveled landing pad. "Are you sure this is the right place?" She wrinkled her nose.

The place smelled of ash and sulfur.

They'd spotted a volcano nearby. It didn't look active. But that might be why McTavish had chosen the planet. Not many would come so close to a volcano, active or not.

A crack came from somewhere near. The noise sounded like a stick breaking, as if a foot had stepped on a branch.

Balt pulled out his weapon. His body tensed, on alert. He pushed Layla behind him. Tilting his head, he listened. No more sounds came his way to indicate anyone was there. Were they stalking them? Who were they?

So many places to hide existed, making it harder to protect his mate.

He looked at the stone building, which had rocks loose and crumbling from it. It looked abandoned. The landscape was all dark rock made from ash and bristly thorns. His eyes scanned, looking for anyone or anything dangerous.

The entire place looked as if it had "Don't fuck with me" stamped all over it.

Layla moved out from behind him.

He growled, trying to keep her to his back. It was the only way he could keep her safe.

She shot him a look without fear.

Such a little thing to be giving him such a look. Despite his knowledge of her abilities, his need to protect her was strong. "Layla."

Her own gaze shifted over the land as she didn't respond to her name. "This can't be the place. It's so barren."

"Doona know what place ya think this is. But, ya've walked into the wrong one." A man's voice came from above them. He stood atop a stone wall. His long black jacket billowed out behind him. Jumping down to land on his feet, he continued as he approached them, "And, ya've nae right ta be calling our place barren."

Balt aimed his weapon. His hands tightened on the trigger. "Stay back."

"I doona think ya wish ta be doing that."

"I think I do." Balt reached with his other arm to urge Layla behind him. She never should've come out in the first place.

The man's green eyes smirked with some hidden joke. "My men won't like it."

As if a floodgate had been opened, men poured out from the stone building. Where the fuck had they been hiding?

Balt counted at least three dozen, maybe more. All of them dressed similarly to the dark-haired man in front of him. And all of them bore arms.

No women existed in the bunch of them.

Balt squared his shoulders while lowering his weapon. He didn't drop it, but took the muzzle down. He could fight, but these odds were stacked against him. He'd have to bullshit his way out of this one.

Fuck, where was Orion when he needed him? Orion was good at that. Balt was good at fighting.

The smirk reached the man's mouth. "Good boy."

"We mean you no harm." Not that they could do much against his mob. Balt tried to look nonthreatening. Not an easy task for an Amador.

"Ya be bringing a mated woman inta our midst." The man nodded at a look from Balt. "Aye. I see the stones. And at such a place as this, it means harm."

Layla shoved herself to Balt's side. "Are you McTavish?"

Balt couldn't make her go behind him again without a shoving session, which he wouldn't do in front of these people. He didn't raise his weapon only by force of will. They'd construe it as aggressive and probably start shooting. *Fuck. This is just great.*

The man's eyes narrowed and his hand drifted to his weapon, holstered by his side. Several weapons came out and up until he waved a hand back at them. They lowered but didn't get sheathed. "Who's asking?"

"My name is Layla. Zelda sent me." She held her head high, voice strong and without fear.

Even with the situation at hand, she was beautiful. And sexy as hell. Gods, what a woman he'd been mated to. His cock hardened, watching his woman do what she did best - go into the heat of the fire.

Balt's other hand tightly clenched around itself. She'd better know what she was doing, or this would go badly. Mated or not, a woman going into a midst of men who hadn't seen one for a time wasn't a good thing.

The man's hand went away from his own weapon. "Layla. Had Zelda sent ya, she'd have sent ya with proof. I doona know who ya two are. But you made a dire mistake in coming here."

"You mean this proof?" Layla reached in her pocket.

Balt hadn't known Zelda had sent any kind of evidence.

A weapon charged.

Balt tensed in response. He had to protect his mate.

The man grunted something.

The weapon powered down.

Whoever he was, this man was in charge. And he held his men with words of iron. Did they fear him? The way Ansel ruled? Or did they respect him, the way Zelda ruled? "Look…"

The man interrupted him. "Bring it out nice and slow." The man took a step closer. "If ya mean ta pull a weapon, you're dead."

Fuck. Balt looked at the three dozen men surrounding them. Anything he did could set them off and on Layla. His jaw tightened. He stayed still. Should anyone come after Layla, then he'd act. Until then, best to keep his cool. Another hard thing for him. His eyes kept up their scanning for their aggression.

Layla slowly pulled her hand out of her pocket, taking her time. She tossed something to the man.

A rock.

A fucking rock.

Balt rolled his eyes. Wonderful. Did they believe in killing first? Or fun? He readied himself to spring to his mate. What would they do? Whatever it was, he'd die trying to protect her from it.

The man caught the rock. He rolled it around his fingers. It shimmered in the red sun. "Lovely stone, Layla." He didn't pull a weapon. His stance relaxed.

Balt kept alert but didn't move forward, as the man's demeanor had gone off alert. No sense pushing them before he had to. As long as Layla wasn't in danger, he could stay back.

"Are you McTavish?" Layla pushed her hair back behind one ear. "Are you a Scoonor?"

Balt frowned. What was a Scoonor?

"Mayhap I am. Mayhap I ain't." The man continued to roll the stone between his fingers. His gaze seemed captured by it. "Why are ya here?"

"I have a chip in my head. Long story, but I want it out."

"Such things are dangerous. Not ta mention expensive."

As if they didn't know that.

Balt had expected something different than this little piece of shit settlement. No way was the man operating on his mate anywhere here. She needed a *real* medical facility. Not a half-assed hospital on a deserted rock. "I think we've made a mistake coming here."

Layla turned her head to glare at him. "It's more dangerous for it to stay in." She reached in her pocket a second time but didn't get the reaction she had the first time. No one seemed to notice. She tossed a bag to the man. "Payment."

The man weighed the bag up and down in his hands for a few seconds. "Tis hardly enough."

Layla reached down her shirt, extracting a second bag from somewhere between her breasts. "After the operation." She dangled it, jingling the coins so the man could hear them. Then she stuck it back inside her shirt. Her hand disappeared before coming back empty. "Do we have a deal?"

The man's eyes blazed something. So did several other men's eyes.

Her motion had called attention to her enticing breasts.

Balt's nostrils flared. No man should look at his mate this way. Something feral went off inside him. With effort, he called the possessiveness back down. "This isn't a hospital, Layla. He's a rogue, hardly a surgeon. This is a mistake." He glared at the large man standing before them. The man was almost as tall as he was.

The man laughed easily. "Yar big friend doesn't find us accommodating ta yar request."

She ignored both of them. "Are you McTavish? You never answered. If so, do we have a deal?"

Balt's teeth gritted. He'd been casually dismissed by his woman - not anything he was used to. And he didn't like it. He didn't offer anything further. But later, he'd remind his woman that she was his mate. She belonged to him. Her heartstone linked them. Nothing could ever break the link. Except the death she risked.

The man executed a full bow to Layla. "Aye. Ta both. A Scoonor as well. Most have nae heard of my race." He motioned to his men. "These people are guests. We'll treat them as such. This woman is his mate. See the stones. They glimmer the closer they are. Few rules of the Alliance do I follow. But mates are sacred. Touch her and die." The bite of his tone left no doubt. His word would be the law. McTavish was a man used to being listened to.

McTavish nodded his head to Balt. "And, ya will find it quite satisfactory. That, I promise." He extended a hand to Balt to shake. "I'm McTavish."

"So I gathered." The man had a grip of steel. Balt let his own hand grip as tightly. "Balt."

After they'd finished shaking, McTavish offered Layla his arm to take. "Layla, let's go to my hospital. I'll show ya two around. I promise, tis a state-of-the-art facility. It'll allay all yar fears."

Layla accepted his arm. "I'm sure it is. And will."

Balt frowned. He didn't like his mate touching another man besides Orion...no, he wouldn't think of the Kurlan right now. After this was over, they'd search for him. And find him. This adventure had told Balt something he never would have admitted. He needed Orion.

McTavish struck out, leading Layla. "Tis a dangerous thing ya ask. I'll not lie to you. But, ya've come to the right surgeon for the job."

Balt hurried to catch up to them with one look back at the men watching them. That remained to be seen.

* * *

Orion pulled himself out of the shuttle wreckage. Blood streamed down one leg. He gritted his teeth as he assessed the damage to his body. Not too bad considering his shuttle had been shot down and crash landed.

The shuttle was toasted. Metal parts had been twisted and tweaked in ways they hadn't been meant to go.

He licked his dry lips.

Merc would be there soon.

He'd pursued Orion with the tenacity of a Madarian dog. Merc's ship had the advantage of speed. Orion's had maneuverability, but that hadn't saved him. Superior fire power had taken him down.

Orion got to his feet, ignoring the fire bomb pricking up his leg. He looked around the rocky brown planet. A few gnarled trees dotted the landscape. Cave entrances punctured the mountainside. If he could reach them before Merc set down his ship, then maybe he could out-hide him. Until he'd healed, he couldn't rely on attacking. Time for a strategic retreat. Plus, the more time he kept Merc here, the less evidence would lead him to the pod.

Where had Merc gone after he'd shot Orion down? He should have been on the planet by now. He had to know he'd shot Orion down.

His heart seized up with a cramp even as he set off at the fastest pace he could manage for the caves.

Suppose Merc had figured out about the pod? And was right now on the trail of Balt and Layla?

Orion could do nothing about that situation, left shipless and in the shape he was in. Gills wouldn't make him fly. All he could do was pray.

No. His teeth gritted harder. They had gotten away. They'd find McTavish. Layla would have a successful surgery. She'd be out of danger. Balt would see she was safe. They'd both be safe.

Those thoughts kept him climbing for the caves despite the rocketing pain shooting up his leg.

He'd reached the halfway point when the click of a weapon sounded behind him. "Freeze, Orion."

Orion didn't turn around as he stopped. He couldn't run fast enough to get away. Merc sounded too close. How close was he?

"Hands up in the air."

Orion's hand hesitated on his waist by his phaser. His fingers itched to draw the weapon, but he needed to know exactly how far away Merc was. No sense drawing it, if he was only going to piss off the insane bounty hunter.

The blast came within two inches of his leg. The heat singed him.

"Don't do it."

Orion didn't raise his hands, but moved them away from his weapon. "Why shouldn't I? I'm dead anyway, aren't I?" But dying later was preferable to sooner. He concentrated on planning what came next.

"Turn around."

Orion turned to face Mercurior. His hands still rested near his weapons. Maybe an opportunity would present itself. He'd take it.

Merc tapped his gun on his other hand as he moved closer.

He had been too far away for Orion to get off a decent shot. Orion mentally urged him closer.

"I hope her pussy was worth it."

"She's worth more than you'll ever know."

Merc's pale blue eyes lit with humor as a sneer twisted his face. "Tell that to Ansel. I'm sure he'll want to hear all about how you helped his property escape."

Orion growled. "She's not his."

"You know, I thought Layla was alone on the shuttle until I saw you crawling out. I had no idea you'd gone with her." A dry snicker left Merc's lips. "Wait until Balt hears this. He'll jones to see you in Ansel's clutches. Probably pay money to be in the audience."

Orion kept his lips closed. If Merc didn't know Balt was with Layla, Orion wouldn't supply the knowledge. Orion's fingers balled up, making a fist around a weapon. His knife. Primitive but effective.

His hand sprang out, tossing the knife at Merc's chest. Rolling over and over, it embedded with a *thwock* where Orion had aimed. Dead center. *Got him.*

Only Merc looked down at his chest and tsked. "As if I wouldn't be wearing body armor. You stupid shit." And, he fired.

Electricity jumbled through Orion's body as he fell to the ground.

"It's a switch gun. Neat, ain't it?" Merc's voice came for far away to reach through the haze clouding Orion's senses. "Goes between phaser and taser with a flick."

Orion's body shook with volts rushing through him. He couldn't move. His muscles had been paralyzed. "Ngh." Even his mouth muscles wouldn't stretch correctly. His spine straightened then tried to twist as he rolled on the ground.

"Oh, yes." Merc had reached him without Orion seeing him or hearing him approach. He took out cuffs and slapped them on Orion's wrists.

No. Orion could do nothing but watch. His brain functioned but the rest of him had shut down, except for the spasms. His gills flapped, helping to draw in more air. His lungs didn't like the zap of electricity. Trapped. Bloody hell. Merc had him. Orion could do nothing to stop him.

Layla got away. Balt got away. Layla got away. Balt got away.

Merc took out chains and fastened them on Orion's ankles. He wiped Orion's blood from his hand on Orion's leather pants. "Where is she? Where did she go?'

Orion couldn't help a chuckle. Spittle flew from his mouth as the snicker came out as more a gasp. Dumb bastard had tasered him, affected all his muscles, and now wanted to ask questions? Answers would not be happening for a while. Not that Orion would tell him anything. *Layla got away.*

"Where. Did. She. Go?" Merc punctuated each word as though it was a sentence.

More spittle leaked from Orion's mouth. *Balt got away.*

Merc found the wound on his leg to press in on it.

Orion groaned. The taser might have affected his ability to move. But it did nothing to his ability to experience pain.

The question asking while knowing Orion couldn't respond was deliberate.

Orion breathed deeply, trying to work through the agony.

Merc liked to cause pain.

Focus on Layla. Layla and Balt. Think of your time with them. How good it was. They got away. Thank Goddess, they got away.

His hand clenched, nails biting in the flesh.

He could move.

Not that it did him any good now. The chains and handcuffs had taken care of that.

Merc's voice sounded amused. "You recover quickly, Orion. Much faster than most."

It's a talent.

Merc moved in closer.

Orion could hear his heavy breathing.

"I'll have to work quickly then."

The tip of the knife pierced Orion's elbow.

"Ansel said not to hurt Layla. He didn't say anything about not hurting the one who got her away from me."

The tip stayed in, creating a burning sensation as it turned around and around the bone.

"Where is she? Where did she go?"

"Hell." Orion finally managed to get out a word between his cracked lips. *Go to hell.* He'd never tell them anything.

Merc laughed.

The horrible sound raised hairs on Orion's neck. The taser effects were almost completely worn off.

"I don't know about her. But, that's where you are." Merc leaned in closer. "Now you can talk. Let's see if you can scream before I deliver you to Ansel."

Chapter Sixteen

Layla looked out the window over the harsh landscape from her bedroom. McTavish had given them a suite, reminding them that while the hospital wasn't spartan, rooms were. Not a huge room, this one suited her and Balt with its plain, pristine bed and dresser.

What a place McTavish had chosen for his field hospital. His completely decked out hospital was camouflaged by stealth technology. The shuttle wouldn't have detected anything to indicate a building of this nature existed.

McTavish hadn't been humble at all when he'd said he'd called in a few favors in that lilting voice of his.

Balt had kept his hands on Layla at all times during the tour, reminding her of the bond they shared. Letting everyone else know of the bond they shared. She'd enjoyed his touch and touched him back when he let go. She was his. He'd seemed much less tense after their tour when they'd sat down to talk to McTavish, perhaps because of her reaction to his touching.

As McTavish had sat them both down to explain the risks, he'd become businesslike. Almost hard to believe that the man with the free-flowing black hair and coat was the same severe man who'd sat down to highlight every risk of the surgery.

Death wasn't the only, or biggest, risk.

Two millimeters to the right or left, she could be left an unmoving vegetable who wore a diaper for the rest of her life.

That was not the way she wanted to spend her future. Not with Balt and Orion. She had a future with them she wanted to claim. And that involved her body and mind whole.

Her throat constricted at the thoughts of Orion. They hadn't heard from him yet, had no way to monitor what had happened to him. He should have contacted them by now. If he'd gotten away. She clasped his heartstone tightly in her hand. She wore both stones now, to keep her mate as close as she could during this period of separation. If only they hadn't had to leave him...

They couldn't contact Settler's Mine to check in for news. Nor did McTavish have an extensive network of contacts. That left them waiting and wanting news. Nothing she could do right now for her mate. She let out a long sigh.

The big thing to think about was the surgery.

McTavish had told her to take a day and think over what he'd told her. He'd wanted her to be "clear in your own head what's going to happen or can happen. Then and only then, do ya let me know. Though you have nae better surgeon for the job."

Better technology existed to go for the chip. Not anything McTavish could get his hands on. McTavish relied on some of the more old school methods. They worked. They were just more invasive. And her only choice right now. The person who'd died had used one of those less invasive methods. So that gave her no comfort.

She and Balt had sat for a good thirty minutes discussing the risks and possibilities before she'd gotten hungry, and he'd gone to find them food.

A door shut behind her. A few seconds later a voice spoke. "You're going to do it, aren't you?"

She turned to face Balt. She smiled, glad he was back. Surprising how she was learning to depend on him. A tray rested on top of the dresser.

Once he reached her side, his hand dropped to her shoulder.

She clasped it. "Yes." Saying it gave it more meaning than thinking it. Not that she had a choice. The thing had to come out. No matter what the surgery could do to her.

"Can I talk you out of it?"

She smiled, patting his hand. "No. I have to do this."

"I could order you not to have the surgery."

A laugh broke free from her lungs.

He laughed a little, too. "I thought as much. I only wish…"

If only she could ease his fears. But how, when she had so many of her own? She didn't want to die. Or be a vegetative burden on anyone. The things worse than dying scared her more than death. Living with the chip in her head was the most fearsome of the options, though. "I have to, Balt. I can't live the way I have been." Turning, she pressed her body against his. "I can't ask you or Orion to live the way I've been living." She needed the closeness. She couldn't have Orion right now, but Balt could give her the comfort she needed. "But you can help me pass the moments until it's time to go for surgery."

A slow grin worked its way across his face, spreading big like a river nearing an ocean. "That I can do, little one." He grabbed her by the waist and picked her up. He held her close to his brawny body. A salzor chick couldn't have been more safe and sound.

She settled in with a smile, placing her hands around his neck.

He carried her over to the bed. He set her down onto the bed and kneeled down in front of her.

She ruffled a hand through his hair, running the green strands through her fingers.

This could be their last time.

No.

She wouldn't think that way. She'd enjoy this as the first of many. Her head lowered to gently plant a kiss on his lips. What started out gently soon turned into a storm of roving mouths and hands.

When her tongue delicately swept across his lips, he caught it, pulling into his mouth. He placed his hands on either side of her head and canted his mouth over hers. He kissed her mouth as if he wanted to crawl inside it and be one with her. He kissed much as he'd soon be making love to her. Rough. Wild. Fierce.

Exactly what she needed, he'd give her. The knowledge filled her with an abiding passion.

The deepening of the kiss soon turned her body to throbbing. Need pulsated through her. Wetness seeped along her swollen folds. She needed him to be inside soon. Wasn't sure she could stand it if he didn't.

One of his hands left her head to crawl between her legs. It pressed into the space that cried out for his touch.

Her thighs closed around him as he pressed forward, going in as far as the material would allow.

She wanted to rip it off, and grabbed down with frustration.

He broke the kiss. "Open your thighs."

With a whimper, she did.

He pulled her further along the edge of the bed. Pressed her thighs even wider open. Inhaling, his nostrils flared. "What a sweet smell."

Her face heated to match the rest of her. It was as if a summer wind from the deserts of Pol caressed her, making her warm all over.

One finger ran up a thigh before running across the place where her pants chafed and down the other thigh.

She shivered. His touch had been a bare whisper across that most sensitive spot. Not what she wanted. What she needed. Her legs shifted restlessly.

He popped open the snap on her pants before shrugging them down.

She had to lean back on her hands, pulling her legs tighter together, to let him pull down her pants. Coolness swept across her skin. But nothing could cool the heat rising up inside of her. For her mate. Her love.

He pulled the pants off her feet and ankles to drop them to the floor with a soft plop. The fire in his eyes burned her with its intensity. He looked at her as if she were his tastiest treat.

He was hers.

Layla still reclined back on her hands with her pussy slightly shoved up in the air. Her legs had shifted more open as the pants had come down.

His eyes darkened as he stared at her most intimate of places.

The object of his attention heated under his scrutiny to a molten furnace. So slick and needy, for her mate and nothing else.

She could lose herself in this for a little while. Forget the troubles and what was to come. Enjoy Balt and his touches. His possession. She shivered.

If only Orion were here, too. She missed him. Missed his completion of their trio. Even enjoying Balt as much as she did, Orion's absence was palpable. Balt probably felt it, too. She wouldn't let the sadness ripple through her. She would draw as much comfort as she could from Balt's touch.

She lowered herself down to the bed, unable to hold the position and be this turned on. Her swollen sex ached. She spread her legs further, inviting him in.

He put one hand on her left thigh and pressed it back until it flattened. His head dipped in. His mouth dotted kisses along her thigh.

Goosebumps raised along her skin. The warm, wet mouth laved along, making it tingle in eagerness. She held her breath, waiting. Would he plant that loving mouth where it most needed to touch?

He moved toward her center.

Her breath sucked in. It whistled between her lips.

His other hand came up to press her other thigh as the first hand released.

Layla's leg flattened down much the way the other one had under his touch. Why'd he keep touching her legs? She wanted his mouth between her thighs. Her sex wept for his direct stroking. Her muscles clenched in impatient fury.

He kissed along the second thigh.

Her limbs shook. What would he do next?

But his mouth didn't move to her sex. It left her thigh completely.

The loss cooled the drying skin.

About to fuss at him for stopping, she stilled when a finger ran along her slit. It dabbled in her folds. She shifted trying to maintain the contact and press him deeper into her sex.

Leaning back, he brought the finger up to his mouth and enfolded it. He suckled it as she watched.

She groaned as he ran his finger in and out of his mouth. The way he'd be in and out of her in a moment.

Eyes keeping her, he released the finger and lowered his head.

Now they were getting somewhere. Even with hardly touching her, he'd showed his mastery of her. She wanted him now more than ever. Her body had been wrung out, wanting whatever he would give her. Her body ached for his touch. Ached for him.

And, it was about damn time that mouth did some finer things to her sex.

* * *

Balt blew a breath along the sight in front of him. Then he inhaled, turning the warm air colder.

A few more goose pimples erupted at the rush.

He liked the view. So pearly pink and open for his gaze. Layla's wetness shone as her folds dripped for him. Her musky scent invaded his nostrils even harder. Set his soul humming more than it already was.

He wanted to slam into those moist folds and take her. Forget the harsh world for those few minutes.

Balt gritted his teeth, holding himself back. Called on all his willpower not to rush this moment. He had to enjoy it as if it were the last. Though it would not be the last.

He'd see to that.

First, he'd get her to the point where she screamed his name. Then, he could take what needed, what he wanted.

Her. All of her.

His mate deserved that much and more. And he'd give it to her.

His body shook from tensing muscles. Anticipation would kill him.

His tongue crept out to funnel down into her depths. Her cream coated his tongue. Nothing had ever tasted sweeter. He lapped at her insides, much as he would a frothy beer. His tongue clicked against her clit.

Her hips bucked. To lie down would break the contact of his mouth on her. It forced her to stay sitting up even while the pleasures took her on a joy ride.

He took the little flesh into his mouth, sucking it in.

A moan escaped her lips.

He bit down carefully. Not too hard. Not enough to hurt. But he scraped his teeth across her clit. Such precious skin lay bare before him for him to love. Taste. Bite. Whatever he could think of.

The moan continued, reaching a higher pitch.

She liked what he'd done.

But hadn't gotten the reaction he wanted yet. His tongue flicked the nub back and forth under it before his teeth bore down on it again but didn't give her the full nip as he had last time.

This time only her hips rocked up against him.

"Scream for me, little one." He sucked her up into his mouth, drawing her further in. Urging her forward to drive her passion spiraling. Her taste inflamed his senses. He wanted inside of her. But she must be ready. Be primed. *Control.*

More wetness seeped from her swollen folds. Such pretty flesh lay before his eyes.

Balt clamped down with his teeth around the favored flesh that he'd been torturing with his tongue. Careful not to bite hard, he exerted enough pressure to excite.

Her hips bucked, but she remained silent.

Not good enough.

He clamped down harder, pressing his thumb into her open channel. In and out he pressed the digit.

He sucked her clit into his mouth, again, puckering his lips around the sweet morsel.

Layla screamed.

He'd done it. Satisfaction enveloped him. He liked to bring a lover to climax. It always pushed up his own libido.

Pulling away, he looked down to a glorious sight. His lovely mate spread-eagled before him, skin glistening with a sheen of sweat. Her face glowed in the sated bliss that only an orgasm could cause.

He'd caused it. *Yes.*

He ripped off his shirt as fast as he could. A button flew off his shirt and bounced against her chest.

She giggled. "In a hurry?"

He nodded.

She got up, legs quivering as he watched. "Here, let me." She grasped the waist of his pants and pulled her to him. She unsnapped the front of them and pushed her hand down the opening.

His cock leapt up to meet her.

He helped her shrug off the remainder of the pants as she continued to stroke him up and down his length.

Not even the veils of hell could cool his ardor. And the way her hands gripped him, he came dangerously close to spilling.

No, not yet.

Balt grasped her hands, taking them from him, and pulled her over to his side. His mouth tangled with hers to taste its sweetness. He backed her up until she reached the bed and then went down gently with her in a tangle of limbs and bodies.

She could tangle with him anytime.

He wanted to be everywhere. Her breasts moved against his arm and so he attacked there. Such beautiful orbs. He fit one to his hand. One nipple worked between his fingers, and the other slipped in and out of his mouth. He suckled her as he would a Soborian twizzler, drawing her in deep before releasing her to move to the other side. His cock lurched against her.

Her hand found him again. Layla ran up and down the length of him, paying special attention to the tip. She rubbed a drop of wetness that must have gathered there between two fingertips and his crown.

Moving his body up, he groaned. Couldn't think beyond her touch. Her hands did things to him he'd never had happen before. Combustion was so close. She had no idea what she played with. Or maybe she did.

She moved him to her entrance as if reading his mind.

The permission she granted, he had to take. He needed to be in her warmth. Needed to join with her so deeply. He positioned himself at her entrance and found it coated in wetness. The wetness of her. "Oh, Layla." He panted, heart pounding.

He charged into her depths. He tried to take it slow, but when she writhed under him, moving upward to him, he couldn't hold back. She was ready for him. He pounded himself against her, going in and out fast. Deep. Hard.

Her sheath hugged him tightly, like a glove.

Sweat broke out across his body, cooling the cooking embers. He pressed in as deeply as he could and rose up while she matched his rhythm.

They melded into one solid mass. No Balt. No Layla. No beginning and no end.

Stars swam before his vision.

His whole body tensed, concentration pooling down to one little moment.

The orgasm ripped him from the inside out, taking him apart at the seams.

He collapsed on top of her. Her body under his both soothed and turned him on at the same time.

After a moment, he moved from her to pull her against his side.

She snuggled into his chest.

He lay there a moment. Something tickled his nose. What was that smell? Cheese. Fruit. The food. "Shit. The food. I forgot it. You were hungry." He should have let her eat first. He was supposed to be taking care of her. Comforting her in the hours before her surgery.

She moved away from him to grab a piece of fruit. "Trust me. I'm fine." She took a bite of the fleshy peachlike fruit.

What kind was it? He hadn't seen anything like it before.

A drop of its juice drizzled on her lips. A small pink tongue lapped out to clean the sheen from her top lip.

She offered him a bite.

He took it carefully but juice dribbled down his chin from the gushing fruit. Frowning, he grabbed for a napkin.

"No. Let me." She leaned over and snagged the juice. She lapped his chin and lips clean.

His cock twitched. Flaccid now, he wouldn't be for long if she kept that up. He wanted another bite of fruit to keep her at his lips.

After a couple of pieces of cheese, when Layla drizzled the juice of the next bite of fruit on his chest, his cock hardened fully once more.

With a grin, she looked down. "Guess he needs feeding, too."

"Guess so." Balt kissed her mouth, tasting fruit and cheese.

These were her last hours before the surgery. She didn't want to spend them talking. So, he'd comfort her any way she wanted. With his body. He'd let her lose herself in him for a while to forget all their troubles. The surgery. Orion. And he'd get lost too in the sanctuary of his mate's arms.

Reaching over, Layla grabbed a fruit, a passion pear, which had no pit or core. She deepened a large hole in the middle of it with her fingers and slipped the chilled fruit around Balt's erect cock.

The coolness slipped around him, encasing him. His breathing hitched.

"A way to feed both your appetites." She leaned down, touching her tongue to his tip at the same time as she nibbled a piece of pear off. Lifting her head back up, she took a bite from the first fruit and gave it to him by placing her mouth on his.

He didn't answer but laid back to give her access.

Much later, still lodged inside her from another round of sex, he fell asleep to her regular breathing.

* * *

Balt drummed his fingers on the table. Rising to his feet, he paced the small lobby. Then he sat down and drummed some more.

What the hell was taking so long?

McTavish hadn't given a time for the surgery to be over. But it had been at least five hours.

Balt had gotten tired of pacing and drumming hours ago.

One of his mates was missing. Still no word from Orion. He could be under deep cover and incommunicado, but Balt didn't think so. If he'd landed safely, he would have tried to get in touch with Balt or Layla.

Now his other mate could die on the operating table. And he had no fucking news.

He rubbed his face with one hand. Not a good day.

Another fifteen minutes passed.

As the clock ticked off seconds, he got to his feet. He couldn't take sitting here, doing nothing any longer. Time to find his own answers.

He slipped through a door, which led to the back of the field hospital. McTavish had a few other patients. Little security. Balt wouldn't go in an operating room. But he had to see what was going on. He had to know if Layla was all right. Concern for his mate overtook everything. Let them throw him in the jail if they didn't like him coming back there.

He kept his eyes down as he walked down a hall. Peeking up, one of McTavish's men came through the door. He looked Balt's way.

Balt met his eyes without dropping them.

The man shook his head. "Come on."

He took Balt to a small set of doors. And through them came McTavish. He still wore surgical scrubs.

"Zyd, what are you...?"

McTavish saw Balt. "Couldn't wait, could ya?"

Balt shook his head. "How is she?"

"The operation was tricky. Twas a good thing she came to me."

"How is she?"

McTavish pulled off a glove. Bloody ones. Layla's blood. His stomach rolled with a lurch. His mate's blood. "I would have cleaned up more before I came to ya."

Balt's heart pounded. "Fuck it, how is she?"

"She's holding her own. All her vitals are stable. Her involuntary functions are responding well. We'll know more once she wakes up." McTavish yanked off the other one. The scent of rubber and blood hung in the air.

She was alive. Thank Gods, she was alive. His breath came easier. He hadn't even realized he'd been holding it. "How long until she wakes up?"

"A few hours. She'll have ta stay immobile for a while after that."

"Thank you." Balt meant it. The doctor had done the impossible. Balt owed him more than words or actions could express.

"Don't thank me until she walks out o'here." McTavish started to walk away and then stopped. "So, do ya want to see it?"

"What?" Balt frowned. All he wanted to see was his mate. With her eyes open and her brain intact.

"The cause of all the trouble."

The fucking chip. "Sure." He'd see the thing that had put Layla in so much danger. He blew out a deep breath. He'd stomp it under his boot.

McTavish held up a bag. A small electronic chip bounced around.

"That's it?"

"Aye. And Layla told me to take it out functional if I could. It's working. It has a charge so it still functions."

"Ahhm." Layla hadn't said a word to him about trying to keep the chip working. That had been why the surgery took so long. His hands tightened up into fists. She'd taken additional risks, but he couldn't be angry with her. He was too glad she was alive.

McTavish handed the bag over. "It's literally a bargaining chip, Balt. That's why Layla wanted it out intact and working, if I could."

Balt took the clear plastic carefully in his hand, looked at the black and brown microchip. It had caused so many problems, for being so tiny. "You're sure it works?" It could be the thing that saved Orion, if Ansel had captured him. Trading a working chip for Orion might work. A dead chip wouldn't have bought them anything with Ansel.

Layla was a smart woman. And he couldn't wait to tell her so and kiss her lips.

"I'm sure. It has a charge. That means it's intact."

"When can I see Layla?"

"I'm going to clean up now. I'll come back and start her waking up process. I need to know if her voluntary functions work as fine as the autonomic functions. So, in about an hour. Maybe two." McTavish smiled. "Take him out in the waiting room." The smile didn't waver but the face hardened. "Balt, if you ever come back where ya nae supposed ta again, it twill be bad for ya. Remember that next time, mate."

Balt followed the other man back to the lobby. His prison for a time.

Layla had survived the first part. Would she still be his Layla and survive the second?

Chapter Seventeen

Layla took a long look in the mirror for the first time since she'd awakened. Shaved head. A long, thin slice running along the side of it. She'd known she'd look rough after surgery, but hadn't expected to look this rough.

She tried not to look too hard at herself. Because she was alive. And everything worked. That was what mattered. She was free of the chip. It would no longer plague her. Finish this, and she'd no longer have to run.

Headaches had been her biggest complaint, along with the pain of the incision. An aftereffect. McTavish had sliced into her brain and gotten the chip out without cutting any major tissue. After all, the chip hadn't been attached to anything. The recovery had been no different than that from a mild traumatic brain injury. She'd been on forced bed rest for four days now. Another day in bed, and she'd go nuts.

She'd been lucky to have it work out so well.

Her luck had started when she'd met her mates. Before that, she'd possessed none. She fingered her heartstone. *Thank Orion's Goddess.*

The door closed behind her. She turned her body to face Balt.

Balt had been there for her during the whole aftermath of surgery. He'd only left her side when McTavish had made him.

He smiled gently. "Hello, gorgeous."

She snorted, casting a final look into the mirror. "Hardly that." The incision was so ugly. How could he look at her without disgust?

His hands touched roughly on her shoulders. "You are to me." He placed a kiss on her shoulder. Even through the shirt, the contact burned.

He meant it. In his eyes, she saw a much lovelier woman than actually existed. Not just with her looks, but with her whole being. Seeing herself through Balt's eyes was a freeing experience. She allowed herself to lean back into the warm, hard confines of his body. The contact of his body inspired so many different emotions. If only Orion were here, and it were over. But it wasn't. Not until they had him back with them.

A knock came on the door. "Just coming to check on my favorite patient." McTavish sauntered in. "Who I see has a visit from her favorite visitor."

Balt straightened, but his hand rested on her shoulder.

Layla reached down to her bed under the mattress to pull out a small bag. She tossed it over to McTavish. "The rest of the money."

He grinned, pocketing it. "Thank ya kindly. I'm glad ta be able to help. For a fee o'course."

"Of course." She nodded.

McTavish had accepted what she'd given him without even counting it. He could have asked ten times as much for what he'd done and gotten it. And desperate people with no money would probably never be turned away. He was that kind of man. How had he ended up on that barren rock? And with all those men? Who were they? Questions for another time and place.

"Are you sure she's ready to travel?" Balt's worried voice spoke from behind her.

She reached up to squeeze his hand. For the first time in her life, she was fine. Free to do what she wanted. And what she wanted was to go find Orion.

McTavish rumbled. "If I said nae, she'd beat me. But, aye, she's doing grand. I see no reason she's not ready ta leave yet." He rubbed his chin. "I have some medications to give ta ya. If ya get caught, all I ask is that no one tell where ya got 'em. Under pain of death."

Balt released her shoulders. "We won't betray you. Ever." He held out a hand in front of him for McTavish to shake. "Thank you for everything."

McTavish gripped it firmly. "'Tis good ta hear that and yar thanks. Are ya both sure you want to be leaving me so soon? Ya can stay here as long as you like."

Layla shook McTavish's hand and then pressed a small kiss to his cheek, a sign of respect among Natives. She owed him that and more. She ignored the slight growl she heard from Balt. "Thank you. But we must be going. We've mentioned our third mate. And..." She broke off with a deep breath. "He got left behind when we came here. We need to find him." They had to find him. Tears pricked her eyelids. She blinked them back. Since the surgery, her emotions had been peeking through often.

"Yar third mate." McTavish's hand came up to finger the heartstone that lay around his own neck. "The luck of galaxy has found ya, as I said before."

Layla had never noticed his heartstone until that moment. But she didn't miss the wistful expression that crossed his face. It was quickly gone as though it had never been there. "It will when we find him again."

"What's this third mate's name? I doona think ya ever mentioned that when ya looked for information."

"Orion." Balt moved to her side to place his hands back on her. Their comfort warmed her. "His name is Orion. He's a bounty hunter."

"The one who's been taken by Ansel. For betrayal."

Layla put a hand to her mouth. Her worst fear for Orion had been realized. Ansel had him. "He has been taken to Ansel?" Her hands shook.

"Fuck." Balt's hand clenched tightly around her arm. He gave her the comfort of his trembling body. It had been his worst fear, too.

McTavish nodded. "I doona listen to the gossip and news much. But this is all over the place. Came out after yar surgery." He appraised them. "Ya dinnae know."

"We didn't know exactly what happened to him after...we had to leave him." Layla's hands balled tightly into fists. Ansel would have her wrath descend on him. Infiltration had been her best skill. But they'd all had to learn to kill. And for the first time, she'd gladly use that skill. What was her lover going through this instant? Her eyes narrowed as she lowered her head, thinking of Orion. And she prayed to his Goddess to somehow keep him from harm.

"I'll send any more news of yar mate any way that I can. Where are you heading after here?"

Layla's head came up. Where were they heading? They could go anywhere. Damn, they had no way to get there, wherever there was.

"Course ya will be needing a shuttle. That pod won't be going anywhere else. I have one for your disposal. Older, but she runs like a charm."

"That'd be great." Layla looked at Balt for confirmation. "I suppose we'd be heading to Ansel's."

Balt shook his head. "He'll eat us alive we go straight to him. He'll know how much we want Orion. And he'll make us pay."

Layla's voice rose several notches. So hard to keep her emotions under control right now. "But we have to get him. We can't just leave him there."

"I have no intention of leaving him there." Balt's jaw worked. This was as hard for him as Layla. Maybe harder. He'd known Orion longer.

"I know you don't. But how do we get him?"

"We could sneak in. Rescue him. Use your abilities combined with mine."

"I'm good at infiltration, which takes time. Time Orion doesn't have. I'm not as good at breaking and entering." Layla shook her head. "Ansel's place is a fortress. We'd be caught and placed in chains next to Orion. That doesn't help him." Her voice broke.

"Sorry ta interrupt."

They both turned toward McTavish, who arched a brow at them.

Layla had forgotten he was standing there.

"Ya two have the chip, remember? Good ta bargain with."

Balt shook his head. "We go in there, he'll know what Orion means to us. He'll sense it. We'll lose the chip and our lives."

McTavish tapped his chin. "Not that I know Ansel or his ways, but I do know negotiation. And ya have a point. Even with something he wants, he has something ya want more."

Layla looked back and forth between the two big men. They seemed to understand each other. Must be their similarities. "Then what do we do?"

McTavish grinned. "Ya let someone negotiate who has less to lose than ya do. By the way, I've made a duplicate chip."

"A what?" Balt frowned.

"A chip that looks just as the one from yar head did. In case ya want ta bargain without the risk of the chip." McTavish held up a test tube with the chip encased. "No one will be able to decipher it's not the original. Only that it doesn't work."

Balt let loose a large grin. "So, that way, they'll keep working on it to make it functional. Without figuring out it's bogus."

"Exactly." He handed the tube to Balt. "Keep them separate. Don't get them mixed up. They are identical in looks."

It had been a good idea. She'd mentioned it to McTavish when she'd told him to get the chip out in working order. Now that they knew where Orion was, how did it help them?

Ansel couldn't get his hands on that chip. It would be too much power in the hands of a sadist.

Union Alliance would want it back. But they'd never help get Orion back from Ansel. And they weren't lily white either. Layla had seen too much blood spilled in the government's name.

She didn't want the chip. It had caused her too many problems. She was done with it. She'd gleefully destroy it if she didn't need it to get Orion back.

But who could they trust to use the bargaining tool for *their* advantage in getting back Orion? Who'd want the real one? Easy to answer the second question. Everyone would. The chip would give them a distinct advantage, especially in dealing with Union Alliance. But if word got out, the news would cause its own host of problems. The chip would need to be with someone who wouldn't flaunt its power.

"That's all well and good." Layla moved to a chair to sit down as she contemplated the options. "But who do we get to negotiate for us?" They could use the real chip to ply their negotiator into place.

The person to negotiate would have to be someone she trusted. Someone who had balls up to his ass. Someone who... Her head came up. Of course. Only one person she'd met came anywhere close to that and would want the power the chip held without going over the edge with it.

McTavish met her eyes. "I was thinking the same thing."

Balt swiveled a confused look between her and McTavish. "So, where are we heading?"

"Back to Settler's Mine."

* * *

"You want me to what?" Zelda looked back and forth between Balt and Layla. Her chin rested on her hand.

Balt had to admire her calm expression. She didn't look shocked. She looked as unflappable as always as she regarded both them.

Even though part of him wanted to rush in himself and save Orion, he saw the merit to this plan. Zelda wouldn't be on the spot as they would be. She could go to Ansel, offer him the fake chip, and whatever else they deemed appropriate. Ansel wouldn't dare mess with her too much. Not the way he would them. Balt's chest rose and fell. Didn't mean he had to like the plan even if he saw it was good. He wanted Orion back now, not later.

If only you were here to schmooze.

Layla pulled the fake chip out of her pocket. "I want you to go to Ansel. Tell him this is the chip from my head, prove it to him, and then, offer it for Orion. Get Orion out of there as quickly as you can." She handed the chip to Zelda.

"You're willing to give Ansel this?" Zelda rolled the tube with the chip inside around her fingers. "If it's what I think it is, that's a lot of power to bestow on one man. Even to save your mate."

Balt pulled the second tube from his pocket. "That one's fake."

A slight smile graced Zelda's lips as she looked down at the tube resting on her palm. "Interesting."

"This one is real." Balt tipped the tube over and over in his fingertips. "It's functional. It is what you think it is." Time for negotiations to be over. Gods, he hated this part. He drummed his fingers on the side of his chair. Frowning, he stopped. When had he started doing that? That was Orion's habit. What he'd give to hear those irritating sounds again.

"It's yours." Layla leaned forward in the chair.

Zelda didn't change expression. She took a sip of something from a glass. "If I bring you Orion."

Layla nodded. "Yes." Her breath held in her throat.

Balt heard it. Layla had buried her deep emotions when it came to Orion. Though he'd noticed her feelings escaping more often since the surgery. She could only hide so much. Especially around him. Because he was of the same mind. He squeezed her hand where it gripped her chair.

"Ansel has Orion." Her fingers wrapped around the cylinder. "He won't want to let him go. Not without a lot of concessions."

"That chip will change his mind on keeping Orion." Layla spoke with assurance. Not that they knew for sure. What would Ansel do? Orion meant nothing except hurt pride to Ansel. The chip meant more. Even not working, he'd hope that he could fix it.

The chip had to work. It was all they had. Going in themselves would be suicidal, especially as a rescue team. Despite his arrogance, Balt had limitations and was aware of them. They had already talked about going forward with that if this failed. They had to do something. Neither of them could stand inaction.

If a plan even had a chance of working, they'd take it. First, they'd try the plots with better chances of working until they'd eliminated them all. Nothing would be overlooked when it came to getting Orion away from Ansel.

Zelda set the other tube down on the desk. She looked at Balt still holding the real chip. "You're sure it works?"

"Yes. McTavish said it had an electrical charge. Plugged into the right interface, all the information will be there." Layla crossed her legs.

"Ansel will ask about you, Layla. And you've been missing long enough for him to wonder, Balt." She lifted her chin. "What should I tell him?"

"Tell him I survived surgery and you got the chip from the one who took it from my head."

Ansel might still come after them even if he got the chip, but he probably wouldn't, as he'd think he had what he wanted. Balt would be ready for him if he did pursue his woman. And his man. For once, he'd missed Orion. He couldn't wait for the Kurlan to come back. Couldn't wait to make the Kurlan come. Be the brunt of his jokes. See the diplomat against Balt's aggression.

"Will you do it?" Layla continued. She managed to look nonchalant. But her breathing picked up. If Zelda wouldn't, it wasn't going to be easy to find anyone else who would.

Without answering, Zelda picked up a com. "Bren, see to our guests. And ready a shuttle. I have some visiting to do."

* * *

A knock came on the door. Layla jumped to her feet from where she laid on the bed by Balt. Her heart pounded. Could it be time? Had Zelda been successful?

Bren's voice sounded from outside the door. "Layla? Balt?"

After sprinting to the door, Layla pushed it open as though it wouldn't go fast enough on its own. "Has there been word?"

"Yeah." Bren stepped into their room with a brisk step. The door swooshed closed behind him. "They're on their way back."

Their way back. Layla ran a hand across her throat. A lump wouldn't swallow down. "She got Orion?" Relief flooded her. She wanted to sink to her knees and thank Orion's Goddess. She hadn't been sure this would work. She needed Orion back as she needed to breathe. He was on his way back.

Funny how the heartstone worked. It had picked her mates with perfection. She couldn't imagine anyone else in her life but those two. No one stirred her heartstrings as they did. Of course, that was the whole heartstone's reason to be.

"Of course she got Orion. She's Zelda." Bren's eyelashes crinkled with humor shining in his eyes. Then, he sobered. "But, be prepared."

Layla's knees almost buckled. She couldn't speak.

Balt slipped an arm under hers and voiced what she couldn't say. "How bad?"

"Z was tightlipped." Bren's own lips thinned. "But she said prepare you, whatever that meant. Ansel was trying to break him." His head tilted to the side. "And Orion wouldn't break."

Layla had heard of how Ansel tried to break people. Not a good thing. Her strong Orion wouldn't break for him. A shiver raced along her spine. Good thing they'd gotten to him when they did. Or there might not have been much left. How much was left now? At least he wasn't dead. They'd have him back. "When will they be here?" Impatience spiked through her tone.

"Soon. Why don't we wait in the bar?"

The wait for him to arrive after being told he was coming was the hardest part.

Balt tried to make conversation, but Layla couldn't pay attention to any of it. She kept running her hands through her nonexistent hair. She'd covered her head with a cap and had to work not to push it off.

When Zelda strutted through the doors to the bar without Orion, Layla's hackles rose. "Where is he?" She needed to see him

Zelda settled in the chair. "Bren, would you get us some drinks please? Clyde's busy." As Bren rose, she looked at Layla. "Orion's in the infirmary being checked out. Ansel said to thank you for the chip. Though he was interested in whether you survived or not."

"That bastard." Balt's mouth tightened into a thin line.

"I won't argue with that analysis." Zelda leaned back in the chair. "He doesn't know yet that you're Layla's mate. He didn't ask about you at all."

Balt snorted.

Layla thanked Orion's Goddess for that. At least he didn't yet know and hopefully wouldn't care by the time he found out about her second mate.

Bren arrived back, setting drinks down in front of them all. "Clyde said thank you. He's got his hands full without a waitress. He hasn't been able to find anyone like Besela."

Layla's throat tightened more. It had been her first "real" job in lots of ways. "How?" She paused. Her mind kept picturing all the things that could have been done to Orion. She didn't even know what to ask, and had a hard time keeping her tears at bay.

"Orion will survive. He's..." Zelda took a sip of her drink, choosing her words carefully before they left her mouth. "Ansel used a lot of things that wouldn't scar him physically. Apparently, Ansel is practicing with electricity."

Layla blew out a breath. That wouldn't scar him physically but what about emotionally? What would Orion be like now?

How would it all affect him? How would his health be? So many questions. She wanted to run to him. Never let him go.

"He didn't give up anything about you, Layla. He told me that several times once we got away. Or about Balt. He was very determined you should know that. If he didn't make it."

There was nothing Layla could say to that. Even under torture, Orion had kept their secrets safe.

He'd better make it. They had a life to lead now. Before she could ask about going to Orion, Balt spoke up.

"He could have told Ansel about me. I don't give a fuck." Balt cursed.

"He didn't want to expose you." Zelda took another sip. "Ansel will not come after you again, Layla. Or any of your mates."

Layla's eye caught Zelda's. Her sure tone meant it was a done deal. She hadn't told Zelda to make such a deal. And, Zelda had probably worded it in such a way to include Balt once Ansel found out about him. "What did it cost you? I never told you to do that."

"That's between Ansel and me. Want me to go back and renegotiate the terms? To something else?"

Layla's eyes widened. "Hell, no." Whatever Zelda had given up for them, Layla had no wish to turn back the deal. She'd enjoy the peace of mind it brought. Zelda had ensured that they could be free now. All of them. No matter what Zelda wanted in the future, she'd get it from Layla.

Her heart pounded. She was completely free. For the first time since she'd been taken to Union Alliance trainers, she was free of any ties save those of her mates. And they were bonds that she wanted. Thrills ran through her at the thoughts. For once in her life, she had what she wanted.

"Leave it alone." Zelda waved a hand. "But you owe me now. I will collect."

Layla had her doubts that Zelda would come for them for any more than tokens. But she didn't say it. Instead, she took the tube containing the chip out of her bra to hand it over to Zelda's long-nailed fingers. "Here."

Zelda took it, placing it in her own bra. "We both know that's not the only payment. But it takes care of a great deal. Provided I can get the chip to work." Zelda would have a world of knowledge at her disposal. And a great deal of it could be used against Union Alliance.

Bren's eyes watched the movement of the tube under Zelda's brown tunic. He licked his lips.

Layla had always noticed Bren's affection for Zelda and ached with a bit of want for that for herself. Now she had those affections and more. Balt had shown desire for her even with her skull hideously deformed. She had Orion back. No matter how hurt he was, they had him back in their life. "I'll do whatever you ask when the time comes."

"You got that right." Balt tossed back his whole tequila shot in one gulp. "So will I."

Bren touched Zelda's shoulder, stroking it firmly with one hand.

Her hand came up to capture his.

"When can we see Orion?" Layla took a small sip of liquor. "How about now?"

"Let my doctors check him out. I'm sure he's eager to see you. He'll probably spend the rest of the day in the infirmary. Go see him once you finish your drinks. That should give my doctor enough time. He gets cranky if he doesn't have time with his patients."

Layla scarfed down the remnants from her glass. "I'm ready now."

Zelda chuckled as she nodded her head. She squeezed Bren's hand tightly in her own. "Fine. Go see your mate. Keep in mind, my doctor is surly. But he's the best."

As Layla stood up, she whispered, "Thank you."

Zelda bowed her head in response.

Time to go find her other mate. *Please let him be all right.*

Chapter Eighteen

Balt followed behind Layla and Zelda, who set a frantic pace on the way to the infirmary. Bren brought up the tail end of the group. Balt enjoyed watching Layla's hips sway. It kept his mind off what was to come.

As they arrived at the room carved from the rock, Balt didn't know what they would find. He didn't like not knowing. His gut twisted. Orion was tough. But Ansel was a sadist. Electricity had been mentioned. What would that do to him? Balt didn't want to see a strong man broken. To see that in Orion might break him.

Ansel couldn't break him.

He kept repeating that as though it was a shield that would have protected Orion from the worst of it. If Ansel couldn't break him, surely he'd be O.K.

Zelda ushered Layla through the swooshing doors as Balt caught up to be at Layla's side. She might need him as they faced what had happened to Orion together. Balt looped an arm through hers. A simple handhold wasn't enough. He needed the contact. So would she.

"Orion, I have two people chafing at the bit to see you." Zelda moved aside so that they could move to the bed.

Balt looked beyond Zelda, even ignoring Layla, as his eyes sought out Orion.

Orion lay with one arm up over his head. His bare chest rested above a sheet, which covered his hips.

Balt resisted the urge to run his hands over his mate. To check him himself for wounds and other hurts. To try and make them better as best he could. He needed to leave that to the doctor. No matter how much he wanted to hold Orion.

Orion's voice was hushed and halting when he finally spoke. "'bout time you two showed up."

"Wasn't us who got lost." Balt saw a burn mark running down Orion's arm. His jaw clenched. Damn Ansel. He'd caused Orion pain. One day, he'd pay for that. He didn't see any other scars or marks.

Orion sounded weak. Winded.

Balt didn't like that, either.

"Hey, now. Wasn't my fault. Should have ducked when I landed." Orion's grin was ghastly. His lips turned up, stretching his gaunt face. He'd lost a little weight during his ordeal, having little fat from which to draw stores. His ribs now showed at his side.

Layla sat down on the edge of the bed as near to him as she could get. "Course it wasn't your fault. Balt took your map." She laid a hand on his leg. "I have something for you."

Orion flinched but didn't move away. "Wha ith it?"

She took off the heartstone on the rawhide cord. "Your heartstone. I kept it safe." She draped it over his neck. If only she could have kept him safe, from all of this. Her heart hurt from pumping so harshly in her chest.

He winced as though that action hurt him. He looked down at the stone now hanging around his neck. His eyes were full of emotion when he lifted his head. "Your hair is short." His words weren't as slurred though she could tell it took a lot of effort for him to speak correctly.

Layla's hand shook on top of the sheet. "Yes, it is. And yes. We'll talk later about that. But it's done."

"I told him." Zelda folded her arms. "But his short term memory is a little impaired."

Balt released her so he could move by her side.

Yes, Orion had lost weight, because he was a Kurlan. His legs trembled, making Layla's hand quake, as did Orion's.

Balt wanted to stop Orion's trembling, ease the pain he'd been through.

A tall man with dark hair and eyes moved through them, entering from the same door they'd come in. "Not to be rude, but you're in my way." He arched a brow at them, sidling closer to Orion's bed.

Balt moved in to block him, not likely to move.

Layla didn't bat an eye as the man faced her and Balt down. "I'm staying right here. He's my mate."

What a firebrand she could be.

Zelda cleared her throat from behind them. "And he's Orion's doctor, Dr. Castille. If he says move, you'll move. He doesn't like anyone interfering with his patients. Even me."

Balt moved. Orion needed medical care. Still wanted to be near his mate, but he'd let the doctor in to do what was needed.

Layla moved back a step as well but stayed close.

Castille didn't look at them at all, but began attending to Orion. "I can work around her. But if she gets something poked because she's too close, oh well."

"Castille." Zelda's voice sounded stern.

"Zelda." Castille didn't shift his gaze from Orion. "My infirmary. My rules."

Orion struggled to push up. "Let her stay."

The man turned a head to look. His face softened a little at Orion's words. "Fine. My patient wants her to stay. That's the only reason I'll work with it." He leaned back. "Can you go on the other side, please? And this isn't a viewing room. It's an infirmary." He waved his hand. "Privacy please. I'll move him into a room when I get done. Until then, *hasta la vista* to the rest of you." He didn't wait for acknowledgement but kept working.

Layla moved to the other side of the bed as she was told. She sat back down by Orion. "Balt should stay, too. He's our mate. Orion's and mine."

The man injected something into Orion's arm.

Balt winced.

"And I should have a million reams of platinum. Julipers, how many mates do we need in here?"

Orion started to say something but Balt interrupted. "I'll walk to the waiting room with Bren and Zelda." His eyes met Orion's. A flash of something went through Orion's. All Balt wanted to do was ease his lover's pain. Such a switch from a few weeks ago, when he'd derived much pleasure from irritating the shit out of the Kurlan. "Layla can stay. I'll come back when he's in a room."

The doctor didn't turn. "Thank you."

Layla looked across Orion as she took his hand to stroke it. She mouthed, "Are you sure?" at Balt.

Balt nodded back to her. He was sure. Let Layla spend some time with him now. Too many people had to be overwhelming for his injured mate. No matter how much Balt wanted to never leave Orion.

With one last look, he left his mates and walked out to get the details on Orion's rescue and subsequent medical needs. Better to be angry at Ansel than sad for Orion.

* * *

Layla came awake instantly. Her eyes scanned the room. Her heart pounded in her chest. What had woken her? A noise. Someone coming for them. She went on guard, clutching the phaser by her side.

It came again.

A moan.

From the bed.

Orion.

His eyes were closed. He must be dreaming.

With her feet bare on the cold floor, she padded from the chair to the bed and softly touched his face. "Shhh." He settled back down, rolling over on his side.

She stood and watched him sleep.

He rolled over again and calmed.

The doctor, Castille, who seemed nice to his patients and rude to everyone else, had put Orion in a room after about an hour of medicines and tests. There, they had all stayed for several days now. She and Balt took turns staying with Orion at night.

The first day with Orion back, Balt had come back from talking to Zelda looking grim. Whatever she had told him must not have been cheerful.

Castille limited Orion's visitors as much as possible, even kicking both mates out at times. Despite his caustic nature, he knew what he was doing, as Zelda had pointed out when he'd made Balt growl. Castille would rather focus on the patient than the family. Layla had noticed family made him uncomfortable so he lashed out at times. But he was the best settlement doctor in the quadrant. No one better could have cared for Orion.

Layla had to keep looking at Orion and touching him. She couldn't keep her hands from him, needed to make sure he was really back with them.

Thank Orion's Goddess for that.

He moaned again, shaking his head.

Bad dreams.

They haunted his sleep.

The electricity had disrupted his body's natural rhythms. There were signs it had stopped his heart. Not to mention that Ansel had bragged about that to Zelda. The asshole.

But now they were free to live their lives.

Only Orion would probably have some residual effects from the torture. A Kurlan's body had natural electrical charges. The amount of amps they'd pumped through him had shifted his natural ones. It would take time to rebuild. And, not everything might go back as it was supposed to. Only time would tell. The medicine had finally kicked in to ease his shaking, though residual tremors still remained. He might be on the medicine for the rest of his life.

Not a lot of people used electricity for torture. Its effects weren't as well known as some other forms.

Castille wanted to keep Orion there for a month. But there was little more he could do except keep a careful eye on the patient. Nothing except waiting would bring back Orion's electrical rhythms. He had to heal himself. Castille's worry was that the charge would build up in him and stop his heart again.

Another moan erupted.

Layla touched Orion again, gently on his shoulder. Then she lifted the cover up and slid in beside him. The best way to comfort him was by holding him, something she wanted to do anyway. Castille had said body contact was all right, even sexual activity. He'd said he didn't see how it could hurt anything when Orion was ready. Balt had asked. Now, she was glad she didn't have to worry about her body hurting his.

Orion mumbled something, turning his body over into hers.

She stroked along his back with one hand. She lowered her nose close to him, to take in as much of his scent as she could. She loved his smell. His spinal cord jutted into her hand with knobby bones. He'd not had much fat on him to begin with and Kurlans lost body weight faster than some species. Feeding him hadn't been a priority of Ansel's. Not when he could hurt him.

"Ansel." Orion shivered in her arms. "No. No. I won't. Damn you."

She pulled him closer, gently patting his back. Goose bumps erupted under her fingers. "Shhhh. Orion, you're safe now."

His eyes fluttered open. "No safety. All an illusion." His eyes had opened but he wasn't seeing her. Or rather, he was, but not believing it. "No. No. I won't. Won't tell you anything. Bastard."

"Orion. It's Layla. You're safe." She held onto him despite his attempts to struggle free. She was aided by the hospital bed rail up on the side he was trying to go to and by his own disorientation. Otherwise, even with as much weight as he'd lost, he would have escaped her hold.

"You're not real." His eyes looked glazed over. His breaths came erratically. "Not real. Leave me alone."

Her heart pounded a fast beat, as if it split in two. Her proud Orion. Reduced to this by the sadist. "I am real. You're safe." Her voice broke on the last word.

Something she said invaded his consciousness. He looked at her face as if seeing it for the first time since she got on the bed. "Layla?"

"Yes. You're on Settler's Mine. You're safe." She squeezed him closer, relaxing as he came back to himself. She wouldn't have wanted to call Castille and have him sedated.

His breathing slowed down. "I...I didn't give you up."

"I know."

"Or Balt as our mate."

Her smile shook. "I know that, too."

"He told me he had you. I knew it wasn't true. He'd describe all the horrible things he'd done to you. Show them to me. In my head. Before pumping me full of juice."

"He never got me." She ran her hands around his back in circles. "Never." If only it had been her. Instead of him.

A tear trickled down his face. One single one. "Thank Goddess. What he did...wasn't to you."

She leaned over to kiss his cheek. What a pair they were. She'd have gladly traded places with him even as he sacrificed himself for his mates. She tasted the salty drop. If only she could wipe away what had been done to Orion as easily as his tears. Only time and the love of his mates would help to heal him. "I've been safe all along. And now, you are, too. Balt and I won't let anything happen to you."

He didn't acknowledge the tear or her kiss. One hand came up and stroked along her skull. "Your hair. So short."

It had started to grow back. Fuzz had come in. She hadn't expected that for a few months yet but Natives did have fast growing hair. "I'm fine. And Ansel won't bother us again. I swear it. It's all been taken care of." Orion had had some trouble with his memory. Again, something that electrical impulses controlled and would get better with time.

He swallowed. His mouth moved. But he couldn't seem to get words to form. Finally, he just pressed his mouth against hers, which said so much more. He kissed her as if she were the very air he breathed.

Her hands pressed across his chest. She ran them across, enjoying the softness of his skin, the planes of his chest and stomach. Even the ribs, which stuck out, felt good under her hands. Because it was him. She had him back with her.

Orion's eyes hadn't seen some mutant with little hair when he'd seen her for the first time. Neither had Balt's when he'd seen her with none. They'd both had the same look for her as they had before the operation. A look of wonder. What they saw was not what her own eyes saw in the mirror. They saw her as their woman. Their mate. And their eyes found her somehow beautiful, even at her worst.

This was exactly as she now found Orion, despite what he'd been through.

Layla looked at him and found him beautiful. He'd sacrificed so much for her. So much for all of them.

She whispered "Mine" against questing lips.

"Always. Layla?"

"Yes?"

"I need you."

"I need you, too."

He swallowed. She heard the sound in the stillness. "I need to be with you."

Oh. "Yes." She found a nipple to tweak between her fingertips. She tugged on the piercing. The nipple hardened and rolled between the pads.

He grunted in pleasure before finding the air to talk. "I...I'm not at my best. It's been...hard."

Her thigh gravitated in to press against his cock. His hard cock. "You seem pretty ready to me. You are hard." She reached down to slide off his pants. Hospital gowns had gone away after the second day, despite his difficulties with dressing.

His baritone chuckle set her hormones on a fine edge. His voice had gotten stronger from what it had been a few days ago. "You've got me there."

"That I do." She moved against him again, grinding her thigh into him, now bared against her. He bumped against her. Her first contact with him in too long. "And you are at your best. You're safe. With me."

With her body and words, she tried to let him know how much she wanted him. Like her, he'd been damaged and thought it would affect other's reactions to him. He couldn't be more wrong about her. She'd have loved him no matter how he came home, as long as he returned to her. And Balt felt the same way.

His hips moved against her, knocking his cock into her thigh again. He kissed her again too, thoroughly.

She was breathless when he pulled away from the kiss.

"Layla?"

"Ummm?"

"I...can't...can't..."

"Can't what?"

He blew out a frustrated breath as if it were a snap of fingers. "I don't have the strength to be on top. My arms won't hold. I'll crush you." The edge in his voice made her heart wrench.

What had it cost him to admit he couldn't take her from the top as he wanted to? Probably quite a bit. His faith in her to admit that filled her chest with warmth. "I'll do everything. You just lay back and feel. Long as I don't crush you."

"You won't." His voice hoarsened. "You couldn't. You're such a little thing."

She snorted. Few made her seem as dainty as her two mates did. "Are you sure you're up to this?"

He shifted his hips forward. "Didn't you already find the answer to that question? I'm up for anything."

She laughed freely for the first time in a long time. Laughter which bubbled out of her and wouldn't be stilled. Freedom with her mates. She could afford to laugh.

She shucked off her own clothes and got his shirt off.

Layla tilted herself up and climbed aboard Orion's body. She ground her hips against him as he probed her entrance. "Are you O.K.?"

"More than..." His breath caught as she helped to guide him inside her body. He slipped in with ease. "O.K."

Oh, how she loved the moment of him breaching her. He slid against her wetness, back and forth, in and out.

She controlled the penetration and the speed. This position gave her so much control. She ground herself down around him. Inside her so deep. She contracted her walls around him. Then pulled him out of her only to slam herself back down on him. She had to pull back then, trying to stay slow. Wanted him too badly. Couldn't slam down again. Didn't want to hurt him. She concentrated on keeping things light. This was for his pleasure.

His hands startled her when they settled on her breasts. He caressed her, twiddling her nipples into harder points. His rough hands gentled on her but kept up their touching, sending her closer to oblivion.

Too close to the edge, her breath rushed out of her mouth in a long groan.

Up and down, she bobbed, squeezing her walls around him. The pace picked up. He was inside her.

She couldn't get close enough. Wanted something more. So good.

His hands were on her breasts.

And still she wanted more. More of him. More of everything. She trembled in the wake of her desires. Needed to be closer to him. Make herself one with him.

As his body jerked against hers, he moaned.

The sensations built and eddied inside of her even as he went in and out, in and out. Furious motions keeping her grounded in something. In him.

He released her breast and on a downward turn, reached up his head to kiss her. The instant his tongue touched hers, starbursts went off inside her.

He cushioned her mouth with his, even as his body joined hers in the oldest dance of time. His orgasm erupted as much as hers did with all the shaking his body went through.

He'd given her something wonderful, even as she'd tried to pleasure him.

Before collapsing, she quickly moved to his side. "Oh, Orion."

He chuckled. The sound rumbled from his chest against her ear. "Should I go away a lot to get that welcome home?"

"I would smack you, but I can't move." She leaned over, belying her words to kiss his chest. "Never go away again." She couldn't take it.

She heard his smile reflected in his voice. "I won't. Even as incredible as that was, I won't."

What a gift he'd given her. The gift of himself. And she'd given it right back to him in return.

Together, they drifted off to sleep in each other's arms.

* * *

Orion awoke to a soft sound.

Layla's snoring. Light and airy, it was cute rather than annoying—a feat for anyone.

He breathed in a deep breath. Her scent filled his nostrils. How he had missed it. Leaning over on his elbow, he watched her sleep.

Her chest rose up and down. Her long lashes met her cheek. Her skin was still dark. How long until it wore off? Now that they were free, the toner could wear down without being reapplied.

Free.

Last night had been more than he'd ever dreamed it would be. He'd been hurting. And she'd taken him into herself. Given him more than he could have imagined.

He stretched out, wincing. His muscles ached. His neurological faculties acted on electrical pulses, which had gone haywire with all the juice that Ansel had pumped him full of. The constant firing, even when he didn't use his muscles, made him sore.

But, he ached less than he had at Ansel's. And less than yesterday. Yesterday, he'd ached less than the day before.

He was back to his mates. He couldn't ask for more.

His morning erection stretched out from his body. But his arms trembled as did his legs. Hell, even his mouth had a quiver. Even though his flesh was willing, his body was weak. Probably had overexerted himself last night. A grin pulled free on his lips. It had been worth it.

Before he could decide on an action, Balt sauntered through the doors. His gaze took in Layla in the bed with Orion before he winked. "Looks as though you two had a nice night."

Layla was still naked. Her clothes lay spread over the floor.

"Yeah."

"Sorry I missed it. Damn doctor." Balt frowned. "He locks the fucking infirmary doors at night. They aren't pickable."

So, Balt had tried to come back at least once. Smart doctor. If Orion had suspected, he'd have opened them for the Amador whenever he wanted. But Orion had been a little spent last night. "There will be a next time. With you." He swallowed. Thank Goddess, there would be more with his mates. It had come close to not happening. The next time with both his mates would be... It would be incredible.

"I know. Only reason the doctor will not get punched. Well, that and the fact he's taking care of you so well." Balt leaned back in the chair. He didn't meet Orion's gaze, instead looking at the floor. "You O.K.?"

From Balt's tone, it wasn't just about this morning that he asked, but the whole damn shebang. Were things perfect? No. Things would haunt him long after his rescue. But, his mates would make it better. "Yeah. I am." Saying it aloud gave it meaning. He would be O.K. There'd been a time he'd wanted death when he'd been at Ansel's. Only thoughts of his mates had kept him fighting not to die. As he had at Ansel's, he'd continue to fight to live. For a life with his mates.

"Good to hear. You seem more with it today."

Orion nodded. Things did seem a little less fuzzy.

Balt flopped in the chair. His bulk took up most of it. "The chip's out of her. I know we've told you..."

"I heard." Orion cocked his head, still watching Layla. He itched to touch along the lines to her face. "What happened to it?" His gaze shifted to Balt. His hands clenched as a horrible thought entered his mind. "Ansel didn't get it, did he?" Had Zelda traded it for his life? He couldn't remember. Everything was a big jumble.

Balt leaned in after looking around as if to make sure no one heard. "Couldn't tell you before now. He got a fake chip. He thinks it's real but not working. That should keep him busy. We three, Bren, and Zelda are the only ones who know."

"Oh."

"It has to stay only between us."

Ansel would be happy as long as he thought he had the chip, whether working or not. "Fine. But, who has the real one?"

"Zelda."

"The hell you say."

Balt widened his legs. "Hey, she got you out of there. And told Ansel he couldn't hunt you or Layla anymore." His lips tightened. "I'm thinking she could have whatever she wanted for that."

"True."

Zelda had done them a service while he'd been incarcerated. He owed her much.

Orion didn't want the damn thing. The chip had caused too much havoc in Layla's life already. Best to give it to someone who understood its power and wouldn't let it fall in Ansel's hands. Or anyone else like Ansel. Zelda had the power and know how to keep it safe.

Orion looked down at his still slumbering mate. He couldn't take his eyes off either of them. He kept shifting his gaze back and forth. Both were so beautiful. He lifted his eyes to see Balt looking at her, too.

Balt's eyes met his. "Quite a woman."

"Yep."

"And you're quite a man." Balt's smile had mischief covering it. "For a Kurlan, that is."

Orion snorted. Even with the added tease, the words meant a lot. He didn't acknowledge them, but went on. "So, what do we do now? Once I'm out of here." He'd never thought about a future plan. Only continued running. Thank Goddess they didn't have to do that anymore.

Layla didn't open her eyes. "We get a ship. For all three of us. And continue as big, bad bounty hunters."

Orion trained his eyes on his mate, who'd been faking sleep. He looked briefly away to see Balt staring down at her with as much confusion as he was sure he had. "Bounty hunters?" Orion said the word carefully as though he might have misunderstood. Surely he had.

Layla yawned and snuggled into Orion's side. "Yep."

Balt came over to plop himself on the bed on the other side of Layla. Probably because he needed to be touching his mates. "You sure about that?"

Orion would have had to do the same thing. Closeness was something they all needed. Must be part of the bonding process they were all going through as heartmates.

Balt placed a hand on her leg, which lay under the sheet. "You want to be a bounty hunter?"

"Sure. You two are already good at it. And with my infiltration skills, I can help." A soft smile graced her lips. "It's what I want to do."

It made sense.

Bounty hunting was the best gig Orion had ever found. With all his skills and contacts, it put them to good use.

Even when they'd been rivals, Orion had to admit Balt was good at what he did. He could fight and knew weapons as though they were the back of his hand.

Layla would be a good addition. With her skills at disguise, she could scope things out for them before they ever went after a skip. And for the first time, it would be her choice instead of being forced into it by Union Alliance or circumstances she found herself in.

Her eyes opened as she grinned up at them. "But it means you two will have to work together now, instead of competing." She looked back and forth between them. "Think you can?"

Orion's hand closed over Balt's on Layla's leg. He needed to touch them both. "We can do that."

Balt nodded. "Can you handle using your abilities?"

Her face cleared with a smile. "I can. It's settled. We find a three-man ship with a shuttle. And start B. L. O. Bounty Hunting."

"B. L. O. Bounty Hunting. Our initials?" Orion shifted up in the bed. It had a nice ring to it.

"Yep. B for Balt, O for Orion and Layla in the middle of the two." She waggled her brows at them. Her eyes danced with more happiness than Orion had ever seen.

Orion's heart thumped. So good to see her happy. So good to be with both of them again. When would he be up for *both* of them? Soon. It would have to be soon. His cock had been tight since he'd wakened. With the two of them in the room it wasn't likely to go down anytime soon. "I like it."

Balt squeezed her leg. His muscles moved under Orion's hand. "I do, too. Sounds like a good plan."

The door opened. Castille came in. "I see the mates are out in full force today." He cast them a bored look. "The longer you're in my way, the more time until he gets out."

Balt jumped from the bed. "I'm going. I'm going. But only because I want him out of here."

Castille arched a brow at Layla.

She didn't blush but let the blanket down. "I'm a little naked."

Castille rolled his eyes and said a few curses under his breath. "In my infirmary? I know you did not. Fumigation needed stat. I'll be back in five. Be gone."

Layla scrambled from the bed, grabbing her clothes to put on. "I will be back."

Orion smiled, watching his mates exit after Layla had dressed.

They'd both be back.

Epilogue

"Did you see his face when you said 'Busted'?" Orion chuckled, still shaking his head. "He couldn't believe a Hablong would be taking him in."

Layla popped out her mouth piece. "And when you and Balt burst through the door? 'How did you find me?'" She snickered. "The locator on my person, dumb ass." She slowly stripped off her disguise to become Layla.

Balt walked over to the kitchen on their little shuttle. "Our biggest bounty yet. Delivered. I think it calls for a celebration."

"Me, too." Orion settled down in the pilot's chair. The three-man ship had become their home. They'd established comfortable routines, and now had their first successful case. Several more had already been lined up. They'd refused only one person. Ansel. They'd never get near that bastard again.

Watching Layla strip out of the constricting costume, freeing her breasts and legs, made Orion's cock fill further. This was how he liked her most. As Layla. Naked. Stripped of all clothes and disguises.

Balt handed him a drink.

Orion took it, hardly acknowledging. He hadn't even seen Balt move over to him as he was so enthralled by Layla's stripping.

Balt's fingers grazed his.

An electrical pulse zinged through him.

Balt let his hand linger on Orion's. He grinned down at him.

Orion took a swig. "Like the view or something?" A challenge to the big man. They'd never stop teasing each other. Orion wouldn't know what to do if they did.

"The view." Balt's gaze looked pointedly at the bulge in Orion's lap.

Smacking his lips, Orion leaned back to make his erection stand out more. "Gonna do something 'bout it?" Balt better.

Balt's hand dropped to caress him through his tight leather pants.

The first touch had Orion's butt clenching. Pulses of pleasures flew down his pathways. No way to disguise that reaction to Balt's touch, nor did he try to.

Balt's other hand came around as he lowered himself. Both his hands now stroked Orion's length.

Orion laid his head back and enjoyed the sensations from the incredible, firm hands on him. His hips lifted up to put himself more firmly in Balt's hands. Damn confining leather. He wanted the touch on bare skin.

As if reading his mind, Balt lifted one hand to undo the snaps to Orion's pants. His hand pressed into the opening, roughly cupping Orion under the pliant material.

A voice purred from behind them. "Private party? Or can anyone join?"

Balt lifted his hand away. "You're always welcome." He stood up, careful not to hit his head on the ceiling. "Let's take this party somewhere more comfortable." Balt moved away.

Orion loved the sight of Layla in front of him wearing a plucky grin and nothing else.

Her breasts bobbed as she moved to his side. Her hair had started to grow long again and her skin had reclaimed its natural color. It suited her more than Besela's colors.

As always, he couldn't pull his eyes away from her pale skin. Her rosy nipples called for his eyes to stare and his mouth to claim.

Orion shivered as Balt tugged him up to his feet, then back further into the ship's cabin. There was a bedroom, with one large bed. Balt led Orion into their bedroom as Layla trailed behind them.

Orion's mouth dried. They hadn't done much as a threesome. They'd played around, but at first he'd been so weak, he had to rest after too much exertion. Being with Layla that one night, no matter how healing it had been for them both, had exhausted him for days. So both Balt and Layla had backed off. Playing at sex had been all they'd done as a threesome, though Balt and Layla had been together a few times.

As his neurology stabilized, they'd been busy, buying a ship and getting it in working order and gathering clients. He'd been off the boat as much as he'd been on it. They all had. This was the first time they'd all been together in one place for days.

Now he had a clean bill of health, given to him a few days ago from Castille, right before they'd had to ship out on this job. Most of the residual effects of the electricity had passed.

And it was time to be the threesome they were meant to be.

Balt yanked Orion to him and planted a kiss on his lips that was designed to fuck his mouth. He pressed so far into Orion, that it was as though he was trying to become one with him.

Orion dueled with Balt's tongue. Trying to get as close to him as he could.

A hand pressed on his back, tugging his pants down.

Layla.

Orion shuddered as she eased the cloth off his legs, taking off his boots as well by lifting his feet one at a time. The three of them made a good team. In everything. They'd proved it with the case. Now they'd prove it with the loving.

Balt never wavered in his assault on Orion's mouth. He didn't let Orion give an inch, by keeping his hand on the back of Orion's head.

Lost in the kiss, Orion almost started when his shirt lifted up his back.

Bared breasts pressed into his back with nipples like jagged points rushing across his skin. They seared him with their contact.

Balt released him with a grunt and started shucking off his own clothes. "I'm overdressed."

Layla continued her motions against Orion even as she pulled his shirt over his head.

Once the shirt left him, he turned into her so those lovely breasts pushed against his chest. He clasped her to him, pulling her into a kiss. Her warm body melted as if it was butter into his. Goddess, he loved her. Loved them both.

One hand came up to block his lips. "Are you all right for this? I don't want to hurt your healing or tire you out."

"Castille gave him a clean bill of health, remember?" Balt shrugged down pants, his cock ready for action.

"I know that. I'm checking with him."

Shaking off his reverie at seeing Balt's cock, Orion leaned down to kiss Layla's hand. Neither of them would do anything to hurt him. "I'm ready for this." He'd never been more ready. It was time they had sex as mates again. It had been too damn long.

"Good." Balt sat on the bed. "Come to Baltazar, my mates."

Layla shook her head. "You nut." She grasped Orion's hand in hers. To the bed, they both trudged.

She sat in between them.

Just like the name of their company.

He liked seeing her there. Her rightful place.

Orion sat down on the other side of her. His hands, unable to wait any longer, thrust out to touch her. He found her breasts and started stroking.

Her eyes went half-lidded.

Balt leaned her onto her back and both he and Orion followed her down.

Orion touched, rolling his palm along nipples, which hardened more under his touch. It was like touching berries.

She smelled just as sweet.

His eyes looked to find Balt inching his way down her stomach to her pussy.

He'd never understood how seeing someone else doing something to your mate could turn you on more, until he'd acquired both of his. Seeing Balt about to give her pleasure upped his own desire. The way of mates.

Orion sniffed as a scent struggled to his nose. Her arousal was so pungent in the air he could smell it. His balls tightened, aching for release.

He leaned over to kiss her mouth. His tongue met hers in a furious sparring they would both win. Over and over, his tongue circled hers, pinning her down and letting it up again to wrestle with it.

She tasted of elderberries and cream while moaning into his lips. She must have had that while in disguise. Her arousal would taste even more sugary.

Orion broke off the kiss to plant smaller ones along her throat.

Her skin tasted salty and sweet, a taste sensation unbeatable by any food.

He let out a soft growl. It was impossible to be everywhere on her body he wanted to go. Down the soft flesh he moved until he reached her breast.

One nipple sucked into his mouth with a slurp.

He'd never tire of tasting her. Not even after a millennia would he be sick of her taste.

Balt's legs touched his as the man shifted. He overplayed Orion and Layla as his mouth went down on her eagerly.

Balt's hand found him. No clothes to separate to them. A bare touch on bared skin.

Orion's cock jerked. Heat enveloped him.

The man squeezed him but slowly, winding up the pace until Orion writhed, his mouth still on Layla's breast.

Up and down, circle around.

Orion mirrored Balt's hand movements with his tongue. Did Balt do the same motion to her sex?

Layla cried out, her body shuddering in an arc.

They'd brought her to orgasm. Her little cries and moans followed by such a big one took Orion to the edge.

He'd never wanted anything more than his mates right now. Even more than ever before, he needed to be with them. He could wait no longer. "Now."

Layla spoke, breathless and panting. "I want you both."

Balt's hand released Orion even as his mouth pulled away from her. "Yes, little one." His mouth glistened wetly with her arousal.

Orion lifted his head with a shake not from his problems. His breath puffed through a constricted throat.

No more words were necessary.

Balt scrambled to reach down into his pants. He tossed a bottle of lube to Orion. Balt lay down beside Layla and pulled her up to straddle him.

She wiggled around, using her hands to guide Balt into her channel.

Orion watched, awed by his mates' glistening skin and noises of pleasure. So pale against pale. Balt's green hair gleamed harsh under the lights.

She rode Balt while sitting for a few thrusts of her body and then she lay on top of him. She looked back over her shoulder, eyes captivating Orion.

He moved quickly lest the moment be lost. Time to join his mates. Take his place in their love.

He spilled the lube into her butt hole, poured in a generous amount and let it warm against her skin.

She rose and fell onto Balt's thick cock.

Orion could almost see Balt's cock upon her rising. What a sight to see. It entered her, glistening upon every pull out. His own heart pounded. Soon, his cock would make its way into her tightness. A first for them. So many had come and gone. Now it was time for this one. Anticipation made his mouth quake.

Slowly, he prepped her with his finger. First, inserting one, waiting for her comfort and then going in more. One by one, he stretched her out, using the lube to ease his coming entrance. A long process but well worth it. He'd never hurt his hearts. They were too precious to him.

Balt kept the pace slow. Letting her take her time thrusting against him. How did he find his control? He'd been within in her so long and hadn't let pleasure crash against him. The tightness of his face, which Orion could sometimes see, spoke of the severity of his iron hand. It was costing Balt to be there and not come.

It was time to finish this. Down the road of pleasure as mates.

Removing his fingers, Orion leaned over to rim her one time, licking his tongue into the confines of her ass.

She let out a moan. "Please."

Orion was only too happy to oblige. He'd prepped her well, but still she held to him tightly as he pressed in. Centimeter by centimeter, he went within her tight confines. Each gain rewarded him with her gasp.

Finally, all the way in, he stopped.

So did Balt under her.

Orion's arms shook with the force of his emotions and the sensations.

"Oh, please." Her head tossed back in the throes of her arousal.

And Orion did move. Furiously, he thrust against her, not holding anything back. So good, her asshole clenching his cock.

Balt tailored his rhythm to Orion's, thrusting up when Orion came up and down when he came down.

She ran between them, the link that bonded them until they were one.

One mind.

One heart.

One thrust.

Her scream came right as Orion's release found him.

Balt cursed in the hand of his own pleasure.

Their stones glowed, warming to their skin.

Full mates at last.

The man who'd been his rival and the woman who'd been his assignment. An unlikely trio of mates. And Orion wouldn't have it any other way.

ꙮ THE END ꙮ

Mechele Armstrong

Have you ever wondered, "What if crayons have a king-dom?" Mechele Armstrong did at age five. Now, turning the imagination of a wide-eyed child into intense spellbinding stories for adults, she is winning over new fans every day.

Writing stories and poetry as a hobby, she graduated from Virginia Commonwealth University with a degree in Religious Studies and Social Welfare. Although there were challenges with work and family, the need to write and be published, to share her passion for books was always there.

During a rainy weekend at the beach reading several romance novels she fell in love, not with the hero, but with the genre again. So began a two-year adventure of doing what she loved most, creating worlds with strong heroines and enchanting heroes that will keep you turning pages until the end.

Using the Internet and the local Romance Writer's Association, she learned and refined her craft. Living in Virginia with a husband, kids, dog, and fish, she finds time to share her vivid imagination and ability to tell stories of adventure, love, lust, and everything in between.

Check out Mechele's website to see what she's been up to at http://www.mechelearmstrong.com, or feel free email her at mechele@mechelearmstrong.com.

THE BLACKER THE BERRY
Lena Matthews

THE BROKEN H
J. L. Langley

THE TIN STAR
J. L. Langley

THEIR ONE AND ONLY
Trista Ann Michaels

TRY A LITTLE TENDERNESS
Roslyn Hardy Holcomb

VETERANS 1: THROUGH THE FIRE
Rachel Bo and Liz Andrews

VETERANS 2: NOTHING TO LOSE
Mechele Armstrong and Bobby Michaels

WILD WISHES
Stephanie Burke, Lena Matthews, and Eve Vaughn

Publisher's Note: The print titles listed above were previously released in e-book format by Loose Id®.

Non-Fiction by *ANGELA KNIGHT*
*PASSIONATE INK: A GUIDE TO WRITING
EROTIC ROMANCE*